MW01194379

TOTAL DREAMBOAT

Also by Katelyn Doyle

Just Some Stupid Love Story

TOTAL DREAMBOAT

a novel

KATELYN DOYLE

FLATIRON
BOOKS
NEW YORK

This is a work of fiction. All the characters, organizations, and events portrayed in this novel are either products of the author's imagination or used fictitiously.

www.flatironbooks.com

Designed by Jen Edwards

Library of Congress Cataloging-in-Publication Data

Names: Doyle, Katelyn, author.
Title: Total dreamboat : a novel / Katelyn Doyle.
Description: First edition. | New York : Flatiron Books, 2025.
Identifiers: LCCN 2024058650 | ISBN 9781250328069 (hardcover) |
ISBN 9781250328076 (ebook)
Subjects: LCGFT: Romance fiction. | Novels.
Classification: LCC PS3616.E279 T68 2025 | DDC 813/.6—dc23/eng/20241227
LC record available at https://lccn.loc.gov/2024058650

Our books may be purchased in bulk for promotional, educational, or business use. Please contact your local bookseller or the Macmillan Corporate and Premium Sales Department at 1-800-221-7945, extension 5442, or by email at MacmillanSpecialMarkets@macmillan.com.

First Edition: 2025

10 9 8 7 6 5 4 3 2 1

For the real Lauren

1

ABANDON SHIP

Today

NASSAU, BAHAMAS

Hope

If you've never gone to Señor Frog's with a broken heart, I don't recommend it. Drinking a frozen margarita out of a neon plastic tube is demoralizing enough on its own. You don't want to do it while weeping.

You wouldn't know it from the snot in my hair, but there was a time when I was not a crying-alone-in-a-Mexican-themed-chain-restaurant kind of girl.

I used to be fucking cool.

I had the kind of potential that grabbed the world by the throat. A level of talent that delighted people. Confidence you could bring down a room with.

And then my charmed life went sideways and my once-bright trajectory flatlined and my efforts to right myself somehow landed me further and further away from the person I wanted to be. I became *this* person instead:

The one with mascara dripping down her face in a Bahamian tourist trap that smells like nachos, sobbing over a boy she's barely known for a week.

"Another margarita?" my waiter asks, appearing out of nowhere. He doesn't acknowledge my hysteria, but his face plainly says, "You look like you need one."

"No thank you, just the check," I warble.

He runs my card and I wipe my face with a napkin and step outside the restaurant into a wall of humidity as stale and stifling as an overcrowded steam room at a not-very-clean gym.

I crave shade and air-conditioning, but I can't bring myself to walk back to the cruise ship in the state I'm in. Even under the best of circumstances, walking toward a cruise ship—*any* cruise ship—is antithetical to my personality. But in the case of this particular cruise ship, it's where *he* is.

Him, and his arresting face and dark tousled hair and dry wit and the terrible, insulting things that he thinks of me.

I know I have to go back eventually, but I still have an hour of freedom before departure, so I wander toward the city center.

"Miss lady!" a woman selling handwoven crafts out of a stall calls out at me. "Don't be sad. No crying in paradise!"

"I'm fine," I sniffle, despite the fact that I'm still ever so slightly weeping. I stop and pick up a straw hat embroidered with tiny conch shells from her cart. "How much is this?"

"Thirty dollars," she says.

I only have twenty-five.

"Oh, okay," I say. "Thanks anyway."

I start to walk away, but she takes pity on me. "For you, sad girl, twenty."

I thank her, hand her the cash, and shove the hat down so it covers my face.

By now I suspect I need to head back to the port. I reach for my phone to check the directions.

But my phone isn't in my purse.

Belatedly, I remember I put it on the bedside table to charge this morning. I must have left it in the cabin in my fugue state of despair.

Well, whatever. I'll just retrace my steps.

Unfortunately, I am not good at spatial awareness, and immediately get lost.

I walk into a cigar shop to ask for directions, and a man at the counter tells me to turn left, then right, then walk twenty minutes.

Twenty minutes?

"What time is it?" I ask him.

"Time for you to smoke a cigar," he says affably.

"No, really—do you have the time?"

"Five twenty-one," he says.

Oh no.

I thank him and dash out of the store.

"It's okay," I say out loud to myself. "Just find a taxi."

But either there aren't any taxis around or I'm too stressed to identify them.

I keep running, this time with the directions seared into my brain out of terror, and finally make it to the street alongside the beach, a straight shot to the pier. I can *see* the ship, glinting white in the distance.

It's *far away*.

I am not someone who approaches strangers, but in my desperation I run over to a guy getting onto his motorbike and ask him if he knows where to get a taxi.

He gestures toward the port. "There's a stand that way, by the cruise ships."

Not helpful.

He must see my distress. He offers to drive me to the port on his bike.

Motorcycles scare me, his bike does not look big enough for two people, and he does not have a helmet.

I gratefully accept.

The bike lurches forward, and we zoom down the road toward the pier.

Felix

What do you do when the woman you were inadvisably falling for on holiday shatters all your illusions about romance?

In my case, you rent a jet ski in the Bahamas and angrily zigzag back and forth across the bay at top speed, hoping that stirring up a violent wake will exorcise the pain.

It doesn't, but apparently it *is* a good way to run out of petrol.

The jet ski lurches to a stop with such force I almost catapult into the sea. I jam down on the throttle, hoping the ignition will miraculously turn and let me chug back to shore.

It emits a sound like an elephant passing wind.

Right.

I'm only about a thousand feet from the beach, but this being late in the day, there's no one else on the water to turn to for help. I'm going to have to wait for the clerk at the surf shop to notice I'm stalled out and rescue me, or float off to my death at sea.

I refuse to perish on a Sea-Doo personal watercraft. I take off my mandatory orange life vest and wave it above my head whilst blowing the whistle attached to my key for emergencies. After about six minutes of this, someone on shore finally sees me. A guy from the surf shop motors out in a skiff.

"So sorry!" he shouts cheerfully as he approaches. "This never happens! I'll take you back and get you a new WaveRunner. Full refund."

"That won't be necessary," I say. My zest for channeling my depression into water sport has abandoned me.

The man attaches the dead jet ski to a towline and drives toward the beach at approximately three miles per hour.

His speed is making me anxious. I only planned an hour for this excursion, and it's been at least ninety minutes.

I grab my rucksack out of my rented locker and rummage inside for my phone to check the time.

It's 5:09. The boat leaves at half five.

I panic jog out of the shop and in the direction of the port. Six streets in, I realize I don't have my rucksack. I must have left it on the bench by the lockers in the shop.

Fucking hell.

I race back.

It's not there.

"Did someone turn in a rucksack?" I ask the attendant. "I left it here a few minutes ago."

She looks at me blankly.

"Sorry, no," she says.

Which means I am in a foreign country with no money or proof of my identity save for a tasteful blue cruise line wristband embossed with my name.

And it's now 5:16.

Making it back to the ship on time will be somewhere between tight and impossible.

It's fine, I tell myself. Surely there must be a grace period when it comes to a vessel catering to elderly tourists addled with sunshine and rum. My passport is still on the ship. All I need to do is get back to the port and explain my predicament and I'll be off to sea to complete this miserable voyage.

The trouble is that I arrive at the port just in time to see the *Romance of the Sea* gliding out of the quay.

I wave my arms madly. "Wait," I call frantically. "Wait."

Other tourists are watching me, some concerned, some snickering. "Look," I hear a jocular American say to his wife. "A runner."

I skip past the queue at the embarkation entrance and breathlessly corner one of the agents.

"I'm meant to be on that ship," I say, my chest still heaving. "Can you radio and tell them to come back?"

He chuckles. "Once it departs, it doesn't come back."

"Surely they wouldn't just leave a passenger stranded," I say. "Please, there must be a tender, or—"

"Over there," he says, pointing at a kiosk by the gates to the port. "That's where you go when you miss the boat."

Ah. There's a protocol. Mildly reassuring.

I sprint toward it.

"Hello," I say to the attendant. "I missed my ship. That gentleman"—I point to the dock agent—"suggested you might be able to help."

The attendant gives me a sympathetic smile.

"What's your name, sir?"

"Felix Segrave."

He nods. "Yes, the ship alerted us that you hadn't returned."

"So they knew, and they left?"

"Ships are not permitted to depart past the scheduled time. By regulation."

"Can I get a water taxi to catch up with them? I'll pay, of course."

"No, sir. Passengers who fail to embark must meet the ship at the next port of call."

The next port of call is St. Martin, which is technically France. I'm fairly certain border control does not accept cruise ship wristbands as a form of ID.

"I'm sorry, but I don't have my passport," I say. "I *must* get back on that boat."

The man shakes his head. "You'll have to contact your embassy, in that case. I would be happy to provide you the phone number."

"This is absurd," I protest. "I can *see* the ship. It would take five minutes to get there by tender."

The man gives me an apologetic shrug. "I'm sorry. It's the policy."

I am about to argue that surely a policy that stipulates leaving a passenger stranded in a foreign country with no money or identification is a *very bad* policy when I hear a sharp intake of breath behind me.

I turn around to see a beautiful face.

A beautiful, tear-stained face half-hidden beneath a conch-themed sun hat. But not so hidden that I can't see the face is frozen in a rictus of loathing.

I gape at the woman who has arguably caused this whole misadventure.

"*You,*" she hisses.

"*You,*" I hiss back.

2

THE LOVE BOAT

Six Days Ago

SAN JUAN, PUERTO RICO

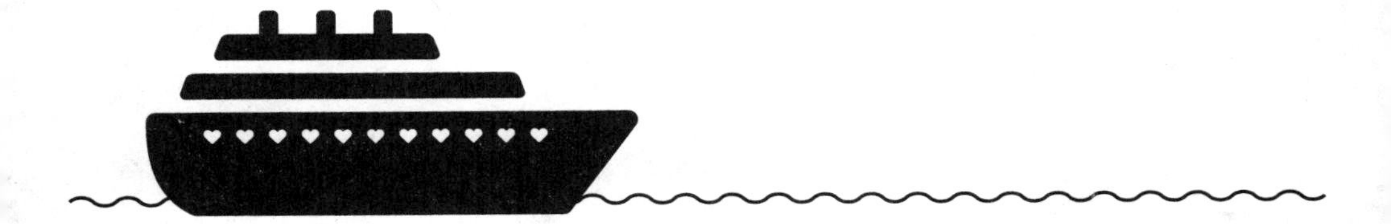

Wonders of the Caribbean, Day 1

Welcome aboard the *Romance of the Sea*!

We are delighted to welcome you to set sail on the adventure of a lifetime! First, check in to your luxurious stateroom, where your private butler will ensure we anticipate your every need. Have lunch at our elegant Windswept Room, where a gourmet buffet will tantalize every palate. At 16:00, meet your crew and fellow passengers at a champagne reception on the Lido Deck featuring the tropical notes of our talented seven-piece Seahorse Band. In the evening, dine at our five-star restaurant, The Starboard Room, or sample the Japanese delicacies at Inagi or the Northern Italian cuisine of Liguria, our signature restaurants. (Reservations required.) And of course, don't miss the electrifying musical revue, *Idols of the Stage*, at 21:00 in our state-of-the-art Cosmic Theater, featuring an all-star cast direct from the stages of Broadway!

We are honored to have you as our guest—and we hope you have a magnificent voyage!

Hope

Imagine being invited to join your best friend on an all-expenses-paid, ten-day tropical vacation. Picture visiting Caribbean islands, frolicking on white-sand beaches, enjoying luxury spa treatments, eating gourmet meals, sleeping in a sumptuous oceanside suite, and doing it all while your every whim is catered to by a personal staff.

Sounds dreamy, right?

Except there's a catch.

This trip will take place on a cruise ship.

And, you see, I am not a cruise ship person.

I'm terrified of norovirus, buffets put me on edge, and I really, really hate water slides.

And yet, here I am, in a taxi pulling into a port lined with gleaming white ships the size of New York City avenues.

Don't be negative, I coach myself. *You are going to fill your creative well with sunshine and luxury and bonding time with your best friend. You're going to stop thinking about Gabe. And then you are going to go home and mount your fucking comeback.*

"What cruise line?" our taxi driver asks.

"*Romance of the Sea*," Lauren, my best friend, says.

I cringe involuntarily, like I do every time she says the name of the boat out loud.

"Stop that," she says. "The name is cute. And oh my stars, look! There she is!" She gestures at the boat towering above us, its side emblazoned with a crest of two dolphins facing each other in the shape of a heart.

"Adorable," I say.

Lauren proceeds to whip out her phone and take a video of herself oohing and aahing over the ship—B-roll, I assume, for the fawning TikToks she's contractually obligated to make in exchange for our passage.

I paste a smile on my face and try not to think of the *Titanic*.

The cab stops at a sign for passenger check-in and a porter swoops in to help with our bags before we've even gotten out of the car.

"Thank you so much," I say, as he effortlessly lifts my beat-up suitcase and Lauren's three enormous Louis Vuitton trunks onto a cart.

"What did you pack in there?" I ask Lauren under my breath. "Your couch?"

"Mostly caftans and ball gowns," she says. "And, of course, camera equipment. Can't go anywhere without my ring light!"

"Naturally," I say.

"Is that an arch tone I detect, Miss Lanover? I thought we agreed you were going to impersonate a basic ass bitch and have fun drinking margs and rotting in the sun with your boobs out."

"Sorry," I say. "You're right. I am hereby excited and bubbly."

"I'm gonna hold you to that."

We make our way through security and are greeted by a man with a European accent and mannerisms so gracious you'd think he was greeting members of the royal family rather than a social media influencer and her plus-one. He inspects our documents and tells us what a fabulous time we will have, and how happy he and the rest of the crew are to host us for what he hopes will be the first of many trips.

Unlikely.

We are then escorted to a seating area to await our turn to board the ship. I gaze out at a sea of silver.

Hair, that is.

"Everyone here is like minimum sixty years old," I whisper to Lauren.

"Yes, darling. That's the point."

Lauren is here for a tactical reason. The *Romance of the Sea* has a new solo package for singles and she's doing a sponsored series on it. "Think about it," she explained to me when she pitched the idea of us going. "You're trapped on a ship for two weeks with eligible men. It's so smart. I'll probably meet my husband."

"Won't that put you out of business?" I ask.

Attempting to meet a husband—a rich husband—is, after all, her entire career.

Lauren Rose Mathison, @LaurenLuvRose to her fans, got her start starring in *Man of My Dreams*, a reality TV dating show in which female contestants submit a list of criteria for their ideal husbands, and are then marooned on an island with "matches" handpicked by producers. The catch? None of the girls know who among the corresponding suitors is their supposed soul mate.

Lauren did not choose correctly, but she did become the breakout star of the first season, after attesting in her charming Texas accent that her soul mate must be "hung like a horse and rich as hell." She parlayed her notoriety into influencer fame, posting tutorials on how to flirt and dress for maximum seductiveness and going on elaborate "missions" to find and fall in love with a wealthy bachelor. Her schemes have included taking lessons at luxury golf courses, moonlighting as a private jet flight attendant, attending cryptocurrency conferences, and infiltrating a high-stakes poker ring.

Before you call Gloria Steinem to complain about the death of feminism, please note that Lauren's schtick is tongue in cheek. Her videos have the breathless style of a reporter embedding herself into a high-stakes investigation and are performed with a wink.

"Oh stop," Lauren says to me. "I do want a husband, and anyway, not *everyone* is old." She subtly nods at a thirtyish Black couple in expensive-looking resort wear who radiate the glow of honeymoon bliss, and then at a pair of stylish white gay men who look about forty and have a toddler in a stroller.

"Token millennials," I say. "The exception that proves the rule."

"Oh look," she says. "Incoming, ten o'clock."

I follow her gaze to a group of four trim men in their fifties or sixties.

"No women with them, and they look moneyed," Lauren says. "And that one in the blue sport coat is super handsome. Maybe *you* should go for him."

"He's dressed like Thurston Howell III."

"Who?"

"The millionaire from *Gilligan's Island*."

"You say that like it's bad. That's our ideal target!"

"Speak for yourself. I'm here for the free shrimp cocktail."

"At least set your sights on lobster, sweetheart. This is a *luxury* cruise. And maybe you'll meet someone. A fling is just what you need to forget about Gabe."

"I'm very over Gabe," I lie.

"You're very not," she says. "You haven't gone on a single date since the breakup, and that was eight months ago."

Well, that's what happens when you fall madly in love with someone who wants to name your future babies on the third date, and then he breaks up with you two weeks after you move in together because he "realized he's not ready."

This type of behavior does not make a girl eager to race back to Bumble.

How do you cauterize a wound that goes so deep? Is it really so unnatural to miss someone you thought would be the father of your children, even if he hurt you?

I *am* moving on. It's just taking longer than Lauren would like.

The bigger problem is that ever since the breakup, I've felt flat. Uncreative. Unmotivated. Unsexual.

And my parents getting divorced is not helping.

But I'm ready to leave that behind. It's time to shake off my depression over my failed relationship and flagging career.

This trip is about recentering myself, powering up, and reminding myself I'm the kind of person who knows how to go for broke.

"I concede a fling might be good for me," I say. "But I'm not trying to canoodle with someone whose diapers I'll have to change in ten years."

"The kind of gentleman we're going for will be able to afford a private nurse for that," Lauren says. "And you'd be surprised at how well a seasoned man knows his way under the covers."

"Um . . . Noted, I guess."

Lauren scans the crowd for other potential suitors, identifying a well-heeled sexagenarian with twinkly blue eyes, a duo of middle-aged guys dressed in head-to-toe golf paraphernalia, and a strikingly handsome gentleman in stylish horn-rimmed glasses walking with an admittedly elegant cane.

And then she gasps.

"Oh my God, look," she whispers, gesturing with her chin toward the check-in desk. I follow her gaze to a middle-aged couple with two very attractive young blond women.

"Uh-oh," I say. "Competition?"

"Not them," she says in a low voice. "*Him*."

One of the girls steps aside, revealing a man who looks to be in his early thirties. He's medium-tall and wiry, with a mop of dark, wavy brown hair. His white T-shirt sets off the muscles of his shoulders and reveals rather artful line-drawn tattoos on his forearms.

He glances over his shoulder and catches me blatantly staring at him. I all but fling my eyeballs out of my head looking away and blush so hard my face stings.

Before Lauren can mock me further, a woman in a pressed white crew uniform walks toward us, smiling.

"Miss Mathison and Miss Lanover," she says. "It's my pleasure to invite you to board. Follow me." She gestures at the gangway, where a photographer is waiting by a step-and-repeat with the ship's cheesy logo.

"Would you like a complimentary portrait?" he asks as we approach.

"Oh, no thank—" I start to say, but Lauren beams at him.

"We'd love one," she says.

She strikes the practiced pose she knows sets off her best angle. I stand awkwardly a few inches away, hands shoved into the pockets of my vintage sailor shorts, waiting for this to be over.

Lauren grabs my arm and tugs me closer. "Tits up, chin to the side," she coaches me. "And smile with your eyes."

I attempt to obey her command as the flash goes off in my face, blinding me.

"Thank you!" Lauren chirps.

As we walk away, the family with the hot son steps forward to take our place.

"Try not to break the lens with the radiance of your poor disposition, Felix," one of the sisters (I assume they are sisters given they are nearly identical) says.

The boy smiles at her pleasantly. "If you continue to antagonize me I *will* see to it that you drown."

They both have British accents.

Oh, God.

Hot and *British*?

I'm the type of Brit Lit nerd who goes weak at the knees for an English accent.

Something inside me lights up for the first time in a very long time.

It takes me a moment to recognize it: attraction.

Lauren elbows me. "Told you."

Felix

I can't believe I agreed to this, I think as I step onto the cruise ship that will be home for the next ten days. It has the vibe of a Las Vegas casino crossed with a very posh care home for the elderly.

"We're on the *penthouse* level," my younger sister, Pear, says as we all pile into the lift to the staterooms. "Thank you, parents."

"If ever there was a time to splurge, it's now," Mum says. "Daddy and I will only have one fortieth anniversary."

"And God knows if we'll make it to fifty," my father says.

"Stop killing us off, Charles," Mum says fondly.

Mum and Dad are only sixty-eight, but Dad's been threatening their imminent demise for at least the last decade.

The lift stops and we emerge onto a plushly carpeted corridor lined with gilded watercolor paintings of the sea.

"We're this one," my older sister, Prue, says to Pear, pointing at the second door on the left. The two of them elected to share a room as their respective romantic partners, Eliza and Matty, were "too busy" to join us on holiday.

Clever Eliza and Matty.

"Let's all have a rest and meet for lunch at one, shall we?" Mum asks.

"See you then," I say.

I walk farther down the hallway, searching for my room, when two women about my age emerge from around a corner ahead of me.

"Eleven fifty-one," the taller of them—a willowy blonde with an exaggerated American twang—says. "Ah, here."

The other girl—the one I accidentally made eye contact with at check-in—nods. She's petite with a curvy figure, creamy white skin, a riotous mass of dark curls, and a sweet, heart-shaped face. I have a thing for curly hair and a thing for, well, curves. I duck into my room before they see me so I don't get caught looking at her again.

I enter a suite so palatial it borders on pornographic. There's a lounge opening onto an oceanfront terrace, a king-sized bedroom with a walk-in closet, and a huge marble bathroom. Everything is in tasteful shades of greige.

I'm accustomed to my parents' taste for luxury vacations—we grew up on first-class flights to the Maldives and Kenyan safaris—but this might top them all.

Someone knocks at the door.

I open it to find a smiling man in a dark suit holding a silver tray of fresh fruit.

"Mr. Segrave," he says warmly. "Welcome to the *Romance of the Sea*. I am Crisanto, and I'll be looking after you on your voyage as your personal butler. May I come in?"

"Of course," I say, moving aside. He sweeps in and places the fruit on my dining table.

"You are from London," he says. "A long journey."

"It was," I agree. He must have memorized the guest profile I filled out online. Impressive.

"Where are you from?" I ask.

"The Philippines, sir."

"Oh, please call me Felix," I say. I've never been particularly comfortable with the trappings of my parents' wealth. Making a butler address me as "sir" is more Little Lord Fauntleroy than I like.

"Very well, Mr. Felix," Crisanto says. "May I show you around your suite?"

"Sure."

He points out a phone where I can reach him and his colleagues twenty-four hours a day, then leads me to the minifridge and wet bar that's been stocked with beer, champagne, and wine.

I can only imagine how quickly my two-years-ago self would have obliterated it.

"A liquor menu is here if you desire—I am happy to bring you whatever you like," Crisanto says.

"No hard stuff, and actually, would you mind removing the wine?" I ask. "I'm more of a Coke Zero man."

Caffeine and nicotine gum are the two vices I've replaced booze and cigarettes with since getting sober. I consume them both with inadvisable voracity. I should probably give them up, given I'm constantly abuzz and have TMJ from all the chewing, but I'm nervous to shake any of the habits upon which I built my sobriety.

It took me too long to get here to risk it, and I've put my family and friends through too much.

A chime rings—the doorbell.

"Ah," says Crisanto, "that must be your room attendant. I'll introduce you."

He opens the door for a smiling young woman in a prim gray dress with a white apron.

"Mr. Felix, this is Belhina."

"Nice to meet you," I say.

"A pleasure," she says.

"Belhina will clean your room twice a day and see that you're comfortable," says Crisanto.

"How do you prefer your pillows, Mr. Felix?" she asks. "I'll bring you whatever you like—firm, goose down—"

"Oh, no worries," I say. "The ones on the bed are just the thing. But thank you."

"Very well, sir. But please let me know if you would like help unpacking your luggage."

"Thank you so much."

"We will leave you to get comfortable," Crisanto says. "Don't hesitate to let us know if there's anything we can assist you with."

"Will do, will do."

They show themselves out and I throw myself down on the bed, which is among the more comfortable surfaces on which I've ever rested my body. I groan in pleasure, then wonder if the neighbors will hear me through the wall and think I'm having a wank.

Probably not. This ship is too grand for thin walls. It's so hushed I can hear myself breathe.

I pull out my phone to check my messages—specifically to see if there's anything from Sophie, my operations manager, concerning my pubs. Like, for instance, that they've burned down in the first eighteen hours without me.

There isn't.

I'm a bit disappointed. I helicopter over my businesses, and fancy myself indispensable to their daily runnings. This is the first time I've left them unattended for more than two days in years.

I didn't want to. My mother coerced me, saying this anniversary trip might be our last chance to holiday as a family before everyone pairs off and has kids of their own.

I owe her too much to disappoint her, but breaking my routine for two weeks is the most frightening thing I've done since entering detox.

I decide to shower before lunch. I'm taken aback by the showerhead, which does an obscene swivel jet maneuver I'm sure several of my ex-girlfriends would have been intimately fond of.

It certainly takes my mind off my pubs.

I slather myself in sun cream and head upstairs to the Lido Deck, where a crowd of waiters in white are serving a handful of guests who have already set themselves up by the pool. (All of them are quite bronze already—it seems the elderly don't believe in SPF.)

I follow the signs to the restaurant, where I'm greeted by a buffet so epic its array of stations requires three rooms. I pass cheeses, a raw bar, salad, pasta à la minute, a lamb roast, and all manner of hot things I don't pause to identify, dished out by men in white chef's coats.

The restaurateur in me shudders at the idea of buffet food. All that labor and waste just to serve mediocre cuisine. But I force myself to withhold judgment. This is, at least, a very opulent spread.

"We're over here," one of my sisters calls. (They have the same voice, the way they have the same hair and figure and capacity for profiting from distressed debt.)

I notice they're sitting a few tables away from the two girls I saw in the hallway.

As I pass them, I hear the curly-haired one mutter "I hate buffets" to her friend.

Clearly, the woman has good taste.

Hope

"I can't believe you're complaining about too much food," Lauren says to me as I side-eye the buffet. "You *love* food."

"I like curated meals," I say. "Not the opportunity to eat camembert, mashed potatoes, and Singapore noodles on one plate, with a side of E. coli."

"Please. This place seems more sanitary than a doctor's office."

"That's because you go to that sketchy place in the dirty thirties."

"They do a fabulous Botox," she says.

"Your forehead does look like it came off an eight-year-old."

"Thank you! Anyway, go pillage the raw bar or something. You're the worst when you're hangry."

I get up to survey the fare. I decide not to risk raw cruise ship oysters, but reason that steamed crab legs probably won't compromise my intestinal tract.

I return to our table to find Lauren tearing into a steak—her primary food group.

"Look who just sat down," she says in what passes for sotto voce if you have the loudest voice in the world, which she does. "Behind you."

I glance over my shoulder to see the British family. I whirl my head back before I get caught looking, but not before clocking, with some disappointment, that the boy isn't with them.

"Don't worry," Lauren says. "He's at the salad bar."

He passes by us, and his plate looks like it was assembled by a professional chef. I would never have thought to dress salmon, feta, and beets with cilantro. I might copy it for my next course.

"I wonder if he happened to have some culinary tweezers in his pocket," I say.

"I wonder what else is in his pocket." She gives me a lascivious wink.

"Please stop before someone hears you."

"You know, the dad is handsome," she says. "Do you think I should seduce him? Then I could set you up with the hot boy and you could get married and I'd be your stepmother." She pauses. "I'd be *very* wicked."

"No, you'd be a great bonus mom to a trio of devastated adult children. So wholesome."

She goes on about the other potentially eligible men in the room, but I'm only half listening because I'm concentrating on extracting the meat from my crab legs, which are buttery and delicious. In my enthusiasm I use too much force and a shell goes flying.

I yelp, turn around, and see it has landed . . . directly in the British guy's hair.

"Oh my God," I cry, leaping up and dashing over to him. "I'm so sorry!"

Instinctively I reach to pick out the shards from his hair, then retract my hand because *what* am I doing?

He gives me a slightly crooked smile, removes them himself, and hands the whole mess back to me.

"Thanks," he says, "but I actually prefer my food plated."

His sisters are laughing uproariously.

"How brilliant of you," one of them says to me. "He deserves it. He's awfully vain about his hair."

"Says the one who gets four-hundred-quid haircuts," he shoots back.

"Can I get you a napkin?" I ask him.

He shakes his head. "You're good. Don't worry. Nothing that hasn't happened before."

"He's a chef," the other sister says. "You wouldn't believe the things he gets all over himself."

"*Offal*," the other sister whispers theatrically. "That means *organs*."

"I'm sure she knows what it means," he says.

"I'm Pear, by the way," she says. "Pear Segrave. And this is my sister, Prue, and our parents, Mary and Charles. And of course you've met Felix here."

They all murmur pleasantries at once.

"Nice to meet you," I say. "I'm Hope."

Lauren has at this point come to join me, and adds, "And I'm Lauren. I'll try to help Hopie here with her aim next time she attempts to eat a crustacean."

Mary laughs. She's plump and pretty, like her daughters, and has a lovely, warm laugh that makes me think of Christmas and hot apple cider.

It makes me long for my own mother, back when my mother was happy.

"We'll be sure to sit far away in the dining room this evening," Charles says.

"Where are you girls from?" Mary asks.

"New York," I say.

"By way of Texas," Lauren says.

"Um, not me. Vermont."

"Where," the one named Prue asks, "is Vermont?"

"Nowhere important," Lauren says at the exact moment I say, "Just below the Canadian border, by Montreal."

"I *love* Montreal," Prue exclaims. "Have you had poutine? Felix does an excellent poutine at his pub. He makes the cheese curds himself."

"Ugh," Pear groans. "Don't say curd. It's a sickening word, isn't it?"

"Where are you all from?" Lauren says, as she has the social graces that seem to have deserted me in my humiliation.

"London," Prue says. "Though Mum and Dad have decamped off to Hampshire in their dotage. Horribly dull of them."

"Well, we'll leave you to your lunch," I say. "Very nice to meet you, and Felix, I'm sorry again about—"

He shakes his head and gives me an affable smile. "It was my pleasure," he says. "But avoid the scampi. No one wants to be pelted with prawn heads."

"You got it," I say.

Before I can be even more awkward, I turn around and return to my seat.

"I can't believe I just did that," I whisper.

"Actually, it was smart," Lauren whispers back. "Now you've broken the ice with him and I won't have to drag you by your armpits to introduce yourself."

"Yeah, instead he'll think of me as the socially inept girl who threw food in his hair."

"Nah," Lauren whispers. "I think he liked you. Did you see the way he smiled? Maybe I won't have to break up the family to get you laid after all."

Felix

It would be an understatement to say I don't care for musical theater. Inviting me to a show at the West End is the fastest way to get a "no" out of my mouth. So, of course, when Prue grabs my hand after supper and announces we're on our way to a Broadway revue, I pry my fingers away.

Pear comes at me from the other side with a death grip on my bicep.

"You *are* coming, dear brother," she says. "You are coming to *everything*."

"Yes," Prue says. "You are going to have *fun* on this trip, or we'll make you walk the plank."

"You wouldn't like maritime jail, I'm sure," I say. "Let me go."

"Oh, I wouldn't get caught. There are *many* unexplained deaths at sea. It's the dark underbelly of the cruise ship world," says Pear. "I read about it in *The Guardian*."

"How tragic," Prue singsongs. "Darling Felix drowned at sea, just like that. Who will take over his pubs?"

"We'll sell them to Pizza Express," Pear says decisively.

"Even you would not turn my life's work into a chain restaurant," I say.

"Oh, I would. Very good ROI."

My sisters are experts in complicated investment-oriented things I read about with minimal comprehension in the *Financial Times*. They're famous in the City of London for their genius aptitude for investing, not to mention their matching blond beauty. They are Dad's pride and joy, while I'm his black sheep who eschewed university in order to "faff about in the pub."

My two gastropubs are both raved about and profitable, but he'll never forgive me for not wanting to raise hundreds of millions of dollars to "reinvigorate failing legacy brands," or whatever it is that he and my sisters are so good at.

It doesn't help that I agonized my family with my drinking, and the fallout, for two decades.

"Fine," I say to my sisters. "I'll withstand a few minutes of show tunes if it means I can end this abuse."

"The show is an hour," Prue trills. "You're going to love it."

We go into a large, dark theater with deep velvet couches arranged around cocktail tables. A waiter comes to take our order. The girls get Manhattans and I order a double espresso and pop a nicotine gum. I'll need fortification to get through this.

The girl who threw crab in my hair at lunch—Hope—sits down with her friend on the sofa in front of us. Prue jabs me in the rib with her elbow.

"Look," she whispers. "It's the pretty crab girl."

I edge away. "I'm going to be bruised tomorrow from all of your manhandling."

"Go cry in the infirmary. Maybe there will be a fit nurse to bandage you up. A little shag would be good for you."

"Please don't talk to me about shagging."

Pear is reading the program for the show and distracts Prue with some babble about Andrew Lloyd Webber.

I hear the American girls chatting in front of us. I lean in slightly. Eavesdropping is rude but I'm curious what two young, beautiful women are doing on a cruise for sixty-year-olds.

"Guess what?" the blond one says. "That handsome Swedish guy, Lucas, asked me to meet him for a drink in the Largo Lounge at eleven while you were in the bathroom."

"Well done," says Hope.

"Ooh, look," the friend says, gesturing at the program. "They're doing a medley from *Chicago*. Don't you just die for Bob Fosse?"

"As discussed, at length, I do not love any musical theater and am here against my will."

"Same," I want to say. But that would reveal that I'm spying on them.

The theater darkens and a man in a crisp white uniform with ostentatious gold epaulets walks onstage in the glow of a spotlight and welcomes us to the show, which he assures us features the finest performers fresh off the stages of Broadway.

He's not lying, as far as I can tell. The singers are spectacular, if you like that kind of thing, and the dancers so lithe and acrobatic that for a minute I forget that I hate this. I would have thought that the cast of a floating theater troupe would be made up of the desperate and talentless, but even I can tell these people are *good.* Not to mention attractive. I work out religiously, but their musculature makes me question the skill of my trainer.

I'm intrigued enough by the mechanics of the performance to make it through excerpts from *Cabaret* and *Phantom of the Opera*, but I draw the line at *The Lion King.*

"See you in the morning," I whisper to Pear. Luckily, even she would not interrupt "I Just Can't Wait to Be King," so I slip out without protest.

As I reach the doors, I sense someone behind me.

I look over my shoulder.

It's Hope.

We both step out of the theater and into the bright lights of the corridor.

She gives me a little wave, wincing against the glare.

As my eyes adjust I see what she's wearing—a retro turquoise cocktail dress that is not obviously clingy but shows off her figure remarkably well. It's prim and alluring at once—something like Joan from *Mad Men* would wear. (I harbor filthy thoughts about Joan from *Mad Men.*)

"Slipping out?" I ask.

"Couldn't take it," she says. Then she seems to feel bad about the bluntness of this statement because she adds, "Sorry. They're very good, but I'm not a musical theater person."

"None taken." I lower my voice. "Can't stand the stuff."

"Sorry again about throwing crab in your hair," she says. "I've never done that before."

"It would be far more impressive if you had."

"Oh, well I can try again tomorrow, if you want."

"I do, actually. The shampoo on this boat is tip-top. Smells like the ocean, you know."

I don't know why I'm suddenly speaking like an Edwardian countess. Am I nervous?

She doesn't seem to notice.

"I love that fake ocean smell," she agrees. "So refreshing."

I like her—she's very dry for an American, and dry is my type. I'm almost about to ask if she'd like to take a stroll on the deck—get some air to shake off the show tunes—when her friend comes bounding out of the theater.

"Hopie!" she exclaims. "You escaped!"

"Headache," Hope says. "I'm gonna call it an early night."

Her friend looks at me. "She's lying. Tell her to go back in."

I raise my hands innocently. "I'd never force show tunes on anyone."

Hope grins at me. "Have a good evening, Felix. If you go back in now, you can probably still catch the medley from *Cats*."

As they disappear, I'm suddenly grateful to be on a cruise ship. Because in the absence of anywhere else for either of us to go, I know I'll see Hope again.

And I want that quite badly.

3

A SUPPOSEDLY FUN THING I'LL NEVER DO AGAIN

Wonders of the Caribbean, Day 2

Enjoy your first day at sea!

Today the *Romance of the Sea* sails the aquamarine waters of the Caribbean. We invite you to enjoy the sweeping views of one of the world's most beautiful seas from our Panorama Lounge, where our staff awaits to pamper you with drinks and gourmet snacks. Our bridge instructor Alan will be on hand for those in the mood for a tutorial, as will our photography guru Clemence, should you wish to improve your skills behind the lens. Or perhaps you prefer to bask in the sunshine on the Lido Deck with a fluffy towel and a cold drink, take in a game of pickleball, or enjoy the array of events that await to amuse, entertain, and enrich you. (You'll find a detailed schedule on your personal in-room tablet.)

And don't miss this evening's electrifying performance, *Dancing the Night Away*, in the Cosmic Theater. But don't stay up too late—for tomorrow we set out for our first adventure on land as we stop on the gorgeous shores of Antigua. (Remember to book your excursions at the Concierge Desk by 16:00.)

Have a wonderful day!

Hope

I'm having quite a nice dream about sunbathing on a beach with a rangy tattooed man with floppy brown hair when the blaring of my phone jolts me awake.

It's a ringtone that cannot be ignored: the one I have assigned to my boss, Magda.

I yank off my sleep mask and look at my phone. It's ten thirty, making it six thirty a.m. in New York. Either she's up uncharacteristically early or, more likely given her party girl lifestyle, she hasn't gone to bed yet.

I accept the call. "Hey, Magda," I say with the extremely false cheer I, and all my colleagues, use to address her. "What's up?"

"Hope, hi," she says in her breathy voice. "Do you have the Conifer Games press release ready to go?"

"Um, yes," I say. "It's in your inbox. I sent it Friday before I left. For vacation."

"Ah, right, you're away. I don't see it, can you resend?"

I scowl and shake my head while brightly chirping, "Sure, no problem."

"And we'll need the media list finalized by tomorrow. You have that, right?"

I freeze. At no point in the last two weeks of me rushing to get all the deliverables done for this project did she mention my being responsible for the media list.

Not that she'll care. Forgetting last-minute deadlines is her specialty. As is foisting her work on other people.

"Oh," I say, "I assumed that was done."

"Never assume, Hope," she says. "You should be all over this."

"I'll have Lana put one together," I say. Lana, our publicity assistant, is very capable of the task. She actually *wants* to work in gaming PR, unlike, say, me.

I don't want to work in any form of PR. But shilling iPhone games for app developers is right at the bottom of the list.

"Fine, just be sure to check it before you shoot it over to me," Magda says. "Rockabye is a *very* important launch for the client."

"Yep, of course," I say.

"Great. Have a nice trip. Where are you? Greece?"

"Um, no. The Caribbean."

"Lovely. Bye."

She hangs up.

Lauren is glaring at me from her bed.

"Was that your boss?"

"Yep."

"You have to be kidding me. She just gave you work on vacation?"

"Yep."

"Can't you say no?"

"Nope." I need this job. I'm financially depleted from my breakup, and my résumé is a mess from bopping around from role to role for years. Magda can smell my desperation and liberally takes advantage of it. She "delegates" so much work to me that at this point I'm doing at least half her job.

"I'm going back to bed," I say, jamming a pillow over my face to block out the aggressive glare of the sunlight reflecting off the ocean.

"No you're not," Lauren singsongs. "We have aquacise in half an hour."

"Aquacise? Are you joking? Can't we just sleep until noon and then lay out on deck chairs and read books?"

She comes over and pries the pillow off my face. I shout and turn over.

"Come on, up and at 'em, sunshine. I've already done a livestream and gone to breakfast. Met an oil man from Houston named Cliff. Bald with good glasses."

One of Lauren's lessons to her followers is to cultivate a taste for bald men.

"Well, go flirt with him. Have his babies. I don't care, just let me sleep."

"Hope, aquacise is an excellent opportunity to show off our bods. Look, I brought you a latte. Oat milk and two sugars, just the way you like it."

I grudgingly accept the beverage.

"I hate exercise classes," I say.

"Oh, come on. This is in a pool. It's forty-five minutes. And we'll look very alluring and find men to have affairs with."

"Who am I going to have an affair with when you've already cornered every single man on the ship?" I ask.

"Not true. I saw you flirting with Felix last night."

I admit it, I was flirting. That kind of energy hasn't bubbled up in me in months. It felt good.

Especially because, if I'm not mistaken, he was flirting back.

This does nothing to increase my desire to wake up for pool aerobics.

But I know Lauren's not going to relent, so I drag myself out of bed and onto the balcony to sit in the sun with my coffee while she changes. The bright light and stunning view of the ocean wake me up.

Cruises do have their upside.

Lauren sticks her head out the door. She's wearing a white string bikini with bottoms that barely cover her spray-tanned ass.

"You're wearing that to work out?" I ask.

"The point is to see and be seen, my dear innocent. Can't do that in a Speedo. Unless you're a man of course. With a nice package."

I don't have the energy to talk about men's packages before lunch, so I refrain from commenting. I go inside and pull a black-and-white, polka-dot one-piece from my bag. It's got a retro vibe and a ruched waist that flatters my figure. It's not exactly sportswear, but it's more appropriate than my other option—a crimson bikini that hoists up my boobs in such an aerodynamic way it borders on the obscene. I do not wear two-pieces—since puberty, I've had the kind of breasts that precede you in a room and give you back problems. Lauren, who is flat-chested, is obsessed with them and often sneaks up on me and pokes them when I'm not looking. It is she, in case you did not predict this, who sourced and purchased the bikini.

"You're wearing *that* one?" she pouts when I emerge from the bathroom.

"Yes. If I try to exercise in the other one I'll drown."

"Good. Then some handsome man will try to save you."

"And his elderly back will go out and we'll *both* drown."

"Come on, Miss Priss. We'll be late."

The Lido Deck is not nearly as deserted as I would have imagined at eight a.m. To Lauren's delight, the group of four gentlemen we saw checking in are stationed near the pool, finishing breakfast. She waves at them—she made sure to introduce herself at the champagne reception yesterday—and you can almost feel the effort it takes them not to gawk at her body as they wave back. (I will spare you a description of Lauren's physique. Let's just say Peloton and Tracy Anderson have both done brand collaborations.)

She goes straight over to them and hands the tallest one her phone. "Todd! Hi! Would you mind taking a picture of us?"

I glare at her. She knows I hate being photographed. Especially in a bathing suit. Especially by a stranger.

"It would be my pleasure," he says, looking delighted at this opportunity to stare at a gorgeous woman in a string bikini.

And me, I guess.

"Thank you so much. We want to document every minute of our trip. We're having *so* much fun, aren't you?"

"Time of my life," Todd says. "And it's only day two."

Yep. Eight to go.

Have fun, I remind myself. *Free. Vacation.*

Lauren throws her arm around me.

"Smile, girls," Todd says.

Lauren flirts with the camera—and therefore Todd—and I try not to roll my eyes. My only consolation is that I have made Lauren solemnly swear never to post photos of me on the internet.

I hate social media, and I refuse to be B-roll.

"I took a selection," Todd says. "You look great."

"You're so sweet," Lauren says.

She pauses thoughtfully.

"Actually, would it be too much trouble to take a quick video of us while we're exercising?"

This is one of the lessons she's always reinforcing on TikTok—find a way to get a captive audience. Now he'll have a free pass to watch her as she gambols about in the water.

"Of course," Todd says, seeming genuinely honored.

By the pool, a group of mostly women are chatting with an instructor in a modest one-piece handing out pool noodles. Here I will digress to say that if you're imagining out-of-shape middle-agers, this is not that crowd. The vast majority of the people on this ship are nipped, tucked, and exercised into the picture of late-in-life fitness. I suspect they will be much better than me with the pool noodles.

"Hi there!" Lauren says to the instructor. "We're here for aquacise."

"Welcome, girls!" she says. "I'm Sue, the fitness officer. We have a few minutes. Let's all do some stretching while we're waiting for the others."

She leads us in shoulder rolls, backbends, and toe-touches, which Lauren uses to waggle her ass in the air.

"Ready to get in the pool?" Sue calls.

"Yes!" everyone choruses back.

I'm expecting we'll tread water or something—how strenuous can pool aerobics be?—but she starts us with a high-knee jog under water, which requires you to hoist your legs up all the way to your sternum.

It's really, really hard.

"A little faster now!" Sue coaches. "Kick those legs out behind you. Work those quadriceps!"

I don't know what quadriceps are, but I do know I'm not enjoying "working them." She makes us add our arms—clapping underwater—then makes us swivel to stretch out our hips, then squat to activate our hamstrings. By the time this sequence is fully underway I'm out of breath, and it's only been five minutes.

"Now grab your noodles, everyone," Sue calls. "Time to pick up the pace!"

I glance around for someone to commiserate with, but my fellow exercisers all look excited to increase the misery.

"Let's do some jumping jacks!" Sue says. She folds her noodle into an arch and starts leaping up and down.

"How is this so difficult?" I pant to Lauren.

"It's not," she says, flashing a big grin at Todd, who's recording this diligently.

"It's killing my legs," I say.

"If you smile it will be easier."

"That would expend energy I don't have."

Sue adds in turns, lunges, leg tucks. At this point we're making such a ruckus that most of the assembled denizens of the pool deck are watching us. It must be quite a show, because many of them are smirking.

Including, I notice with horror, Felix.

He's sitting in the shade in swim trunks and a T-shirt reading a book, but he catches me glancing at him. He arches one brow at me as if to say, "Oh, is this what you're into? Very cool stuff."

"Higher!" Sue shouts. "Last set, make it count!"

I don't want to be seen being *bad* at jumping over a pool noodle, so I leap up with more force than I've used in the whole class.

One of my entire breasts bounces out of the top of my bathing suit.

Like the whole fucking thing.

The correct thing to do in this instance would be to duck underwater before anyone notices, but the problem is I'm still holding a pool noodle under my body.

So what I actually do is squawk and drop the noodle, which flies up out of the water and bounds into my face—all while my boob bounces around and I try to catch it and shove it back into my suit. Which is not easy as the top is tightly boned for support and I have to flatten my breast like I'm preparing for a mammogram.

Lauren has noticed my struggle—as has, I assume, most of the people within a fifty-foot radius—and, helpfully, is doubled over with laughter.

I shove myself back into a semi-clothed state but I know—I *know*—that Felix caught this whole incident.

Sue is pretending nothing has happened and is shouting out cool-down instructions, but I've had enough aquacise for one lifetime. I doggy paddle to the steps and pull myself out.

I would like to run off to my room in shame, but I'm soaking wet, out of breath, and don't want to abandon my stuff. Which, conveniently, I left on a chair a few feet away from where Felix is sitting. And in the interim between spotting him and making my grand display, he has removed his shirt.

He's all lean muscle and those sexy tattoos, and I find him *incandescently* hot.

I grit my teeth and wave.

Felix

Hope is heading straight for me, hair clinging to her neck and swim costume askew. She looks like a voluptuous, angry, wet Labradoodle.

I hope she's not angry at *me*.

I didn't *mean* to look at her topless. It was just that I happened to be looking in her direction, and the whole slow-motion disaster was so riveting it was impossible to turn away.

That, and her breast was magnificent.

She stops four chairs over and I realize she doesn't have a towel. I spring up to offer her my unused one.

"Thanks," she says, taking it. "Did you see that?"

"See what?" I ask innocently.

She rolls her eyes at me. "Uh-huh."

"Right. Fair. I think everyone saw it," I admit.

"Humiliating," she says.

"Just a wobble."

"Literally."

She towels off and sinks down in her chair. She's incredibly pale, in a nice milky way that contrasts with her dark hair.

"Was it at least a bit of fun?"

"Exposing myself?"

"Aquacizing."

"Well, I learned it's possible to sweat in a swimming pool."

"The wonders of homeostasis."

She rummages in her bag to pull out suncream and shades, which I take as my cue to leave her alone.

I return to my book.

"Oh my God," she says suddenly. "Are you reading *Middlemarch*?"

"Uh, yeah," I say.

She holds up a fat, tattered paperback. It's also *Middlemarch*.

"Oh shit," I say. "You too?"

"It's my favorite book! This is my mother's copy from when she was in college. She almost named me Dorothea."

"A bullet narrowly dodged."

"Have you read it before?"

"First timer."

"Ooh. What part are you on?"

"Casaubon's dying. And not a moment too soon, in my opinion."

She laughs. "Just you wait. He gets worse."

"No spoilers, please. I'm reading it for the thrills."

"You don't like it?"

"I love it, actually. I'm trying to get through the classics, belatedly. Just finished *Anna Karenina* and was looking for something a bit more uplifting."

"You must love a doomed bourgeois marriage."

"Very much."

"Not based on experience, I hope," she says. And then she winces. "Sorry. That was rude."

"Not at all." I hold up my bare ring finger. "I'm as yet unwed."

"Ah," Hope says.

She doesn't seem to know what to say next and I don't want to stop talking to her so I say: "Are you?"

"Unhappily married?" she asks.

"Divorced."

"Neither," she says, "but I'm young yet."

"Compared to the rest of the chaps on this boat, anyway."

She laughs. She has a great laugh—full and earthy.

"So do you read a lot of nineteenth-century literature?" she asks, gesturing back at my book.

"I do lately. I started last year with the Brontës, then moved on to Jane Austen. Dickens will be next, when I finish the greatest hits of George Eliot."

"Oh, you have so much to look forward to!" she says. "I'm a massive Brit Lit nerd. Studied it in college."

I'm immediately self-conscious. As a man who did not even get through his A-levels in a family of people who all went to Cambridge and Oxford, I am, I'll admit, insecure about my intellectual interests. It's not that I don't think I'm smart. It's just that I know I'm not educated.

"Flattered on behalf of my culture," I say.

"It's funny we both have actual books. I usually read in audio."

"Me too," I say. "Gives me something to focus on while I'm cooking."

"Same."

"You cook?" I ask.

"Well, not professionally, but I love it. It relaxes me."

"What do you do professionally?"

"This and that," she says, waving away the question. "Nothing interesting. Mostly PR." She says this apologetically, like her job is embarrassing. "I'd much rather be a chef. Sounds exciting."

"It has its pleasures. Next time you're in London you can come by one of my pubs and I'll put you to work in the kitchen."

"I wish," she says. "I haven't been there since grad school. Haven't been abroad at all, actually."

"You're abroad now, I think. International waters."

"Soaking up the rich culture of this cruise ship, yes," she says, gesturing at our elderly compatriots sleeping in their lounge chairs.

"Well, don't discount the excursions," I say. "You can absorb the vibrant culture of luxury beach clubs. What are you planning on doing—"

I'm trying to see if she's going on any of the scheduled outings at port, so I could perhaps conveniently join her, but her friend comes bounding toward us and plops down at Hope's feet.

"Felix!" she says. "It is Felix, right?"

"Indeed. And you're . . ." I wince. I don't remember her name.

"Lauren," she provides, unoffended. "I'm starving after that. Want to join us for brunch?"

I consider accepting even though I gorged myself on (very good) pastries an hour ago, but I don't want to come on too strong.

Or maybe I'm just nervous.

It's been years since I've had a crush on a girl.

"I'll leave you to it," I say. "I've already eaten."

Hope starts gathering her things.

"Nice chatting," I say to her.

She smiles at me. "Yeah, see you around." She gestures with her chin at my book. "Can't wait to hear what you think of the ending."

I've never wanted to finish a novel so badly in my life.

I spend a few hours reading and pounding back iced teas. Hope is correct that Casaubon gets worse—the bloke is even a controlling asshole from the grave. Why is everyone in nineteenth-century novels so miserable?

By midday it's grown intolerably hot, even in the shade. I'm about to pack up and retreat to my room when my entire family comes down the staircase from the Recreation Deck, dressed in tennis whites.

"We just bollocksed the girls at doubles," Dad reports to me cheerfully.

Prue and Pear both scowl at him.

"Unfair victory," Pear says.

"The wind was against us," Prue adds.

Prue and Pear hate losing at anything.

"No whinging, girls. We handed you your arses," Mum says.

"I believe I saw beginner lessons offered with the pro on the activities schedule," I say to my sisters. "Maybe a refresher course on the fundamentals will help you beat our elderly parents?"

"No time," Pear says, her demeanor transforming from sullen to puckish. "We're taking our brother to cha-cha lessons, remember?"

"I remember informing you that won't be happening."

I, emphatically, do not dance.

"Let's all go!" my mother exclaims. "Cha-cha! How fun. When's the class?"

"Two o'clock," Pear says. "Just enough time for us to have lunch first."

Pear leads us to Picante, the "Latin fusion" bistro. It has surprisingly authentic tapas.

"Don't eat too much," Prue says as I reach for a third ham croquette. "You'll be too bloated to move and embarrass yourself in front of the gentlemen ambassadors."

"Gentlemen ambassadors?" I ask.

"You know! The men they pay to entertain single ladies on the cruise."

"Saucy," my father observes. "Behave yourself, Mary."

"Don't worry about me, darling," Mum says mildly. "You're the only man I want to fraternize with."

My sisters and I exchange long-suffering looks. Our parents love to traumatize us by alluding to their sexual chemistry.

"Anyway, let's get going or we'll be late for our lessons," Prue says.

"Fine," I concede. "I want to see the moment you decide to leave Matty for a gentleman cruise ambassador."

"I would only leave Matty for the captain. Did you see him at the welcome reception? So handsome in his epaulets."

"You do love seamen," I say, because the joke writes itself.

"Yes, Felix, I do," she says. "Would you like me to tell you just how much—"

"No, I rescind the comment. Let's go."

We take the lift to an expansive lounge with a panoramic view of the sea. In the middle of the room is a grand piano and a gleaming parquet dance floor. Two of the glossy, impossibly fit dancers from last night's musical performance are standing at the center, in salsa outfits, chatting with a group of mostly older women, with a few men mixed in. Another group, a passel of attractive elderly gentlemen in blazers with name tags, stands by the piano.

"Those must be the ambassadors," Prue whispers to me. "Go see if one of them will be your date."

"Hello, everyone!" the female dancer says into a wireless microphone. "I am Svetlana, and this is my colleague, Sergio. Please, gather round."

We walk to the dance floor and listen attentively as Svetlana and Sergio explain the origins of the dance and the basic steps.

"It's a Cuban dance similar to salsa, so if you already know salsa, you're in luck," Svetlana says.

I guess I'm not in luck.

"The dance gets its name from the sound of our steps—*cha cha cha*—when we do the core triple step," Sergio says. He and Svetlana demonstrate a back-and-forth shuffle.

"Just like this," Svetlana says, doing it again. "Easy!"

It does not look easy. My mother forced us all to take dance lessons as kids. As with most structured education, I failed miserably and dropped out.

I'm about to leave when a familiar Texas drawl calls, "Oh no, are we too late?" I look away from the dancers to see Lauren and Hope rushing in.

Hope is wearing a short, red polka-dot sundress that looks right out of a 1950s pinup calendar, with her curly hair piled on top of her head. It's all I can do not to stare.

"You're just in time," Sergio says to the girls. "Please, come join us."

They make us practice the steps, all of us calling out "cha cha cha" as we move on the balls of our feet.

Most everyone picks it up quickly. Hope, I notice, takes to it naturally.

I, however, am baffled.

"Beautiful! Well done!" Svetlana exclaims, like we're toddlers she's very proud of. "Now everyone pair off, and we will practice."

I skulk off behind the piano, alone. We're an odd number, so I'm hoping this is my excuse not to embarrass myself. But Svetlana comes over and offers to partner up with me.

Maybe this will be less disastrous under the direct tutelage of the instructor.

Sergio calls out time as we all practice the moves to music.

"Forward one, two, three, *cha cha cha*, forward six, seven, eight, *cha cha cha*. Left side, one, two, three, *cha cha cha*. Repeat right, two, three, *cha cha cha*."

Combining these movements makes absolutely no sense to me. Sergio may as well be demonstrating how to perform knee replacement surgery for all I am able to replicate the process.

Svetlana's Slavic stoicism is impressive, but she's beginning to look as miserable as I feel.

I decide to leave, if only to spare her.

But I feel a tap on my shoulder.

"May I cut in?" Hope asks Svetlana.

No woman has ever dropped my hand so fast.

Hope

"Thanks," Felix says to me. "But you don't want to do this."

"On the contrary," I say.

I love dancing, I'm good at it, and after embarrassing myself in front of him at the pool, I want to prove I am not a fumbling klutz at everything I attempt.

"I can't dance," he says.

"I can see that. May I?" I offer him my hand.

He reluctantly takes it. "If you must."

I weave his fingers between mine and guide him to rest his other hand on my hip.

I'm momentarily distracted by how good it feels to be touched by him.

He glances up into my eyes. I wonder if he feels the spark too.

"My hand is sweating," he says apologetically. "From stress."

"First of all," I say, "stop caring about this. It's a dance lesson on a cruise ship. The stakes are low."

"Not if I stomp on your foot and break it."

"Surely the infirmary has wheelchairs. Now then. I'll lead."

"Please do."

"Every time I tap your left hip"—I demonstrate—"put your left foot back. And every time I squeeze your hand, right leg."

"Perhaps even I can handle this level of simplicity," he says, following my instructions.

"Beautiful work," I say. "You'll be on *Dancing with the Stars* in no time."

"Oh good. That's my dream."

"I thought so. Next we do the same thing except side to side. Ready?"

"Ha."

I count out "one, two, three" and guide him. He gets confused and steps forward instead of sideways, bumping into me.

I laugh. "Your other sideways."

"You seem to be enjoying this," he observes.

"I like bossing men around. Okay, now we'll try the 'cha cha cha' step. Are you ready?"

"No. It makes absolutely no sense to me."

"It's three steps on two counts," I explain. "But you don't actually move your feet. You just balance on the balls of them." I demonstrate, shuffling my weight. "See?"

"Cha cha cha," he says darkly. But he dutifully attempts the move, and I nod approvingly.

"Perfect. Now we put it together."

We practice about fourteen times until, between my taps and squeezes and whispers, he gets it down well enough to complete the full sequence without stumbling.

"Look at you!" I say. "You're a natural. Now we're going to put our hips into it and do the dance with the Cuban flair our Slavic teachers are so good at. And let's be daring and try doing it to the actual beat of the music."

I hold up my hand, listening for the rhythm. When the right note sounds, I nod at him, tap his hip, and step to the side.

Miraculously, he does the whole thing correctly.

He grins.

We're kind of getting into it, hips brushing near each other's quite pleasantly, when the music stops. Felix looks a little disappointed.

I hope it's because it means he is going to have to stop touching me.

"Thanks," he says. "That was almost . . ."

"Enjoyable?" I provide.

"Yes, weirdly."

"We'll have to come back for ballroom. I'll teach you to waltz."

"Oof," he says. "Hard pass."

"Break my heart."

We're still holding hands.

From across the room, Lauren catches my eye and nods approvingly.

I'm beginning to agree with her: maybe I *do* want to have an affair on a cruise ship.

It's on the tip of my tongue to ask Felix to go with me to the ice cream parlor. This is something the old, charming, confident Hope would do: ask a boy on a date.

But just then Felix's sisters come up, chattering about which one of them is a better dancer, and he gets pulled into the conversation, asserting that *he* is in fact the best dancer.

I feel self-conscious asking him out in front of an audience, so I wave goodbye and invite Lauren to ice cream instead.

I order vanilla soft serve in a cone with rainbow sprinkles—my go-to since childhood—but Lauren takes her time sampling dark chocolate huckleberry crunch, coconut key lime swirl, and crème fraiche with salted caramel.

"I'll let you in on a secret," says an Irish voice from behind us. We turn around to see a grinning man built like a bullfighter. He looks to be in his forties, and has dark, silver-flecked hair, playful arched eyebrows, and the twinkliest blue eyes I've ever seen.

"Please," Lauren breathes, instantly going into ingenue mode at the sight of a handsome stranger.

"The pistachio Stracciatella is the best I've ever had," he says.

"Oh, amazing," she coos. "I'll have a cup of that," she tells the clerk.

"Best get two scoops," says the man.

"So we can share?" she asks innocently.

He laughs from deep in his barrel chest. "I'm afraid I'll be needing my own."

We take our ice cream and sit down at a table by the open windows to catch a breeze.

"That man is giving me Tom Selleck and I'm obsessed," Lauren whispers.

"He is kind of hot," I agree.

"I'm going to invite him over here," she says.

"I had no doubt."

As soon as he accepts his ice cream from the clerk, she waves him down.

"You were right," she calls out. "This is transcendent."

He grins. "I aim to please."

"Come join us,"

He ambles over, openly delighted by the invitation. I notice he's not wearing a wedding ring.

"Colin," he says.

"Lauren. And this is Hope.

"I like your accent, Lauren," he says.

"Oh, no, I speak like a yokel," she says with a laugh, even though she's well aware that her drawl is part of her charm. "You can take the girl out of Texas, but you can't take the damn Lone Star twang out of the girl."

"Texas, you say," he says. "Whereabouts?"

"Outside of Waco. But Hope and I live in New York now. What about you? Is that an Irish brogue I detect?"

"'Tis that. I'm from a little town near Cork you wouldn't have heard of."

"And what do you do in a little town near Cork?" she asks.

"I make whiskey."

"I love Irish whiskey!" she exclaims. "I prefer it to Scotch. Too peaty. What's it called?"

"Killcurragh," he says.

"Well, color me purple. It just so happens that's my favorite."

He laughs. "Is it?"

"It is now," she says.

He cracks an infectious grin. "I'd forgive you if you've never heard of it. I've only been at it six years or so. I sold my company, left Dublin to look after my mam, and needed something to do to keep from going mental."

"You'll have to give me a tour next time I'm across the pond."

"You often find yourself passing through County Cork, do you?"

"Constantly," she says. She licks her ice cream off the back of her spoon like a cat.

She's clearly enjoying herself, and he is clearly eating it up.

"Well now, Lauren and Hope, I'm late to meet the lads for a game of snooker. I don't suppose you'd like to join a group of sad Irish corkers for supper this evening?"

"I'm afraid we're spoken for tonight," she says, very obviously regretting accepting an invitation from her cha-cha partner. "But perhaps you and the sad Irish corkers could teach us snooker some other time?"

"I don't suppose you'd want to give me your number to arrange that?" he asks.

She holds out her hand for his phone. "It would be my pleasure."

Once he's excused himself, she locks eyes with me and waggles her eyebrows. "That was promising," she says.

And for the first time in ages, I detect genuine excitement in her voice at the idea of a potential date.

She doesn't even get out her phone to post about it.

Felix

"You like that girl," Prue announces as we leave the dance class. "You should ask her out."

"Out where?" I ask, not bothering to deny it.

"You could take her to the fancy Italian place for dinner," Prue says.

"Invite her on an excursion," Pear suggests, elbowing into the conversation.

"It doesn't really matter what you do, does it?" Prue says. "You just have to let her know you fancy her."

I know she's right. I haven't so much as invited someone on a coffee date since getting sober. Nor wanted to.

But maybe this is a good chance to try something casual. After all, the remaining eight days of this cruise is too small an interval to risk a dalliance disrupting my life and sending me back to the edge.

And I'm drawn to Hope in a way I haven't experienced in a long time.

Which leaves the question of how to approach her.

The previous version of me would have downed a few drinks first. Liquid courage.

I suppose the current version will just have to white-knuckle it and express interest.

I resolve to do this the next time I see her.

This happens earlier than I expect, because when we arrive at the dining room, she's seated alone at a two-top a few feet from our table, playing Wordle on her phone.

Surely I am a better dining companion than Wordle.

"Mind if I ask Hope to join us?" I ask my family in a low voice.

"Please!" Mum says. She's the kind of gracious hostess that believes any table that doesn't have at least six people around it is depressing. She also thinks I spend too much time alone, and should start seeking out female company.

My father, by contrast, worries that I'm better off by myself. That my previous girlfriends were partiers who enabled me at best and at worst pushed me closer to the brink of destruction.

But he doesn't object.

I walk over to Hope, praying I seem confident and casual even though I feel like I'm a six-year-old telling a girl I like her on the playground.

"Not dining solo?" I ask.

She looks up from her phone and smiles at me. "My dinner date ditched me for her cha cha cha partner."

"Well, what if you dined with *your* cha cha cha partner? And . . ." I gesture at my table, "his annoying immediate family."

"You're really selling it."

"No worries if you don't want company."

"No, I'd love to. Thank you."

I try not to look as inordinately pleased as I feel as I escort her over to our table.

"You all remember Hope," I say to my family, as though we weren't just discussing her. "She'll be joining us."

"Only if you don't mind," Hope says.

"Of course not," Dad says in a jolly voice. "Our children don't bicker as much in front of company. We'd be grateful."

"We actually do bicker just as much," Prue says to Hope. "We all have dreadful manners."

"Weren't raised properly," I agree.

"Sit down, sit down," Pear says, gesturing at the lone empty chair.

Which, conveniently, is directly next to mine.

"So, Hope," Mum says, "are you enjoying the cruise so far?"

"I am," she says, in a tone that rings surprised to me. "I wasn't sure what to expect, but it's fun."

I didn't expect to enjoy it either. But then I met her.

The sommelier comes by with "tonight's featured wines"—a bottle of red and a bottle of white—and asks us which we'd like. I decline a glass. I notice Hope does too.

I wonder if she drinks. And if she does, how much.

The waiter takes our orders. Hope goes for yellowtail crudo and the filet of sole. I was going to order the same thing but on the spot I pivot to French onion soup and a ribeye to seem . . . I don't know . . . more manly?

Christ, I'm out of practice.

When the orders have been taken, Hope asks us if we have any plans for tomorrow when we stop in Antigua.

"We girls are riding horses on the beach," Pear says.

"We're hopelessly horsey," Prue adds. "Mum keeps a stable in Hampshire. Do you ride?"

Hope sucks her teeth. "No. When I look at a horse all I can think about is falling off it."

"They've fallen hundreds of times," I say. "It explains a lot about them. Head injuries, you know."

"Oh, you should talk," Pear says. "You rattle your brains head-butting the football so often I'm shocked you can function."

"His ability to function is debatable," Prue says.

"Try to be polite, children," Mum says. "Hope, what are you doing tomorrow?"

"The Caribbean cooking class," she says.

"So are Felix and Charles," Mum says. "How nice."

I take a sip of water to hide how pleased I am.

Hope turns to me. "A chef taking a cooking class?"

"Never hurts."

"He never went to culinary school, so he needs the help," Pear says.

"What she means is he's self-taught," Mum says, because Mum is an angel unlike her demonic daughters. "Worked his way up from a dishwasher, didn't you, love?"

"He's actually quite brilliant," Pear says, probably because she can tell she's annoyed me. "He's always being written up in the papers."

"We keep trying to convince him to let us invest, so he can expand," Prue adds. "But he insists on doing it all himself."

"What kind of food is it?" Hope asks me.

"New British, mostly," I say. "All locally sourced, seasonal."

"Sublime," Mum says. "If you're ever in London, you *must* try it."

"What are they called?" Hope asks. "Your pubs."

"The Smoke and Gun, in Canonbury. And the Fatted Calf in Stoke Newington."

"We grew up in West London but he's abandoned us for the North," Pear says. "He's much too edgy for Notting Hill."

"I've only been to London once, during grad school, but I actually stayed with friends in Canonbury. It's so beautiful. I wonder if we passed by your restaurant."

"Well, if they'd ever like to go, send them my way. I'd be happy to look after them," I say.

"Take him up on it, dear," Mum says. "It's impossible to get a booking."

"Give him your contacts now, so you don't forget," Pear says.

Hope rummages in her bag for her phone. "Do you mind?" she asks, handing it to me.

Mind? I have never been so thankful for my sister's interference.

"Not at all," I say. I take it from her and enter my number, and then my email for good measure. She immediately sends me a text:

Unknown: Hi! It's Hope Lanover, your new friend from the cruise ship.

Her full contact details, down to her home address, are attached.

I save them and send a text back.

Felix: Enchanted x.

She shoots me a smile. "Me too," she says.

"So, Hope," my father says, "not to be a bore, but what do you do for work?"

"I'm a publicist," she says. Her face takes on the same sheepish expression she had when she mentioned her job this morning.

"Is that what you went to grad school for?" I ask.

"God no." She laughs. "You definitely don't need a master's to write press releases. I did an MFA in fiction. I actually had hoped to go to Cambridge to study English literature, but it didn't work out."

"We went to Cambridge!" Pear exclaims. "Daddy made us go to business school before he would let us take over his company."

"We do private equity," Prue adds. "Consumer brands. Have you heard of Maquille? That's our latest. We're expanding globally. We just opened a flagship in New York."

"I've been there!" Hope exclaims. "Bought an eye cream I really shouldn't have splurged on, but my God is it good."

"It's brilliant, isn't it?" Pear says. "We're obsessed. I'll send you a box with the whole line."

"Why didn't you make it to Cambridge?" Dad asks. "I'm an alum myself. Could speak to someone for you, put in a good word."

"Daddy's famous in the UK," Prue whispers theatrically. "*Very* good connections."

I want to die of shame at this pronouncement, but Hope seems unfazed.

"Oh, thank you," she says. "But I was accepted to the program. I just had so many student loans already that moving overseas didn't make sense in the end."

"The American education system is ghastly," my mother says. "Not to mention the healthcare."

The conversation turns to the wonders of the NHS, which leads Dad to itemize his health problems, which leads Prue and Pear to gag, which leads Mum to say her life's work was raising them and look what happened, what a waste. Hope seems highly amused by all this. I like watching her laugh—she really does have the best laugh—and I'm relieved she finds my family's antics funny rather than alienating.

When our mains are taken away, Hope rises to her feet.

"I hate to run," she says, "but I promised to meet my friend for the dance show in the theater."

"Oh Felix!" Pear cries. "Are you performing?"

I glare at her.

"Thank you for putting up with us, Hope," Mum says.

"Heroic," says my father.

"It was a pleasure," Hope says. She touches my arm. "See you tomorrow?"

"Yep," I say. "Have fun tonight."

I'm a bit disappointed that she doesn't ask me along to the show, but I don't want to invite myself and elbow into her girls' night. I spend the evening at the piano lounge with my family, watching my sisters dance to Billie Holiday and Cole Porter with cruise ship ambassadors. Prue's is a seventy-one-year-old retired firefighter from Calgary. Pear's sold used cars in Manchester and decided to join the cruise circuit when his wife died. My mother gets jealous that her daughters are enjoying such scintillating life stories and abandons my dad for a former wrestling coach from Minnetonka, Minnesota.

My phone pings with a new message from Hope.

Hope: Thanks for letting me crash your dinner.
Hope: Your family is a riot.
Felix: Is that American for "disaster"?
Hope: No! They're lovely.
Hope: I'm a bit jealous. Only child. No one to spar with.
Felix: My dream.
Hope: Speaking of, I'm going to bed.
Hope: See you tomorrow. Hope you can handle the cooking class without a degree from Le Cordon Bleu.
Felix: It will be desperate but I'll give it a go.

She doesn't reply, so I add:

Felix: Sleep well x.

4

TROUBLED WATERS

Wonders of the Caribbean, Day 3

Welcome to St. John's, Antigua, and Barbuda!

Today the *Romance of the Sea* alights on the sparkling shores of St. John's. Adventure awaits eco-lovers, be it snorkeling with stingrays on a sandbar, hiking the Shekerley Mountains to Rendezvous Bay, or boating to the famed Great Bird Island. Beach buffs can sun the day away at a five-star seaside hotel or explore the scenic shore on a guided horseback tour. (No experience required!) And for the gourmet, indulge in an authentic Caribbean cooking class, where you will experience the scents and tastes of the islands, including a three-course meal. (And, of course, a rum tasting!)

In the evening, make sure to attend our unforgettable show, *Elvis Extravaganza*, featuring the legendary Garrett Montcrieff accompanied by our Seahorse Band. Wear your blue suede shoes—this will be one rockin' night!

Have a wonderful day!

Hope

I awake to the dulcet tones of Lauren recording a video about the courtship opportunities provided by ballroom dancing, along with tips for assembling an outfit suited for cha-cha. (Chiffon frills and sparkles encouraged.) I would love to spare myself the details by falling back asleep, but I have to check my work email to make sure Lana sent me the media list.

She has.

There is also, horribly, an email from Magda herself:

Hope—Where is the speech for Xeni to give at the TGE Games Investors Day? Not seeing it in the shared drive. Need ASAP!!!

Fucking hell. I don't even work on the TGE Games account. Rather than pointing this out, which will only piss Magda off, I dig through the drive until I find it and send her the link.

"Are you working?" Lauren asks with a look of profound distaste.

"Yes," I sigh. "Magda's being needy."

"I can't believe she's bothering you on vacation. You *never* take vacation."

"In part because she harasses me when I try."

"Shouldn't you get dressed?"

"Yes," I say, shutting my laptop. "What should I wear to a cooking class?"

"Um, given your boy is going to be there, something fetching, obviously."

She's not joining me for the class—she opted for an arduous mountain hike to see if she can meet "someone jacked" instead.

I don my cutest sundress—a flared blue vintage number with a flattering sweetheart neckline. I'm tempted to wear my wedge espadrilles—I like how they tie up my legs and give me a little more height—but they aren't terribly comfortable and I doubt Felix finds hobbling sexy, so I opt for sneakers.

Lauren takes one look at me and immediately says, "No way."

"What?" I ask.

"You are not hanging out with that boy wearing Keds. They don't go with your dress."

"I need to be able to walk," I say.

"You also need to look hot. What else did you pack in that tiny little bag?"

I let her rummage in my suitcase, and she comes up with a pair of high-waisted white shorts with a flouncy tropical-print top that ties at the midriff.

"Better for showing off your legs," she says. "But you still can't wear those shoes."

She examines what I brought—the sneakers, the espadrilles, a pair of heels, and some surprisingly cute Tevas—and scoffs at me. "Nope."

"Shall I go barefoot?"

She sails over to the walk-in closet where our butler, Crisanto, meticulously arranged her seventeen pairs of shoes when he unpacked her bags. She selects a pair of pointy-toed flats.

"They look uncomfortable," I say.

"They have a rubber sole and are made of recycled plastic bags, so they mold to your foot."

"Let me guess. Brand partner?"

She nods. "And they paid *very* well."

I slip them on. They're actually quite comfortable, and they do nice things for my legs.

"Perfect," Lauren says. "By the end of the day you'll be married."

"Is there a chapel on the boat?"

"No clue, but there's definitely an Elvis impersonator, and I think they're required to be wedding officiants by law."

"I would actually love to be married by an Elvis impersonator."

"I'll start making a Pinterest for your wedding. I assume you want the cape and rhinestone jumpsuit era?"

"Obviously. Okay, I have to go."

"Wait," she says. She pops into the bathroom and comes out with a tube of lipstick. "Wear this."

I open the cap and am blinded by a nearly fluorescent shade of coral.

"What is this color? Hot orange?"

She winks at me. "It's Dior Cruise. And I get two thousand dollars every time I post about it."

"I can't wear this outside. I'll look ridiculous."

"No, you'll look glamorous. Just *try* it."

I put it on and gape at myself.

It's amazing. My skin has never looked creamier, and my eyes have never looked greener. It perfectly complements my top.

"Wow," I say.

"Told ya. Take it with you so you can refresh every two hours. And don't lose it or I'll make you reimburse me for lost income."

God knows I already owe her enough money. I hold the tube protectively to my chest.

"I'll treat it like a bar of gold."

She holds up her phone. "Let me take your picture for posterity."

I'm so happy with my appearance I actually *want* a photo. I turn to her and vamp for the camera. She takes several shots.

"You look like a goddamn pinup," she exclaims, holding out her phone.

They might be the most flattering shots ever taken of me.

"Wow," I say again.

I'm sure this lipstick is like eighty dollars, but I make a mental note to buy one next time I get paid.

"You need these on your dating profile," Lauren says. "I'll text them to you."

"Okay, thanks," I say, even though I don't currently have a dating profile. "I gotta go. Wish me luck."

"Bonne chance, sugar."

I leave and head down to the lounge where we're meeting our guide for the excursion. I feel a bit self-conscious being this dolled up for a cooking class, but whatever. I want Felix to notice me.

No. I want him to *covet* me.

He's already there when I walk through the doors to the lounge where we're meeting our guide. His hair is damp, making me imagine him showering.

"Hi," he says with a lopsided smile. He holds out a to-go cup. "I got you a coffee. Just in case."

"You absolute prince," I say, accepting the cup.

"I wasn't sure how you take it so I went for an oat milk latte."

"Lucky guess."

He holds out his own coffee. "Cheers," he says.

"Where's your dad?" I ask, looking around.

"He bowed out. Ever since he retired he's the king of the lie-in."

I'm pleased to hear this. I want Felix all to myself.

"I guess we'll have to get by on our own," I say.

"I'll warn you that I'm quite boring."

"Oh good, so am I."

He reaches into his pocket and pops a piece of gum into his mouth.

"Can I have a piece?" I ask, worried about coffee breath.

He flashes me a guilty look. "Yeah. But only if you like nicotine."

"You smoke?" I ask, dismayed. I can't stand the taste of cigarettes, and I've decided that I want to make out with him.

"No, not for two years," he says. "Switched to gum to wean myself off the Marlboros and got hopelessly addicted."

"What does it taste like?" I ask.

"Spearmint and mild euphoria."

"Maybe I'll borrow a piece if I need a kick."

"You can keep it. My treat."

The tour guide calls us and our six fellow participants to gather around, and reminds us to make sure we have our IDs and cruise wristbands. We follow her out the door and down a flight of stairs to the gangway, where a tender awaits to take us to shore.

The sea is choppy—the boat lurches up and down so forcefully it makes my ass hurt, and we all get sprayed by water. A woman runs to one of the windows and gags. Which is when I realize I forgot to pack the seasickness patch my doctor recommended.

Oh well. I've never gotten motion sickness before, and I feel fine.

A large, open-air Jeep meets us at the port to take us to the class. We pile in, three to a bench, and it's extremely tight.

So tight that my entire right side is molded onto Felix's left one.

His body is lean and hard, whereas mine is ample and soft, and we melt together.

The ride is bumpy and involves tight turns over terrifyingly vertiginous cliffside roads.

I wish it would go on forever.

Felix

Hope is smushed up against me. Our bodies fit so naturally it's like we're lovers who've been together for years. And this close, I notice she smells exactly like the magnolia in my parents' garden.

It takes everything I have not to bury my face in her neck and inhale her.

I am determined: I will not let this day end without kissing her.

But for now, we lurch to a stop.

The cooking class is in a stately Colonial-style house on a wooded property. An Antiguan couple comes out to greet us, and they introduce themselves as Sarah, our teacher, and Joseph, who distills rum on the property. We all chat for a minute about where we're from, and then they show us inside to a large kitchen. Sarah explains that we'll be making saltfish and fungie, Antigua's national dish, as well as jerk chicken, conch salad, and tamarind balls with ripe Antigua Black pineapple for dessert.

She asks us to divide ourselves into groups of two.

Hope snatches my hand. "I claim the professional chef," she says.

"All yours," I say. As if there was any doubt.

Sarah asks if we have preferences about what we cook. The others shrug but I ask if we can make the saltfish and fungie. I love salted cod. We sometimes serve baccala fritters at the Smoke and Gun, and I'm curious about the Antiguan preparation.

Sarah leads us to a station with the ingredients. The cod has been soaked overnight to remove some of the salt, and it's our job to boil it and make a sauce. We also need to prepare the fungie, a mixture of okra, cornmeal, and butter.

"You have to take care with it," Sarah says. "If you don't whisk it enough, it will clump. And no one likes clumpy fungie."

"Sounds like that's your job," Hope says. "I can't be trusted with a whisk."

"I thought you liked to cook."

"I do," she says. "But I didn't say I was good at it."

"I'll . . . whisk you off your feet."

She groans. "You're in charge, chef. What first?"

We set to chopping the ingredients to make the base of the sauce—onion, garlic, capsicum, celery, Scotch bonnet, tomatoes, and fresh thyme. The veg is beautiful, grown right here in Sarah's garden.

I give Hope an onion to dice while I work on the tomatoes. When she presents it to me, I see she's done a beautiful job.

"Wow," I say. "Impressive knife skills for a civilian."

"I confess I'm not *that* bad in the kitchen. I just don't like to whisk. What next?"

"Want to chop the capsicum?"

"The what?"

"Oh. You speak American. The bell pepper."

"Excuse me, your majesty," she says in a faux-British accent that sounds like Dick Van Dyke in *Mary Poppins*.

"What an uncanny impression of me."

She gets to work on her task and I do the Scotch bonnet and garlic. I'm warming oil to sweat the alliums when my eye starts watering from the sun cream I put on my face, which is sweating into my eyes from the heat of the kitchen. I reach up to wipe away a tear.

"Fucking fuck," I hiss, as my eyeball screams in protest.

Hope looks at me in alarm. "What's wrong?"

"Got chili in my bloody eye."

I cook with Scotch bonnet all the time. I cannot believe I've done something so asinine. I was paying more attention to Hope than the food.

Sarah hears me hissing and rushes over.

"Don't worry," she says. "Beginner's mistake."

"I actually own two restaurants," I admit through the pain. "I'm just an idiot."

"Should you wash it off with some water?" Hope asks, gesturing at the sink.

"Won't help. I don't suppose you have any milk?" I ask Sarah.

"You're going to put milk in your *eye*?" Hope asks.

"No, my hands are covered in Scotch bonnet. *You're* going to put milk in my eye."

Sarah brings us a bowl of it and a clean towel. Hope washes her hands up to the elbows as I try not to jump around in agony, and then dabs a bit of milk onto the cloth. I sit down so she can reach.

She carefully smooths the hair out of my eyes.

"I'm going to drip it in," she says. "I don't want to scratch your cornea."

"Couldn't feel worse than this."

She squeezes milk from the cloth directly into my eye, and I blink and rotate my eyeball.

Very attractive, I'm sure.

"Does that feel any better?" she asks.

"It does. But my pride physically hurts."

"Yes, I'm not terribly convinced of your talents in the kitchen. I blame it on the lack of culinary school."

"You'd best hurry back to tell my sisters."

"Never. Your secret is safe with me." She gestures at the dining table in the center of the room. "Do you want to chill here and recover and I'll do the rest?"

"No. I intend to redeem myself."

I throw myself into cooking with my entire life force. I'm determined to make the best dish of Hope Lanover's life, even half blind. I sauté aromatics with the tomatoes and celery, stir in vinegar and tomato paste, taste for seasoning, balance the salt.

It's good. Very good. I take it off the flame and leave it to rest. I'll finish it off with some lime when we're ready for service.

Hope, meanwhile, chops the okra for the fungie and measures out the cornmeal.

"Your turn," she says when she's done. "I don't want to ruin it. I'll cook the fish."

I boil the okra until it's soft, then whisk cornmeal into the water in a thin, careful stream. I swear to holy hell if there is one clump in this goddamn dish I will wander off into the woods and never return. I stand obsessively stirring in butter and water until Sarah pronounces it perfect.

I feel like I just won a Michelin star.

Sarah goes over to Hope to help her flake the cooked fish into the sauce.

"Felix, come taste," Hope says. "It's ludicrously good."

I do, and it's almost there, but it could be better. "Needs acid," I say. I cut open a lime and juice it with my bare hand.

"Do *not* touch your eye," Hope says. "I can't go through that again."

We bring all the food to the table and take our places. Joseph comes around with rum punch for everyone. I politely decline.

Hope takes the rum.

"Yum," she says, after we toast to our hosts. She holds her drink out to me. "This is amazing. Want to try it?"

"No thanks. I don't drink," I say.

"Ah," she says. She doesn't ask me why. I'm grateful for that. There's nothing like being interrogated over declining a drink, especially in a room full of strangers.

All the food is amazing. Hope eats it with relish, asking questions and licking jerk seasoning off her fingers in a way that makes me even more obsessed with her cupid's bow mouth.

God, I want to kiss her.

And I think she wants that too.

It's so terrifying and exhilarating that I'm jittery.

They say in sobriety you have to relearn the pleasures you felt before you started drinking. But I started drinking purloined vodka with the older boys at boarding school when I was thirteen, and immediately developed a taste for it. I was never a good student, never a high achiever like my father and sisters, and the camaraderie and drunken confidence booze gave me made me feel like I finally had something to offer.

I was the popular, charming partier who could always secure forbidden substances. The one who held wild weekend-long parties at my parents' country house when they were away. The bad boy good for a laugh and a shag.

This must be what it feels like to have a goofy, boyish crush on a girl, unmediated by being fucked up.

I rather like it.

When we move on to dessert, Hope takes a huge bite of the pineapple and rolls her eyes back into her head. "Oh my *God*," she moans. "How is this real?"

I take a bite of mine. It is the platonic ideal of pineapple. It is the pineapple you would find growing in the garden of Eden, and risk original sin just to taste.

Makes my sauce seem a bit less impressive.

Sarah and Joseph are laughing at Hope's ecstasy.

"Antigua Black," Joseph says. "Sweetest pineapple in the world. Want some more?"

"Yes!" she says. He cuts three more slices and she eats all of them, juice running down her fingers. I'm addicted to watching. All I want to do is take her to my kitchen and prepare her things that elicit such heady joy. I want her to react to *my* food that way. To be the reason she's moaning.

I need to calm fucking down.

When we're done with dessert, Joseph invites us to join him on the veranda for the rum tasting. Everyone stands. I feel awkward, as there is going to be little to do as a sober person amongst a group sampling high-proof liquor.

Hope grabs my hand and turns to Sarah. "Would you mind if the two of us skipped the tasting and went back to the kitchen?" she asks. "We're dying to learn how to make that conch salad."

It's such a kind gesture.

I try not to show that I'm melting.

"Thanks," I say to Hope, under my breath. "I was dreading that. But don't feel like you need to miss out on the rum, if you want to leave me to it."

She shrugs. "I'm good. I don't drink much. Went a little too hard last year after a breakup and it made me . . . off." She says this in a way that makes me think there is more to the story.

With drinking, there usually is.

Same with breakups.

"I went a little too hard for about two decades," I tell her. "I'm in recovery. Two years."

"That's amazing!" she says. "Congratulations."

I can tell by the warmth in her voice that she means it.

Hope

Usually when I have a crush, I feel pressure to make myself seem more cool and mysterious than I actually am. To be bold-print alluring.

With Felix, I forget to put on the femme fatale act. I'm just myself—and he seems to dig that.

Normally I might be nervous at how much I like him. I have the bad habit of getting infatuated too quickly. But the fact that there's an automatic end date between us makes me feel safe to relax.

Besides, I feel more like myself since I met him. I used to pride myself on being captivating and sexy, but since Gabe, I've felt like a drab little mouse. A girl with no real career, no real prospects, and nothing to offer.

I came here to shake that feeling. Granted, my intention was to do it by soaking up books and sunshine, not canoodling with a boy.

But the canoodling is helping.

I feel desired. It makes my brain sharper.

When we get back to the port, the water in the bay is markedly darker than it was when we arrived, and there are waves lapping up along the edges of the pier. The captain of the tender warns us that the wind has picked up and tells us to hold on to the posts inside the boat.

The woman who got sick on the way here goes ashen.

She's probably regretting ingesting three kinds of rum.

Felix and I sit down on a bench in the middle section of the tender to avoid getting splashed. As soon as the boat leaves the dock, I go lurching forward and almost fall over.

Felix puts his arm around me to steady me.

When I'm steadied, he doesn't remove it.

All thoughts of seasickness vanish.

We stay that way for the entire ten-minute ride back to the ship.

"What are you doing tonight?" Felix asks as we walk back onto the boat.

My breath catches. Is he going to ask me to hang out, even though we've spent all day together?

I really, really hope so.

"Lauren and I have a reservation to do the tasting menu at the Italian restaurant," I say. "And then after that, definitely Elvis."

"Definitely Elvis," he agrees. "My sisters have already made me promise to go. Want to meet us there?"

"Sure," I say, trying to infuse my answer with chill rather than the five exclamation points I actually feel.

He grins at me. "See you then."

I float back to my room.

My joy must be apparent, because as soon as I walk into our suite, Lauren looks at me knowingly.

"Well I'll be," she says. "I guess the lipstick worked."

I throw myself down on the bed, smiling. "He's so nice. We hung out all day. And he asked me to meet him at the Elvis thing after dinner."

"Shipmance!" she squeals. "Can I interview you about it for my Insta?"

"Absolutely not. You know the rules."

"Come on!"

"Don't you have your own exploits to talk about? How was the hike?"

"Arduous," she said. "I'm so sore. But I met a new beau. He's sixty, divorced, lives in Fort Lauderdale, and does Muay Thai. He invited me to go for a jog around the deck tomorrow morning before breakfast."

"Sexy."

"Some of us have to suffer for our art." She gestures at a shopping bag with the cruise ship logo sitting on our dining table. "By the way, I got you a prezzie."

"Lauren, no!" I say. Gifts are her love language, and she's constantly giving me things. But on my budget, I can't reciprocate, and it makes me feel terrible.

The gulf between her wealth and generosity and my constant financial straits has begun to cause us tension. Not because she resents helping, but because it embarrasses me that I need it. We were two broke girls making our way in the city for years. And then, all of a sudden, her reality show changed her life, and she ran with it. She's very, very good with business.

I'm really proud of her.

I'm just ashamed I'm still floundering.

"Hopie, open it," she says, waggling the bag over my lap.

I pull out the tissue paper and look inside.

It's an emerald green wrap dress made of impossibly delicate silk. Just from holding it up, I can see the cut will be perfect for me—long sleeves, low neckline, cinched waist, fluttery skirt. I can also see that it must have been very expensive.

"Where did you get this?" I ask.

"One of those boutiques on the Metropolitan Deck."

"Thank you, it's beautiful. But there's no way I can afford it."

"Just lean into the glam, darlin'. They gave me a ten-thousand-dollar credit to use however I want on the cruise. I also booked us a spa day tomorrow. You'll be nice and relaxed for your man. Now try on the dress."

I do, and it's magnificent.

I usually go for vintage clothes, as they tend to have silhouettes that flatter my figure. But this shows off my boobs, hips, and ass to perfection.

I can't wait for Felix to see me in it.

Lauren goes to shower and I flat iron my hair into smooth waves I hope a certain boy will find alluring. I'm interrupted by a FaceTime call from my dad.

I go out on the terrace to answer it. When I accept the call, he looks haggard.

Old.

It breaks my heart.

"Hey dear," he says. "You look pretty."

"Thanks. This cruise is so fancy. I have to doll myself up to fit in."

"Had any fun adventures?"

I tell him about the cooking class and the otherworldly pineapple. I leave out Felix. After my meltdown over my breakup, my parents fear for me in any romantic relationship.

Their divorce no doubt has something to do with it. They'd been together since college and seemed happy my whole life. Until somehow, last year, they fell apart.

I still don't understand why. No one cheated or had a midlife crisis. It just . . . stopped working. Just like that.

They had one of those love-at-first-meeting stories everyone longs for. It always gave me confidence in my own tendency to fall fast and hard. After all, they did, and for forty years, they were rock solid.

Now that seems naive.

It terrifies me that people can fall out of love as quickly as they can fall into it.

But it shouldn't surprise me.

Not after what happened with Gabe.

Mom and Dad have already separated—they sold my childhood home in Burlington a few months ago and both moved to smaller apartments. Now the only thing left to do is empty out the cottage, put it on the market, and finalize their divorce.

They've divided up the month—two weeks each alone there to take what they want and split up the packing. Dad got the first shift.

"How are you holding up?" I ask him.

He blows out a breath. "A lot to do," he says.

He's dodging the real question. My parents are New Englanders to their core—kind and loving, but undemonstrative and uncomfortable talking about anything too personal. I credit my friendship with Lauren for helping me to open up. She *only* wants to talk about the personal.

"I don't want to bother you on your vacation," Dad says, "but I wanted to check in because I'm going to start packing up your room tomorrow. Wondering what you want to hold on to."

He doesn't need to tell me it can't be much. Both of my parents' apartments are small one-bedrooms. And there is not the slightest extra inch of storage space in my studio.

"Can you keep my quilt from Granny?" I ask.

"Of course. Anything else?"

"Hmm, let me think."

I try to picture the room—the antique dollhouse my great-grandfather made for my mom. The handsewn cushions on the window seat. The old brass bed in which I have spent so many hours and days and weeks of my life reading.

The books.

My entire youth's worth of books, many passed down over generations. Some so beloved that I have parts of them memorized.

It devastates me to think of them being tossed out.

"I have a small storage space in town," Dad says. "I'll keep the books for you."

Tears spring into my eyes.

"Thank you."

"Yep. All right, dear. I'll let you go. Have fun."

"Thanks, Dad."

He hangs up before I can tell him I love him. My small, broken family makes me feel achingly lonely. I'm envious of Felix's.

Maybe that's part of his appeal.

Lauren emerges from the bathroom. "Oh no!" she exclaims. "Why are you crying? You're going to mess up your makeup."

I inhale, centering myself. "Just my parents," I say. "My dad called and he looks and sounds terrible."

She clucks sympathetically. She's become close to my parents since her own father died our freshman year of college. She's estranged from her mother, so I took her home with me for a week and we all gathered around her and helped her plan the funeral.

She and I were already best friends—we bonded the first day of school when she flounced into our randomly assigned dorm room and immediately gave me a makeover—but that week, she became family.

"They're going to be all right, my love," she says.

"I know. It just makes me sad to see them both so unhappy."

"Well, we're going to make you beautiful and then carbo load your pain away."

She grabs a makeup remover wipe from the mess of cosmetics we've both strewn along the vanity table and gently dabs mascara away from my eyes.

Then, biting her lip, she reapplies concealer with the skill of a professional makeup artist.

"Perfect," she pronounces. "You just need the magical lipstick."

She dabs it onto my lips.

"Ooh, hold still for a sec. That light is perfect."

She snaps a picture of me with her phone and holds it up. It is indeed a beautiful photo.

"That could be my funeral portrait," I observe.

She glares at me. "Stop being macabre and come on. It's time to OD on pasta."

Felix

My family has supper at the Japanese restaurant, and my parents insist we do the full omakase experience. I've never been so impatient to finish a perfect filet of miso-glazed black cod in my life.

I *must* not be late to Elvis.

"I think we need to duck out before the green tea semifreddo," I tell my sisters.

"Why?" Pear asks. "It sounds delicious."

"Elvis is on in ten minutes."

Prue snorts. "This morning you were complaining it's too camp for your delicate sensibilities. Now you want to be early?"

I hesitate before confessing my motivation, as I know my entire family will either mock me (my sisters), worry about me (my dad), or fawn over me (my mum) for inviting a girl somewhere.

"I told Hope I'd meet her there," I confess.

Cue the mocking and fawning from the ladies, and the grimace from my father.

"Hope," Mum says. "How nice. Isn't she a lovely thing."

"Far too lovely for Felix," Prue says.

Meanwhile, Pear is singing, "When the boat is a rockin', don't come a knockin'," in a very poor imitation of Elvis's voice.

"That's not an Elvis song," I tell her.

"Just be careful," Dad says. "Don't . . . you know."

"Oh, let him have his little cruise flirtation, Father," Prue says. "It might make him nicer."

"I agree," Pear says. "I haven't seen him this bubbly in months."

"I am not *bubbly*," I protest.

Prue stands up. "Well, come on then," she says. "We can't be late. Poor Felix may never have another date again, with his looks and attitude."

We dash out of the restaurant but are confronted with a scrum on the way to the lifts, as the corridors are congested with fellow cruisers strolling about in evening finery—many a bow tie, many a sparkly frock. The ladies also seem fond of a heavy spritz of perfume. The lift smells like the cosmetics department at Selfridges.

Our pace is not helped by the fact that the ship is listing a bit, and people are moving more gingerly than usual. Which is good, as there will be a bottleneck if someone falls over and breaks a hip, and then we'll certainly be late to meet Hope.

By the time we navigate to the theater, we only have three minutes to spare. I'm worried Hope will have given up on me and gone inside. But Pear elbows me and stage whispers: "Ooh. She dressed up for you."

I follow her gaze to the doors, where Hope's waiting with Lauren. She's looking in the opposite direction, which gives me a moment to take her in. She's got on a fluttery green dress that swishes around her hourglass figure, her hair is smoothed out into waves that fall down past her shoulders, and she's wearing bright lipstick that radiates old-school glamour.

It's like someone asked me to imagine my dream girl, then plucked her straight out of my brain.

I walk ahead of my sisters and say her name. She doesn't look up—it's loud amidst the crowd milling into the theater and she's chatting with Lauren—so I tap her shoulder.

She jumps.

"Sorry!" I say. "It's just me."

She smiles softly, not at all hiding that she's pleased to see me. "Ah. Just you."

"Well, and my sisters," I say, because they are now hovering six inches away from me, grinning.

"Hi, Hope and Lauren!" they singsong in unison.

I wish they'd given me thirty-five seconds to tell this woman how smashing she looks before barging up.

It's fine. I'll be sure to tell her later.

"Hey!" Hope says, flashing Prue and Pear a warm smile. "How are you?"

"Ready for the King!" Pear says. She switches to her fake Elvis voice and sings: "We're gonna rock around the clock tonight—"

"Also not an Elvis song," I interrupt.

"It is!" she protests.

"Bill Haley and His Comets," Hope says. "My dad has the album. But Elvis covered it. So you're both right."

"Wow, good intel," Prue says. "Are you a music buff?"

"She's the daughter of a man with a *very* extensive vinyl collection," Lauren says. "She's like a human jukebox, just wait."

We make our way into the theater and find a group of seats together near the back. My sisters and Lauren graciously slide in first, allowing me to sit next to Hope on the aisle. The lights dim right away.

The band steps out on stage, dressed in tight, shiny black pants and white blazers. They're followed by two backup singers in shimmering gold dresses who take their places behind microphones on the other side of the stage.

"I wasn't aware Elvis impersonators traveled with a full entourage," I say to Hope.

"We're not in Reno anymore."

"Do you spend much time in Reno?"

"Oh, sure. It's the Monte Carlo of America. Can't keep me away."

"You'll have to take me some time."

"Only if you let me blow all your money on the slots."

"Do you have a gambling addiction?"

"Yes."

"I know a great rehab."

A spotlight shines on the stage, and a heavily tanned middle-aged man with a mane of dyed-black hair steps into it. He's wearing a bell-bottomed onesie with gold boots and a heavy gold chain.

"Oh my *God*," Hope whispers. "I think I'm in love."

"I must say, I was hoping for rhinestones."

"Maybe he does costume changes."

We can't talk further, because without preamble, he launches into "Hound Dog."

"Whoa," Hope whispers. "His voice is amazing."

"Shockingly so. And he has the hip-swivel down."

"Is it wrong that I'm attracted to him?"

"The heart wants what it wants."

Elvis hits the bridge, and the backup singers encourage us to stand and clap along over our heads. The audience leaps to their feet. Despite the mature demographic, they're surprisingly spry.

Hope grabs my hand to pull me up. "Listen, you're not too cool for fake Elvis," she shouts into my ear above the music.

"I'm actually not cool *enough* for him."

But I get up, because I'll do anything to keep holding her hand.

Elvis strikes up "You're the Devil in Disguise," and Hope bops along with the music, mouthing the words. I smell her perfume again, and the magnolias are much nicer than whatever the women were doused in on the lift. She bumps me with her hip.

"Dance with me," she says.

"Glutton for punishment?"

She takes my hand and does a cute little twirl into my arms, rocking her hips toward mine.

This, I can get into without lessons.

I put my hand on the small of her back and she smiles approvingly.

Unfortunately, that's when the song ends.

"How are you enjoying paradise, ladies and gentlemen?" Elvis asks in a very fake Southern drawl.

Everyone cheers.

"Well, since ya'll love to cruise, I'm gonna take you sailing on this magical night to a pretty little place I like to call . . . Blue Hawaii."

The band strikes back up and everyone starts swaying along as Elvis croons the ballad. I'm disappointed that we've transitioned to a down-tempo number, as I was looking forward for another excuse to press close to Hope.

One of the backup singers hands Elvis a heap of white and pink orchid leis. He steps into the crowd, stopping to put leis around the necks of several ladies as he sings to them about their dreams coming true.

The way they swoon, you would think he was the real deal.

And then he stops in front of Hope and drapes a lei over her head. She accepts it with pure delight. He throws an arm around her. "Sing it with me, pretty lady," he says.

She joins him for the chorus, and I'm shocked by the loveliness of her voice—a clear soprano. She hits every note, harmonizing off the cuff with Elvis's baritone. The whole room erupts in applause, and she laughs and curtsies. I'm oddly proud, like I have something to do with the star turn of the woman I'm standing next to.

"Isn't she amazing?" Lauren whispers into my ear.

"A marvel," I whisper back.

Elvis walks back on stage and does a powerful cover of "Unchained Melody" that I'm pretty sure makes Hope tear up. And then he transitions to "Bridge Over Troubled Waters."

"Is it bad luck to sing about troubled waters on a cruise ship?" Hope asks over the music.

"Almost certainly."

"I hope he doesn't do the theme from *Titanic* next."

"No? Personally I'd love to hear an Elvis version of Celine Dion."

A woman in front of us turns around and frowns, so we stop talking.

The next forty-five minutes is hit after hit. "Blue Suede Shoes." "All Shook Up." "Heartbreak Hotel." I had no idea I knew so many Elvis songs, and by the end I'm singing along to "Suspicious Minds" at the top of my lungs with the rest of the crowd. Hope pulls me toward her and sings the lyrics directly to me, so I sing them back to her, both of us belting about how we *love you too much, baby.*

She collapses into me with laughter as the song ends, and I'm not sure if it's because the ship is tossing or because she wants a hug.

I err on the side of wrapping an arm around her shoulders.

Hope

I have always loved Elvis for his kitsch factor. Now I love him for allowing me to cuddle with Felix.

By the time the fake King takes his final bow, I feel so light I'm unsteady on my feet.

But as Felix and I walk back into the lobby with Lauren and his sisters, I realize my wobbliness isn't just crush endorphins. The boat is rolling—gently but noticeably—back and forth.

And then it surges to one side dramatically. A senior with a walker in front of us grips the wall for balance.

"Shit," I say.

"Something wrong?" Felix asks.

"I meant to get one of those seasickness patches and I forgot."

"Give her yours, Felix," one of his sisters says. (I feel terrible, but I'm completely baffled as to which one is Prue and which one is Pear.) "You know the rules of the sea," she goes on. "Save the women and children first."

"I'm not sure that's hygienic," he says.

"I'm refusing to wear one," the other sister says. "They can make people go mad."

"You're already mad, so that shouldn't have scared you off," Felix says.

"I'm serious," she says. "Sophie Blyth wore one last year on Mungo Roland's yacht and went completely off her head. Shouted at everyone all week and refused to eat anything but raspberries. Mungo said he was tempted to leave her in Mustique to find her own way home."

To me, the most remarkable part of this story is that she knows someone named Mungo. Followed closely by the fact that Mungo owns a yacht.

The ship rocks again.

"Am I imagining it, or is the rolling getting worse?" I ask.

"It's definitely getting worse," says the sister who knows Mungo. "Do you get seasick?"

"I don't think so. I'll probably be fine." I hope, anyway.

"I'm sure they have patches at the infirmary," Felix says. "Shall we go see if we can find one?"

"Yeah," I say. "Good idea."

"I'm off to the casino," Lauren says. "There's nothing like saucy conversation with a handsome stranger at a craps table."

"Ooh, can we join you?" an unidentified sister says.

"Of course," Lauren says happily. "Do you two want to meet us there after the infirmary?"

"We'll see," Felix says. "I hear Hope here has a gambling problem. Not sure she can be trusted."

"Is that true?" Prue/Pear asks.

"No, actually. Betting terrifies me." As someone with no financial cushion, the proposition of losing money is not something I equate with "fun."

"No!" the sister exclaims. "You *must* learn! We're absolute whizzes at blackjack. We can teach you. Prue once won forty grand in Vegas at a hen do."

Ah. So the one talking is Pear. She has slightly shorter hair and a mole just under the left side of her mouth. I commit this to memory.

"Promptly blew all the money on a handbag," Felix says.

"I did not 'blow' the money," Prue says primly. "I bought a Birkin. They appreciate."

She looks at me as though for corroboration.

I nod, trying not to give away my horror at the idea of a purse costing more than half my annual salary. Even Lauren does not traffic in that level of luxury.

Yet, anyway. By the way her eyes have lit up at this story, I'm sure she aspires to.

"Well, good luck at the casino," I say. "Maybe we'll see you there in a bit."

Felix and I walk down the hall toward the elevators.

"Sorry about Kitty and Lydia," he says when we're out of earshot.

For a second, I'm confused.

And then I am incredibly delighted.

"Was that a *Pride and Prejudice* reference?"

"I'm told you like British literature."

"Does that make you the Lizzie Bennet of this metaphor?"

"Hmm. Always fancied myself more of a Jane, actually. Because of the tattoos."

"Oh, that's right. Jane had the two full sleeves."

"And M R . B I N G L E Y across her knuckles."

"That's how he knew she was the one."

"Do you have any tattoos?" he asks.

"Afraid not."

"I have a few."

"I actually noticed."

"Weird. They're subtle."

"Yes, very understated. How many do you have? Sixty?"

"Hmm. Twelve, I think. But if you'd prefer more I'm sure there's a tattoo parlor at the next port."

"Good idea. What will you get?"

"What do you suggest?"

"How about the *Romance of the Sea* logo?"

"Just that?"

"Yes, but forty-eight times."

"That might hurt."

"I'll hold your hand."

He grabs my hand and squeezes it.

"Deal," he says.

He doesn't let go.

We pass a couple in the corridor and they say hello to us, smiling at our joined hands like *aww, young love*.

"Would you happen to know where the Cigar Lounge is?" the woman asks.

"No, sorry," I say.

"Are you two on your honeymoon?" she asks.

"No," Felix says. "It's our first anniversary."

"Oh, how wonderful. She's such a beautiful place to celebrate."

It takes me a second to realize the "she" in question is the cruise ship.

"She sure is," Felix says.

"Well, enjoy your evening," the man says with a wink.

"We certainly will," Felix says with a wink back.

"Oh no," I say once they pass us. "Now we have to be in a fake relationship every time we see them."

"Tragic," he says. "How will we convince them it's real?"

"Maybe we could make out," I suggest, because I have fully bought into my own narrative that it's fine to throw caution to the wind on a cruise ship.

"What a compelling idea," he murmurs.

He stops walking, pushes me gently against the wall, and kisses me.

It's just a brush of the lips, but it is a *good* brush of the lips. A brush of the lips that portends additional pleasures to come.

Felix takes a deep breath. One that freely admits he felt it too.

"Was that all right?" he asks softly, smoothing a strand of hair off my cheek.

"No," I say. "Apologize."

"I'm sorry."

And then he does it again.

And had the boat not shifted suddenly under our feet, I suspect he would have kept doing it. But I stagger on my heels, and he has to brace me to keep me from toppling over.

Which I like. But I'm worried this is going to get worse, and I've heard that motion sickness medicines don't work if you already have motion sickness when you take them.

"So, about that infirmary," I say.

"Right," he says. "Let's go."

We find it at the end of the corridor.

The door is locked. Felix points to a sign on the window that says it will reopen at nine in the morning.

"Apparently ship doctors keep banker hours," he says. "Maybe we could check at the boutique."

"Pretty sure they only sell designer caftans and fine jewelry."

"Do you think a designer caftan would help?"

"I'm good on caftans. Lauren packed about thirty of them."

He looks at me with concern.

"Do you feel sick?"

"No, I think I'll be fine," I say. In truth I am beginning to feel a little off, but I don't want this night to end. "Do you want to go up to the casino?"

He considers this. "Not especially."

I'm a little deflated, until he says, "I'd rather invite you to my room for a cup of tea."

I laugh. "Tea, eh? Subtle."

"Not a line!" he protests. "A nice peppermint tea is good for the stomach. But if that's a no, I'll walk you back to your room."

"It's a yes."

We take the elevators up to the Penthouse level.

"This is me," he says, pointing at a door a few away from my room.

"We're neighbors," I say.

"I know. I figured out where you were staying and requested a room nearby so I could run into you."

"Really?"

"No."

"You didn't need to. I would have found you anyway."

He grins at me. "Come in."

His suite is so neat that were it not for his copy of *Middlemarch* sitting on the dining table, I would think no one was occupying it. But then, all our rooms are cleaned twice a day, so I'm not sure if this is a sign of his habits or just the strength of the *Romance of the Sea*'s housekeeping department. I'm tempted to pretend I need to pee so that I can go into his bathroom and examine his toiletries.

It's not that I want to snoop. But it's odd to meet someone on vacation, out of their usual context. Were we in New York I'd be able to infer things about him based on what neighborhood he lives in, or where he suggests meeting, or what restaurants he likes. But knowing he "lives" on the Penthouse Deck and "dines" at the ship buffet doesn't give me much to work with.

I want to know everything about him.

"Mint is okay?" Felix asks, filling an electric kettle. "There's also chamomile."

We don't have a kettle in our room—just a Nespresso machine.

"Mint is good," I say. "Did you bring that from home?"

"What, the tea? No. Came free with the cruise. Though I did stash some PG Tips in my bag if you prefer."

"The kettle."

"Oh. Well, yes."

"You were worried the ship wouldn't provide hot water?"

"Not all hot water is created equally, dear Hope. My kettle here has temperature controls. You'll be getting an herbal tea brewed to exactly eighty-five degrees Celsius, like nature intended."

"And that would be different from a tea brewed to, let's say, ninety degrees Celsius?"

"Herbal teas become bitter at too high a temp. Now, for a black tea, you'll want to nudge it up to ninety-five. Same for oolong."

"Ah," I say.

"I can go on," he offers, pouring hot water into our cups. "Green? White? Tisane of lemon and turmeric?"

The ship rolls, and he curses sharply.

"You all right?" I ask.

"Burned my hand," he says.

"You're rather clumsy in the kitchen for a man who makes his living in one," I say.

"Pretty girls make my hands shake."

I want to banter back, but I feel my stomach flip-flop.

"Is it just me, or is this getting worse?" I ask.

"My corny attempts at flirtation?"

"No, the waves."

"They are becoming rather ominous, now that you mention it."

"Oh my God," I say. "I just remembered your last name is Segrave."

He nods solemnly. "Me too."

"I wonder if that only dooms you to a watery death, or if I'm cursed by proximity."

"Let's get you into a life jacket, just to be safe."

"It doesn't go with my dress."

"And it's quite a dress," he says softly.

So softly, so intentionally, that I blush clear down to the pads of my feet.

He walks over to me and puts a hand on my shoulder.

"You look *perfect*," he says, looking into my eyes. "You look so perfect it's making me nervous."

I let out a breath. "I'm nervous too," I confess.

It feels good to say that. To be honest with a boy.

"Like, I'm trying to play it cool here," he says, "but actually . . ."

"Yeah. Same."

He opens his arms to me. "Maybe it would help to just . . ."

"Yeah," I say again, stepping into them.

He wraps me in a hug.

Not an erotic, gropey kind of hug. A steadying one. One that feels like we're telling each other, *It's okay. This is okay.*

"Better?" he asks into my hair.

"Better," I whisper.

"Me too."

We separate, and he smiles at me. "Tea," he says decisively.

"Oh! Yes! Quick, before it cools down to eighty-three degrees."

He takes the two mugs and walks carefully to the sitting area, putting them down on the coffee table. Despite his efforts, they slosh.

As does my stomach.

I sit down on the sofa, hopeful I will feel better if I don't have to work so hard to stay upright. Felix sits down beside me.

And then he leans over and kisses me. Softly. A bit more lingeringly than he did in the hallway.

I melt against him, and there's that feeling again: *it's okay*.

Except now there's more to it. *This is lovely. You're lovely.*

I put my fingers in Felix's hair, which is soft and tousled and so nice to touch, and draw him closer to me.

"I like you," I say, when our lips part.

"Good," he says. "Because I like you too."

His eyes go down to my lips, and he's going to kiss me again, and then—

"Oh fuck," I say, lurching away. "I'm going to throw up."

Felix

Hope jumps off the couch, her hand over her mouth, and staggers to the loo. It takes me a few seconds to react, and then I run after her. She slams the door shut, and moments later I hear retching noises.

I don't know what to do.

I want to help her, but how? Going in to hold back her hair seems like a disgusting cliché, rather than something someone would want you to do in real life. If I were the one vomiting, I emphatically would not want her to watch.

It sounds bloody awful.

Poor girl.

After a few minutes the noises stop. I knock tentatively on the door.

"Hope?"

"Don't come in," she cries.

"Can I do anything for you?"

"I'm okay."

But she's not; the gagging resumes immediately.

I feel responsible. Perhaps if I hadn't invited her here, she would have gone to sleep, and the nausea wouldn't have claimed her. And I'm worried. Tomorrow is a day at sea, and who knows how long the swells will last. She could be sick for ages. I get a selfish twinge of disappointment. I was hoping to spend time with her tomorrow.

Not to mention tonight.

Feeling helpless, I pour her a glass of water and stand sentry outside the door. The retching stops again, and then I hear the tap running. Hope pokes her head outside. Her lipstick is smeared. She looks absolutely miserable.

"Here, love," I say, offering her the water.

"Not sure I can keep it down."

"Just try. You need to stay hydrated."

She accepts it and takes a tiny sip, then swallows very cautiously.

"Do you think I could borrow a robe?" she asks. "I, um, made a mess of myself. If you don't mind, I'm going to just take a quick shower so I don't have to subject anyone in the hallway to . . . well."

"Of course," I say, tremendously relieved that I can do *something*. I go to the closet and grab a plush white *Romance of the Sea*–branded bathrobe and bring it to her.

She takes it and closes the door, and I pace around googling seasickness remedies. Unfortunately, most of them have to be taken *before* the nausea sets in. But several articles suggest that eating ginger and lying down help. I go to the phone, dial the number for Crisanto, and ask for ginger ale.

"Of course, Mr. Felix," Crisanto says. He pauses. "I hope you aren't seasick."

"Not me. But my friend is ill."

"May I suggest something that may help?"

"Please."

"Green apples can calm the symptoms. I will bring you some."

"That would be wonderful. Thank you."

He arrives within minutes, carrying a tray of apples and bottles of ginger ale.

"I also brought some ginger lozenges," he says. "We keep them on hand."

"Thank you so much."

"Can I do anything else for you, Mr. Felix?"

"No, thank you. Have a good night."

I lay out the supplies on the table.

Hope emerges from the bathroom. Her hair is wet and her face is scrubbed clean of makeup. Her bare face is stunning, but without the makeup I can see how pale she's become.

"I got you some ginger ale and lozenges," I say. "And this sounds bizarre, but Crisanto said that green apples help."

"You're so sweet. Thank you. Although not really sure I want to risk an apple right now."

"WebMD says lying down is good. Do you want to . . ." I gesture at my bed. Then I realize that this could be interpreted the wrong way. "I mean, for a rest," I clarify, "until you feel a little—"

"Puking in your bed is not how I had planned to seduce you," she says.

My heart jolts.

"You planned to seduce me?"

If she didn't look so ill, I would take her into my arms.

She smiles wanly. "Eventually." She holds her hand to her stomach. "Oh God. I need to get back to my room. Can you grab me a laundry bag for my dress? It's a biohazard."

I duck into the closet and find her one. She goes to the bathroom to gather her clothes and I get her some slippers, as I doubt she wants to totter down the hallway in a bathrobe and heels.

I hand them to her when she emerges.

"Thank you," she says. "You're so thoughtful."

"Let me walk you back to your room."

"You don't have to do that. It's twenty feet away."

"I want to. And I'll carry your medicines, feeble though they may be."

I gather up the apples and sodas and we walk slowly down the hall. Hope unlocks her room, then pauses at the door.

I lean in and give her a kiss on the cheek. Her brow's a little sweaty. I get a bad feeling that her respite from vomiting will not last the night.

"Text me if you need anything," I say.

"Thanks, Felix. Good night."

She closes the door and I go back to my room.

I get in bed, but I'm wired from the events of the past hour. I occupy myself by continuing to research seasickness cures.

A text pops up from Hope.

Hope: I risked the apple. It actually helped.
Felix: I'm so glad.
Hope: I had so much fun with you today. Vomit episode notwithstanding.

I smile.

Felix: Me too.
Felix: Do-over when you're not sick?
Hope: Absolutely.
Felix: Get some sleep xx.

5
BOATMANCE

Wonders of the Caribbean, Day 4

Rest, relax, and recharge at sea!

Today the *Romance of the Sea* sails the crystalline ocean on our way to St. Lucia, affording you a day of fun in the sun and luxurious pampering.

The Coral Spa welcomes you to leave your cares behind and delight your senses with our signature Mermaid Treatment. To indulge in luxury, head to the Seahorse Gallery for a presentation on diamonds by Ludo Bianchi, head jeweler of the Treasure Chest Boutique—and perhaps treat yourself to a gift.

For some time in the shade, visit the Game Room at noon for a rousing Scrabble tournament, stop by the Fitness Center for a gentle Pilates class with instructor Jen, or learn to paint the blues of the Caribbean Sea while enjoying the libation of your fancy at our Watercolor Sip and Paint.

At sunset, local culinary delights and delicious cocktails await you on the Lido Deck for a special al fresco Caribbean Feast. And afterward, night owls can stay and dance until the wee hours at the Silent Disco.

Have a wonderful day!

Hope

The green apples backfired.

I got up so many times in the night that Lauren decamped to the couch in the living room to avoid being awoken by my retching. I consumed such a large quantity of ginger that I never want to taste it again. It was dawn by the time we sailed out of the swells and into calmer waters. I finally fell asleep at six a.m.

I wake up at nine feeling frail and dehydrated.

I lie in bed, nervous to get up in case walking reignites my queasiness. The need to pee eventually overtakes my anxiety. But going into the bathroom, after the dark hours I spent there last night, nearly gives me PTSD. I force myself to get into the shower. The hot water makes me feel vaguely human, but I resent the sea-scented bath products. I never want to think of the ocean again, let alone smell it.

Lauren is waiting on the bed when I emerge.

"My kitten!" she cries. "How do you feel?"

"Like I survived the plague. But just barely."

"Poor baby. At least the turbulence stopped. I called down to Guest Services and they said they don't expect any more rough seas. You should start taking Dramamine as soon as you can keep something down. I'll go get you some. And they can give you an IV in the infirmary."

"I don't think I need an IV. Just water."

She passes me a giant bottle of Evian. I'm thirsty enough to want to gulp it down, but also fearful of what will happen if I put too much of anything in my stomach.

"I'll go and get you the pills," Lauren says. "Do you want anything else? Maybe some dry toast?"

"No thanks. Pretty sure I'll never eat again."

I curl up in bed with the water and look at my phone.

There's an ominous text in all caps from Magda.

Magda: WHERE IS THE MEDIA LIST?

Fuck. I got distracted with my dad's call yesterday and completely forgot to send her the list from Lana. Now it's a day late.

I drag myself over to the desk and email the list to Magda. Then I send her a text.

Hope: So sorry for the delay.

Hope: It's in your inbox now.

Hope: Let me know if you need anything else before I'm back at the end of the month.

I'm hoping this line will remind her, once again, that I'm on vacation. I assume I won't hear back due to the time difference, but she writes back immediately.

Magda: You sent me the wrong draft of the speech yesterday. If Heidi hadn't caught it we'd be completely fucked. Totally unacceptable.

I freeze.

Hope: I'm so sorry! I don't work on that account so I just pulled the latest file from the drive.

Magda: Why would you send it when you don't work on the account? Get it together, Hope.

I flinch. I know that I don't deserve this—I was only trying to help—but I am too desperate for this job to advocate for myself.

Hope: Won't happen again.
Magda: You're set to send out the launch press release on Monday?

I stare at my phone. Why would *I*, a person several time zones and many countries away, send out an important press release?

Hope: I was going to task Lana with the distro since I'm abroad.
Magda: I'd prefer you be on it.

I frantically grab our cruise ship tablet programmed with the ship's schedule. On Monday we'll be in the Bahamas, so at least I won't have to rely on ship Wi-Fi. Rockabye is Conifer's first new product in sixteen months, and they are among our biggest clients. Magda will fire me if the release goes out late.

Hope: No problem.

She doesn't respond. I very badly want to throw my phone out to sea, but instead I program in ten reminders to myself to send out the press release.

While I'm doing that, a new text comes in from Felix.

His name, after being bombarded with Magda's so many times, is like a balm to the soul.

Felix: Hey, let me know when you're awake. Worried about you x.
Hope: I'm ok. Rough night but feeling better now.
Felix: Can I come by your room? I have something for you.

I look at myself in the mirror and am not at all pleased with my reflection. But I suppose if he saw me last night after puking, this will be an improvement.

Hope: Sure

I don't want to put on actual clothes and don't want to answer the door in my bathrobe, so I borrow one of Lauren's many silk caftans. Usually I try to avoid dressing like an aging Texas socialite, but if ever there is an appropriate time for a caftan, it's while convalescing on a cruise ship.

Because I don't want to look like I have a wasting illness, I also dab a few dots of concealer over the dark circles under my eyes and apply a little blush to my cheeks. I'm still disturbingly pallid, but there's a knock at the door before I can figure out what else to do about it.

When I open the door, Felix is standing in the hallway looking remarkably stressed.

"Good morning," I say.

"Is it, though?"

"I've had better."

"Were you able to sleep?"

"A little. Not my best night of REM."

He holds out a pill bottle. "I brought you these. Just remembered this morning that I packed them or I would have given them to you last night."

"What are they?"

"Electrolyte tablets. For hydration. You just put them in water. They're a bit vile, to be honest, but they work."

"Much better than Lauren dragging me downstairs for intravenous fluids."

"It was that bad?"

"I'll spare you the details." A yawn overtakes me, and I realize I should lie down. "I think I need to go back to bed."

"And miss poolside Pilates?" he asks with mock horror.

"Tragically, yes."

"Well, text me if you need anything. I'll check on you this afternoon." He pauses. "Unless you now associate me with nausea and would prefer never to see me again."

"I was worried it would be the other way around."

"Nope. I'm afraid we're permanently trauma bonded."

"Can't wait to spend a beautiful, codependent life together."

"Great. I'll buy you a ring at the gift shop. Apparently they have really good diamonds."

"Are you love bombing me?"

"I think you're the one who proposed."

"Mrs. Segrave would actually be an appropriate name for me after last night."

"Flattered you're taking my name."

I yawn again. I want to keep flirting with him but suddenly I can barely hold my eyes open.

"Sorry, I'm keeping you," he says. "I'll go. Get some rest."

"Maybe we can hang out later?" I venture. "Plan the wedding?"

He grins at me. "Yes, please."

I start to close the door but he says, "Hey, wait." He leans in and gives me a kiss on the cheek. "Feel better, yeah?"

I float back to bed and drink electrolyte water like it's a love potion. Lauren returns a few minutes later with Dramamine.

"They said it might make you sleepy," she says, handing me two pills.

"Already am."

"Good." She closes the blackout blinds. "Go back to bed."

I drift off immediately and sleep, hard, for so many hours that when Lauren pokes me awake, I have no idea if it's the middle of the afternoon or the middle of the night.

"Hopie?" she whispers. "Are you alive?"

"What time is it?" I ask.

"One thirty. Our spa appointment is in half an hour. Are you still up for it?"

A massage sounds perfect after crouching over the toilet all night.

"Yeah. Can you open the curtains?"

She does, and the afternoon light hits me like an assault.

"Gah!" I yell. "You're blinding me!'

"You told me to!"

She takes the huge black sunglasses she has clipped to her coverup and tosses them to me. I put them on and gulp down some water.

A wave of hunger hits me, unwelcome and terrifying.

"I'm scared to even ask this," I say, "but do we have any food?"

"I grabbed you some muffins and an apple at lunch."

I nearly gag at the thought of apples.

"I'll take a muffin."

She brings it to me on a plate, and I eat it in bed. She snaps a picture of me with her phone.

"Hey!" I protest. "What are you doing?"

"Capturing your vibe. You're giving glamorous 1970s invalid."

She shows me the photo. In it a woman with big, tousled hair wearing a turquoise caftan and oversized sunglasses dines off fine china in a fluffy white bed.

"Very Princess Margaret," Lauren says. "Can I post it?"

"No."

She texts it to me instead.

We gather bathing suits and reading material and head upstairs to the spa. We're greeted by a lovely smell—a combination of lavender, rosemary, eucalyptus, and sea salt. The lobby's at the bow of the ship on the top deck, with floor-to-ceiling windows. It has the best views of the ocean I've seen yet. I peer out distrustfully. The waters are so blue and placid that it's shocking they were fierce enough to make me violently ill last night.

"Welcome to the Coral Spa, ladies," the receptionist says. "I'm pleased to let you know your treatments have been upgraded on the house to the full Mermaid Package, with our compliments."

Lauren squeals. "Thank you *so* much. That's just what we need. Hope was up all night. Seasick."

"Oh no, Miss Lanover! Would you like a ginger tonic?"

My mouth goes dry at the idea of more ginger.

"No, thank you. I'm feeling much better."

They give us champagne instead. I donate mine to Lauren.

We change into bathing suits and robes and are taken into a warm, cave-like room made out of pink Himalayan sea salt. There are two copper tubs in the middle. They look like bathtubs, but they don't have taps and are half-full of fine black sand.

"This is volcanic basalt sand from Montserrat," one of our two spa attendants, Lucie, says. "It's incredibly mineral rich and contains detoxification properties that purge impurities from the body. It's heated to 104 degrees Fahrenheit for a warming treatment that will stimulate your circulatory system and awaken your senses."

This sounds *very* hot to me but I obey Lucie's instructions to take off my robe and step inside. The sand is soft and pleasantly warm under my feet. I sit down in the tub and stretch out.

Lucie and her colleague Chanlina then proceed to bury Lauren and I in a layer of hot sand up to our chins. They turn on soft New Age music and tell us they'll return in half an hour.

Lauren groans rapturously. "This feels amazing."

"It's like if a hot tub were a weighted blanket," I agree.

"I'm never getting out."

"How was the casino last night?" I ask her.

She sighs. "Well, first it was promising. I ran into that guy Ralph I met hiking and we played roulette. But then he totally granddaughter-zoned me."

I snort. "What does that mean?"

"He completely missed all my signals and started giving me life advice and talking about his kids. Then he offered to set me up with his grandson in Arkansas."

"Maybe the grandson is nice?"

"I'm not moving to Arkansas unless it's to marry a Walmart billionaire. The grandson works at a nonprofit. No *thank* you."

"Yeah, people who devote their lives to nonprofits must be terrible."

"You know what I mean. Anyway, then I went up to the cigar bar to see if I could meet someone else, and sat down next to this very handsome guy who was alone and not wearing a wedding ring. I said hello and he was friendly enough and he asked what I was doing and I said I was hoping he'd buy me a drink. And do you know what he said?"

"What?"

"He informed me that *drinks are free*. Like hello! I know that, sir! I'm hitting on you?"

"Ha. Suave."

"So then I ordered a cigar and went to sit by the piano to smoke it and look beguiling. Cuz like, who is not going to chat up a beautiful girl smoking a cigar alone, right? It's sexy and a perfect conversation piece."

"Right."

"Well, guess who came over and joined me? A group of three *women* on a girls trip. So I had to talk to them about tasting notes of Cuban versus Nicaraguan tobacco, which obviously I know about because you have to in my line of work, and they kept asking me questions and it took me like an hour to extricate myself. And by then I was all stinky from smoke so I decided to go upstairs and shower. And that's when I found you half-dead in the bathroom."

"I'm sorry it was a bust."

"It's fine. I made plans to meet Colin, that Irish whiskey distiller, at the outdoor dinner thing tonight. Do you want to come? He's extremely charming and has cute friends."

"Maybe. I'm going to see what Felix is up to."

"*Felix*, eh," she drawls.

I can't stop myself from grinning. "We went back to his room after the Elvis show last night and—"

"Hopie!" she cries. "You didn't!"

"No, not *that*. But he kissed me, and it was . . . lovely. Until I puked in his bathroom."

"You *didn't*."

"I did. At length. He was so nice about it. He gave me his bathrobe and got me ginger ale and then this morning he came over with electrolyte tablets. He's nice. I really like him."

It feels so good to talk to her like this. Just shooting the shit on vacation, without all the heaviness of my stalled-out life or the guilt I feel about overrelying on her. I smile to myself, until I notice she's gone oddly quiet.

"Something wrong?" I ask.

"Just be careful," she says.

I look over at her and she's frowning at me.

"Why do you say that?" I ask.

"You know what you do."

"What do you mean?"

"You meet sexy guys and go nuts over them immediately and then they turn out to be troubled or sleazy and you get your heart broken."

So much for easy breezy girl talk.

She is, of course, correct about my pattern.

But this crush is the first thing I've enjoyed in months. Can't she just . . . let me have it?

"Okay, I admit I've been guilty of that in the past," I say, "but I'm talking about *kissing* someone. I'm certainly not going to end up devastated over kissing a guy on a cruise ship. We're only here for ten days."

She side-eyes me. "I'm pretty sure you moved in with Gabe after ten days."

"Oh my God. It was three months! And excuse me, but you literally *told me* to hook up with Felix the day we met."

"Fair. Sorry. It's good for you to dabble with someone else. I was just imagining more of a fuck buddy situation, and I worry when you get all swoony like this. I'm really glad you're having fun."

I'm relieved she's not pressing the point. Lately, we've been bickering over our respective life choices. I get irritated with her incessant filming of every moment of her life, and while she doesn't outright say it, I think she thinks I'm too passive.

"I am having fun," I say. "Thank you for inviting me. I know I was a bit skeptical about this, but I'm having such a great time."

She smiles at me. "Good. It's nice to see you less hung up on Gabe."

"I'm not hung up on him," I say immediately.

She snorts. "You've been in mourning for him for months, Hope."

I consider this.

My feelings for him are still so complicated.

I loved him madly. From our first date, he enchanted me with long, intimate talks in which it felt like he could magically see inside my soul and was entranced by what he found there. And it was flattering, because of who he was.

He's an influential book editor, and he told me that despite my disappointments, I still had vast potential. That by our combined powers we could conquer the world. That feeling was magnetic. That feeling dulled my real life—the writer's block, the thankless deadlines at work, the constant low-grade financial anxiety, the dread that I'll never stop floundering.

I fell in love with that feeling as hard and fast as I fell in love with him.

But he panicked and fled when the smallest part of the fantasy he spun for us became real. And the way he did it—so abruptly, with so little regard for how it would upend my life—was, frankly, cruel.

I *should* hate him.

And yet I still miss him, a little. I miss our Saturdays at the New York Public Library, him scribbling on manuscripts in his glasses with his shirtsleeves rolled up, me toiling over the stories that I finally felt inspired to write. I miss the wine-drenched dinner parties we threw, the dazzling conversations with authors and artists that before I'd only known from the fiction pages of the *New Yorker* and exhibitions at the Guggenheim. I miss his solicitousness, his enthusiasm for introducing me to his friends and family, his intelligence and wit.

I miss believing in the fantasy of that life being my happy ever after.

That, more than anything, is what I'm in mourning for. The version of myself I might have been if the dream had actually come true.

"I'm not sure that's right," I say to Lauren, choosing my words carefully. She loathes Gabe, and thinks I should too—unilaterally, viciously, without mercy.

But I'm just not there.

And I'm tired of her lecturing me about it.

"I'm not pining for him anymore, per se. It's more like without him sugarcoating my life, I feel stuck."

"We have to get you out of that PR job," she says, perhaps tacitly agreeing not to dwell on this topic. "It's not healthy for you to work so hard at something you hate."

I do not inform her that I'm still being harassed by my boss, and on the hook to send out a press release on vacation. The spike in her blood pressure will undo the spa treatments.

"I know," I say. "But I'm so tired of bouncing around in entry-level positions trying to find something that sticks. I want to be *great* at something, you know?"

"You *are* great at something," she says. "You just need to start writing again. It's what you love. But it won't happen if you don't try."

"I know that," I say. My tone sounds defensive.

I hate that we're back in this dynamic. Her wanting more for me. Me falling short.

"Sorry, I don't mean to sound all harsh and judgey," Lauren says. "It's not like I'm living my dream life either."

This startles me.

"I thought you were," I say.

She sighs. "I like the money, obviously. I love being creative. But I'm a little over trotting around being a fake pickup artist, if I'm honest. I know it's my bread and butter, but I'm ready to meet someone for real."

It touches me that she's being vulnerable. Lately, I've been so emotionally shaky that she's acted almost like she's my mom—like she has to protect me from any of her problems. Sometimes her soft heart gets buried under all that bravado.

"I hope you let yourself," I say, thinking of the pleasure she took in flirting with the Irish guy from yesterday. "It would be so nice to see you in love. And you can always pivot to being a tradwife."

She snorts. "Honey, I don't have the birthing hips to make eight babies, and I spent enough time on the farm back in Texas."

"Well, your following adores you. You could post about your favorite cereal brand and you'd still get ten thousand likes."

"Actually," she says. "I might have a new opportunity. I didn't want to tell you until it was more concrete, but I'm in the running to host the Australian version of *Man of My Dreams*."

"Oh wow," I say. "That's fucking amazing. Why didn't you want to tell me?"

She looks at me out of the corner of her eye, wrinkling her lips. I realize she's worried about me.

"I'd be in Melbourne for a couple months," she says. "And if it works out, they'd potentially consider me for the UK version too."

"Oh," I say, realizing the implication. "So you'd be gone a long time."

"Yeah," she says. "And I'd really miss you."

It's sweet that she cares about me so much she doesn't want to leave me on my own. But I know what it's like to have a dream you don't pursue. I don't want that for her.

"I'd miss you too," I tell her. "So much. But you can't hesitate about big opportunities just because you're worried about me."

"You're right. I know you're right. But like, we've been two peas in a pod forever. It would be weird not to be in the same place."

"You have to go for it, my love," I say. "You're meant for big things."

"You are too," she says. "I mean that from the bottom of my heart."

"Love you," I tell her.

"I love you too, Hopie," she says. "I would hug you if I weren't buried in twenty pounds of sand."

The spa ladies come back and exhume us, then lead us to a steam shower where they scour us with sea sponges native to the Caribbean. We emerge pink and tingly, wrapped in fluffy robes, and are escorted to a room facing the ocean, where we lay on massage tables and have our faces daubed in serums and then wrapped in actual kelp.

"We're gonna smell like sushi," Lauren says when the facialists leave us alone to absorb chlorophyll. "And then how will we inveigle our suitors?"

"I thought my suitor was off limits," I said.

"Changed my mind on that. I'm just being overprotective. Maybe a good ol' fashioned makeout is just what the doctor ordered." She pauses. "If you *guard your heart*."

"I will," I promise. "If you swear you'll stop guarding yours."

Felix

So-called days at sea have a very strong resemblance to rehab. Gentle exercise, fresh air, board games, art classes. The only thing missing is the group therapy and twelve-step meetings.

I amuse myself with a long workout in the gym, a Codenames tournament with my family, and a very frustrating painting lesson my mother drags me to. We're supposed to capture the horizon over the sea, but my attempt turns into a sodden blue rectangle with a watery yellow line across the middle.

"Hmm," Mum says, inspecting my work. "Were you attempting a Rothko?"

"You know I don't excel at the arts."

"That's not true. You're fabulous at drawing."

This is not fully accurate, but I can sketch passably. I designed all my tattoos.

"And," Mum adds, "you were always so good at the tuba."

"Oh God, don't remind me." I was assigned the instrument at school, where we were all required to participate in the orchestra. It didn't take. Thank Christ it was an all-boys school, as my red-faced attempts would certainly not have helped with the ladies.

"Have you seen Hope today?" she asks, unnaturally casual. It's clear she's now invested in my four-day-old relationship. There's nothing like trying to get to know someone while under the constant surveillance of your immediate family.

"I saw her this morning," I say. "I might ask her to have supper, if you can survive one without me."

"I think we'll manage."

I pull out my phone and open my text chain with Hope.

Felix: How's the health?

Hope: Feeling *much* better.

Hope: Just left the spa.

Hope: Got my whole face wrapped in kelp.

Felix: Hot.

Hope: As I made clear, I'm trying to seduce you.

Felix: Care to continue that process over supper?

Felix: I hear there's a Caribbean feast.

There's a long pause while she's typing, then nothing. I worry I'm about to be rejected, until the phone vibrates again.

Hope: TBH, not sure I'm up for a whole luau vibe . . .

I'm glad we're typing, so she can't see my disappointment. But then she adds:

Hope: Would you want to hunker down and order room service instead?

Would I ever.

Felix: I'd be honored.

Felix: Why don't you come over to mine so we're not in Lauren's hair?

Hope: Is soonish ok? I know you're a European and probably prefer to dine at 10 p.m., but I'm beat.

Felix: Hate to tell you this but Brexit happened.

Hope: Oh, right, sorry for your loss.
Hope: How's 7?

That's in forty-five minutes.

Felix: Perfect. See you then xx.

I stand up. "I have to go," I tell Mum. "I have a date."

She smiles at me. "Have fun."

I stand up to go. "Darling!" she calls to my back.

I turn around to see her holding up my work of accidental abstract expressionism.

"Don't you want to give Hope your beautiful painting?"

I laugh. "I see where Prue and Pear get it from."

Back in my room I dial the number for Crisanto.

"Good evening, Mr. Felix," he says.

"Hi there. Can I ask a favor?"

"I'd be delighted to help."

"I'll be dining in my room tonight with a friend and I was wondering if there's a way to track down some fresh flowers."

"Certainly. Would you prefer roses or tulips?"

"Roses, please."

"A wonderful choice. Would you like me to come prepare your table?"

"If you wouldn't mind. Is it possible to set something up outside?"

"Of course, sir. It will be a beautiful sunset."

"Do you have candles?"

"I do."

"Thanks, Crisanto."

I take a quick shower while I'm waiting, then change into jeans and a T-shirt. I'm tidying the lounge when Crisanto and Belhina arrive with a cart laden with flowers, china, and a charcuterie board I didn't even ask for. They take it all outside and get to work transforming my veranda into a scene from *Beauty and the Beast*. All that's missing is a clock singing "Be Our Guest."

The old me would have cringed at myself for putting so much obvious effort into a date. My style of courting women was to let booze and chemistry do all the work. But one thing I've learned in recovery is that sincerity is healthy. That it's okay to be a bit vulnerable about the things you want.

And if you go after it armed with effort rather than chemical courage, your odds of fostering connection are stronger.

I'm not looking for a drinking buddy, or a fuck buddy.

Eventually, I'm looking for a lover.

A partner.

I'm not ready for that yet.

What I want with Hope is something light and sexy and, above all, temporary.

But being earnest with her, however fleetingly, feels like good practice for becoming the type of man I want to be.

Hope knocks at the door at seven sharp which, as a chronically punctual person, I appreciate. She's wearing a long, gauzy, Grecian-style white dress and her face is totally bare. She's radiant.

"Wow," I say.

"Sorry, I didn't have it in me to dress up."

"This isn't dressed up? You look gorgeous."

"Must be the kelp."

"Come in," I say, stepping aside.

"I'm shocked you're letting me back in here after last night."

"Stockholm syndrome. Um—" I grab the vase of flowers off the wet bar. "I got you these."

"Felix!" she exclaims. "You don't have to butter me up."

"Right. Well then technically Crisanto got them for you."

"I guess I'll go have dinner with Crisanto then." She turns around like she's going to leave.

"No, wait. It was my idea. Also, I thought we could eat outside. That all right?"

I gesture at the open veranda doors. Dusk is beginning to fall, and the candlelit table looks quite nice, even if the vibe is more "Club Med ad" than would normally be my style.

"You, Felix Segrave, are a gentleman and a scholar."

"Minus the scholar bit."

We walk outside. I have beverages chilling in an ice bucket.

"Want a sparkling water? Or some champagne?" I had Crisanto bring a bottle of fizz.

"Sparkling water is great."

I point at a charcuterie board set up between the two chaise lounges.

"There are nibbles, but I didn't order food yet—I thought you might want to look at the menu first."

"In a minute. Let's sit." She stretches out on one of the loungers. "Wow," she says. "The sunset is going to be amazing."

I sit down on the other chaise. There's a breeze, and her scent floats over to me.

"You always smell incredible," I tell her. "Like magnolias."

"Good nose. My perfume is literally called *Eau de Magnolia*. Far too expensive but a girl's got to live."

I note this is the second time she's mentioned her finances. I hope she's not in dire straits, but the Brit in me cringes at frank talk of money, so I don't ask.

"My parents have a big magnolia tree in Hampshire," I say. "I associate the smell with my childhood."

"I thought you grew up in London."

"I did, but we have a family house in the countryside. Spent summers there."

"Do you have an ancestral manor?" she asks wryly, like she expects the answer to be no.

"Uh, yes, actually," I admit. I always feel sheepish revealing my family's aristocratic background. The way I grew up is absurdly privileged.

"*Really?*" Hope asks. "How ancient?"

"Eighteenth century–ish."

Her eyes widen. "Does it have a name?"

"Downton Abbey."

"Be serious."

"It's technically called Elswale Court. But no one calls it that."

"Next you're going to tell me you're a duke."

"Definitely not a duke." I hesitate, not sure whether to tell her the full truth. But if she finds out later it will be strange that I didn't. So I add: "Just the lowly son of a baronet."

"*Wait*. Your dad's a baronet? Really?"

"Yep."

"So that means in the event of his unfortunate passing . . ."

"I will become a baronet, yes."

"This is incredible. Now I want to deviously marry you for your title."

"This is the most stereotypically American you've ever acted," I say, ignoring the marrying me for my title part. People have, unfortunately, wanted to do just this in the past.

"You're a British gentleman with an eighteenth-century manor house called Elswale Court and *I'm* the caricature? Anyway, Lady Hope Gertrude Segrave has a nice ring to it, don't you think?"

"Your middle name is *Gertrude*?"

"I'm afraid so."

"I wasn't prepared."

"No one ever is."

"Is it a family name?"

"No. My mom's obsessed with Gertrude Stein."

"Ah."

"Are you named after anyone?"

"Felix the Cat."

"Mmm, that tracks. You look just like him."

"Thanks."

"You know, I was wondering," she says. "Why is it that you're named Felix when both of your sisters have 'P' names? Why not Percy or something."

"Felix is actually my middle name."

"What's your first name?"

"Peregrine."

Hope throws back her head and laughs. Not like "ha ha." More like a full-throated cackle. "No it's not," she says. "Stop."

"I don't see what's so funny. My full name is Peregrine Charles Felix Segrave."

"Am I in a regency romance novel right now? Because that's the only place I've ever seen the name Peregrine."

"I don't know about regency. But I can provide the romance part, obviously," I say, gesturing at the overblown tablescape.

She smiles at me.

"Obviously," she says softly.

"Before we get to that part," I say, "do you want to order food? I'm starving."

"Yeah, me too."

I hand her the room service menu. "Want to take a look?"

"Sure. What are you in the mood for?"

"Surprise me."

She takes the menu and walks inside. I hear her speaking on the phone, but I can't make out what she's saying. She comes back and spreads some brie onto a cracker.

"So, Sir Peregrine," she says. "I want to continue to interrogate you."

"Sounds relaxing."

"First, how old are you?"

"Thirty-two."

"When's your birthday?"

"November third."

"Oh no, a *Scorpio*. How terrifying. Are you as vindictive and secretive as they say?"

"Yes, but I make up for it with my romantic passion."

"Speaking of which, you're single, right?"

"Very much so."

"And why would a handsome boy like yourself not have a girlfriend?"

"I could ask you the same question."

"You think I'm a handsome boy?"

"I do."

"You first."

"I was engaged a couple of years ago. Before I got sober. It flamed out in a pretty spectacular way."

"Spectacular how?"

"We had a huge drunken fight three weeks before the wedding and I woke up on my restaurant floor in a pile of glass and my own vomit. That kind of spectacular."

She sucks in her breath. "Ouch."

"Yeah. I went to rehab and canceled the wedding. She stopped speaking to me. Bad show. I haven't been with anyone since."

She's quiet.

"Sorry you asked?"

"No, not at all. Sorry that happened to you."

"It was inevitable. I'd been out of control for years, and our relationship was chaotic. Nonstop partying, nonstop fighting. I loved her a lot, but we enabled each other's worst tendencies."

"And you haven't been with anyone since?"

"I've been focused on staying healthy, getting stable. My business was an absolute shambles, all my relationships were dysfunctional. So now I'm that guy who works out and does therapy and drinks two liters of water a day."

"It looks good on you."

"Thanks. Now it's your turn. How on earth are *you* single?"

She sighs deeply.

"I had a bit of a heartbreak last year. I've been avoiding men."

"Can I ask what happened, or is it too fresh?"

"No, it's fine. Classic story. Girl meets powerful book editor boy who promises to help fulfill her writerly dreams. Boy sweeps her off her feet with visions of their perfect life together. Girl moves in with boy and he immediately decides he's in over his head and breaks up with her."

"Damn. How long ago was this?"

"Eight months ago. I'm okay now, but things got hairy after it happened. I was blindsided, and leaned hard into drinking away my sorrows at night, and then dabbling in uppers to stay awake and do my job. Rinse, repeat."

"Definitely been there," I say. "I'm so sorry."

"Yeah, it was dark," she says. "But I've been putting myself back together. I moved in with Lauren for a while. Stopped drinking like a fish. Went to therapy. I'm, uh—" She hesitates, like she's suddenly at a loss for the right word. "Over it."

That brief pause makes me wonder if it's fully true. Eight months is not such a long time to heal from a cataclysmic breakup. But I'm not going to ask her follow-up questions—it's not my business.

"Sounds like we've had a similar ride," I say.

"How lucky for us."

"I'm grateful, actually. If my life hadn't blown up when it did, I would probably have been dead before I turned forty. I like living this way. I'm terrified of anything messing it up, rocking my routine, you know? That's why I haven't dated."

I hope this disclosure isn't too personal. I don't want to scare her off. But she nods.

"Yes. I totally get that. Though in my case I'm more scared of backsliding into the emotional side of it. I have this preternatural ability to fall hard and fast, get absorbed into other people's worlds, and lose sight of myself."

"Well, aren't we the optimistic pair," I say.

"It's okay," she says. "We're safe together."

"Why do you say that?"

"Because how much damage could we do in a week?"

Hope

Felix's honest, no-bullshit approach to his past—and to mine—is refreshing. This is not a man who intends to seduce me with visions of a better life.

He wants a harmless, fun little cruise fling.

So do I.

I think it will be healing.

The doorbell rings.

"That must be the food," Felix says. "I'll go get it."

"Wait. I have to confess something," I say.

"Uh oh," he says. "What?"

"I ordered a *feast.*"

"Great. I'm starving."

"No, you don't understand."

But he's already walking away.

I brace myself.

He lets in Crisanto, who rolls a two-tiered cart crammed precariously with silver platters. Crisanto calmly arranges everything on the table as though ordering eight separate dishes is not at all weird and gluttonous, tells us to ring him when we'd like it cleared away, and *bon appetit.*

"Jesus, Hope," Felix says when he's gone. "Are you expecting twelve more people?"

"I wasn't sure what you liked, and I didn't want to alienate you with my bad taste," I say. "I'd rather alienate you with my maximalism instead."

"You haven't alienated me. Though I will say pappardelle bolognese, steak tartare, crab cakes, coq au vin, and endive salad are an odd combination."

"Don't forget the truffle macaroni and cheese."

"I blacked it out."

"Good because there's also dessert."

"Dare I ask?"

"Molten chocolate brownies and pistachio cheesecake. I declined ice cream because I figured it would melt in the four hours it will take to eat all this."

"You're a marvel."

"Wait until you see how much damage I can do."

I load up my plate with a generous assemblage of food and dive in, both out of rabid hunger and determination not to put it to waste. Felix, probably just to avoid embarrassing me, does the same.

"What, as a professional chef, is your review of the cuisine?" I ask him, once I'm out of danger of hypoglycemia.

"This Roquefort dressing is delicious. And I'm impressed by the homemade pappardelle. Though the macaroni cheese is a bit too truffley for my palate, and the crab cakes could do with less potato and a sharper aioli."

"A measured response."

"No chef should be judged by room service food. Unless you're doing chicken fingers. Those have to be perfect."

"Do you do chicken fingers in your restaurants?"

"Sadly, no."

"Tell me your specialties."

He describes things like Cornish crab salad with grated egg, aged lamb tartare with pancetta and tarragon crostini, roasted pork belly with celeriac mash, butter-poached Dover sole with cod's roe and sage emulsion.

"I'm dying," I say. "Let's steal a lifeboat and sail directly to London."

"Can you sail?" he asks.

"I can canoe."

"Surely a translatable skill."

"I have other skills."

"Like what?"

"Juggling. Architectural photography. Badminton."

"Really?" he asks.

"Of course not. All I'm good at is writing short stories no one will ever read and college admissions essays for high school students."

"That last part seems unethical."

"Well, I don't technically write them. I just tell them what to say and edit it with a very heavy hand. It's a good side hustle to earn extra cash."

"Tell me more about the short stories part."

I sigh. I don't love talking about my failed ambitions and wasted potential to people I'm trying to sleep with.

"I always wanted to be a writer," I say. "A novelist. I had some success early on—sold a book when I was still in college."

"Wow," he says. "That's amazing."

"Yeah," I say. "But it was with a small press, and they went out of business before the book was printed. My agent tried to find a new publisher but no one else picked it up, and I was so demoralized I turned to short stories. But my MFA collection didn't sell either. I still dabble here and there, but nothing good enough to submit, and my agent has likely forgotten I exist. And I don't really have time to pursue it, between my job and freelancing on the side."

I feel myself wilting. It's never fun to admit that you're living your backup plan. But he takes it all in without judgment. With compassion in his eyes.

"You're obviously brilliant," he says. "I suspect you'll figure it out."

I shrug. "Maybe. I hope so. In any case, this is a nice break from real life."

He smiles. "It is. I'm usually not keen on holidays. Idle hands are the devil's workshop, and all that. Mum nearly had to break my arms to get me here. But I'm having a delightful time."

"All that bingo?"

"Nope. Met a nice girl."

My heart thumps like the tail of an overexcited puppy who's been told he's a very good boy.

"Yeah," I say. "Me too."

I *cannot* sensibly take this conversation forward without swooning, so I change the subject. "What are you doing for tomorrow's entertainment?"

"Zip-lining," he says.

"Ah, too bad. I'm deeply afraid of zip-lining."

"Have you ever tried it?"

"God, no."

"What are you doing?"

"Embarrassing myself on a surfboard."

"I'm sure you'll be great."

"Um, you saw my attempt to aquacise. And that was in a tiny pool with the elderly."

"It was good, family-friendly entertainment."

I snort. "Yeah. I remember. Vividly and deep in my bones."

"Oh, I meant to tell you," he says. "I finished *Middlemarch*."

"Wow. That was fast."

"Trying to impress that girl I mentioned."

"It's working. What did you think?"

"I was relieved to see that love conquered all in the end."

"Well, except for poor Lydgate," I say.

"Yeah, tragic figure, that guy. But it was, in all seriousness, one of the best books I've ever read. What, in your estimation as a scholar of English literature, should I read next?"

"Well, she's not British, but have you fucked with Edith Wharton?"

"I have not."

"Let's get you on *Age of Innocence*. Very doomed-marriage-core."

"On it. One moment, please."

He takes out his phone and starts typing.

"I'm going audio on this one," he says.

"So you can listen while zip-lining?"

"Yep."

We both laugh, and then we're quiet for a moment. It's not an uncomfortable silence, but there's an air of uncertainty. The sun has gone down, the meal has been eaten, and I'm not sure what he's thinking in terms of what happens next. So, in the spirit of our general policy of self-disclosure, I say, "What do we do now?"

He gives me a crooked grin. "You mentioned something about seducing me?"

I'm glad that this is where his mind went. I'm not going to let myself fall for him. But I am very much going to let myself sleep with him.

If I can remember the steps.

There was a time when I prided myself on being quite a pro at this. But after Gabe, and my long abstinence, I feel a bit uncertain of myself.

"Yeah, about that—" I begin.

"Oh, shit," he says. "Sorry, I don't mean to be an asshole. You definitely don't need to seduce me. I was just—"

"No!" I say. "I still want to! I'm just not sure how to go about it. Should I order more food?"

"If I eat more you are definitely not going to *want* to seduce me."

"Roger."

"We could go inside," he suggests. "And maybe I could kiss you?"

"I like this plan," I say.

We stand up and he takes my hand and squeezes it, then walks me into his living room. He turns to me and opens his arms. I step into them.

He leans down and softly brushes my lips.

My entire body radiates approval. I press closer.

He takes the back of my head in his hand and kisses me deeply. And when I lean in to devour him, he puts his hands on my hips and kisses his way down my neck, then lower.

Maybe I do remember how to do this. I grab the hem of my dress and pull it up over my head. I'm not wearing a bra, and I'm aware that this sight is astonishing.

By the look on his face, he is aware too.

I reach for him. "Touch me."

His grabs me and pulls my hips to his. His hands trace my waist, the small of my back, my rib cage, and then, deliciously, my breasts. He's hard, and I grab his ass and press myself against him.

It feels amazing.

So amazing that I let out a jagged sound that gives me away.

"Can I take off your shirt?" I ask.

He does it himself, throwing it onto the floor like he never wants to see it again.

And nor do I, because his body is ridiculous, and all I want is to feel it against mine.

We grab each other and things get frenzied and raw, and I'm grinding my hips into his, and he's sucking my nipples and I'm moaning and he's moaning and his hand is tracing over my panties and I'm so wet I know I've soaked through them and it's so fucking hot that I widen my legs for him and hear myself whisper "Please."

His fingers are warm and assured, and he doesn't stop kissing me as he strokes expertly between my legs, teasing me, and I'm whimpering and I can actually hear the sound his fingers make against me as they caress me, venture inside me, and it's like the most erotic ASMR I've ever heard. He's biting my bottom lip and his stubble is brushing up against my face and I'm grinding myself against his fingers, the palm of his hand, and then I'm breaking completely apart.

I shudder against him and go boneless and wobbly as wave after wave of pleasure rolls through me. He catches me, holds me against him, and I can feel his hard cock and I want it inside me like I can't remember wanting anything in this world for a long, long, long time.

I reach down and unbutton his jeans.

"Hey," he says softly. "We don't have to—"

"I want to," I say, slipping my hand into his underwear and stroking the hard, hot length of him. He pulses under my hand and sucks in his breath. I pause, not sure if that gasp is a yes or a no.

"I mean, if you do," I say, looking into his eyes. They're green, almost yellow around the irises, and the intensity in them says yes at the same time that he does out loud, like he's never wanted anything more in his life.

"Do you have a bed?" I ask.

"As it happens, I do."

"Can I see it?"

He picks me up and I wrap my legs around him and let him carry me into the bedroom.

Felix

I put Hope down on my bed and enjoy the debauched bloody sight of her as I pull off my jeans. She's all breasts and hips and thick thighs and I don't want to objectify her but she's looking at me, sultry and limpid, like she wants me to. And frankly I can't help it.

"Come here," she says.

"Can I just look at you for a minute? Because you are un-fucking real."

"I'm very real," she says, shimmying off her panties. The dark thatch of hair over her pussy is as perfect as the rest of her, and my cock actually trembles. She lies back against the duvet, puts her arms above her head, and widens her legs. "I want to feel you," she says. "Everywhere."

Briefs have never come off my body so quickly.

I crawl onto the bed and pull her on top of me. "I want you inside me so bad," she says, bearing down on my cock and holding herself there, her pussy just grazing my erection. I can feel her wetness against my bare skin and it's so fucking hot that I moan.

And then I remember.

"Fuck," I gasp out. "I don't have a condom. I wasn't expecting to—"

"Yeah, me neither," she says. "Shit."

We lock eyes, panting, pulsing against each other as we consider this, dying.

"I have an IUD," she gets out. "And I haven't been with anyone since my breakup."

"Me neither," I say. "Do you think we should wait, or—"

"I really, really don't want to wait."

That's all I need to hear. I slide into her.

I almost black out from how perfect we fit. I hear a strangled cry come out of my throat and before I can be embarrassed by it, she says, "Oh fuck yeah, moan for me."

I do, again. I can't help it.

My entire body is one desperate erogenous zone.

Hope lifts herself up and starts riding me, throwing back her head and arching her back, giving me an astounding view of her astounding breasts. I reach up and thumb her nipples and she gasps, closes her eyes, rides me faster, squeezing my hips between her thighs like she can't get me deep enough.

I grab her hips and pull her down, flip her over so I'm on top, then slide back into her. "Oh *fuck* yes," she cries. She puts her knees over my shoulders and clenches my cock with her pussy.

"Christ," I groan. "You're going to make me come."

But she's already there. She spasms over and over against my cock, which takes me right past the edge and into an oblivion I didn't know you could reach without drugs.

We're both sweaty and panting as we melt into the mattress.

I fold her into my arms and kiss her.

"That was . . ." I start, but I can't find the words.

"Orchestral," she provides.

She burrows into me and I nuzzle my lips against her temple and stroke her hair.

I feel bizarrely emotional. And then I realize why.

"What's wrong?" she asks.

"Uh, nothing. It's, um . . . I've just never done that sober before," I say quietly.

She pulls back and looks tenderly into my eyes. "Really?"

"Really."

"How did it feel?" she asks softly.

"Intense," I say.

"In a good way?"

"In a really good way. I didn't feel like I was just trying to get off, or get you off, you know? I was fully in it. Does that make sense?"

"Yeah. It does. I'm glad I got to be the one to share that with you," she says. "Thank you, for trusting me."

"Can I trust you with something else?"

"Yes," she says. "Anything."

"I have this fantasy."

"Ooh, a fetish? Tell me more."

"No. My fantasy is to wake up beside you. Will you stay?"

She runs her fingers over my lower lip. "So you can try sober morning sex?"

"And perhaps some sober midnight sex. Maybe a little sober two a.m. sex. But losing my sunrise virginity would also be a perk."

She gets a wicked gleam in her eyes.

"Did you know I've taken four men's virginity?"

I bark out a laugh.

"I think you forgot to mention it."

"Ah, rare oversight. I usually lead with that."

"It's an impressive accomplishment. Tell me more."

"The first time was with my sophomore year boyfriend in high school. First love. Very stressful. Took several tries to accomplish it."

"But you persevered."

"Yes. Then we figured out how to do it, but we broke up. So I went about refining my skills with other callers."

"I had no idea you were such a seductress."

"Why not? It worked on you."

"It worked *very* well."

"When did you lose your virginity?" she asks.

"Fifteen. With Gemma Bertram, in a spare room at a house party, after splitting approximately a liter of Malibu."

"I'm impressed you could get it up after that much coconut rum."

"If alcohol impeded my ability to get an erection, I'd have just been the fifth man whose virginity you've taken."

She laughs, but it turns into a yawn. "I'm tired. Do you really want me to sleep over?"

"How else will I ravish you 'til dawn?"

She wriggles happily against me. "I enthusiastically accept," she says.

"I'm gonna shower," I say.

"With me?" she asks innocently.

"Maybe that's my fetish."

"Let's go."

The shower is spacious as far as the dimensions of a cruise ship bathroom go, but it's tight for two people. Hope has to smush against me.

"Sorry," she says. "My milkmaid boobs take up all the room."

"Your milkmaid boobs are making me astonishingly aroused."

"Touch them," she says urgently.

I caress them with my tongue, drawing her nipples into my mouth. She gasps, and it's so hot I don't want to stop. So I don't. Suddenly she starts shaking and cries out, bracing herself against the wall.

Holy shit.

"Did you just come from that?" I ask.

"Party trick," she says, taking ragged breaths.

"I'm going to expire."

"Let me make you come one more time before you die."

She does.

Once we're clean and sated we towel off and climb back into bed. I turn off the lights and she snuggles up beside me.

It always takes me at least an hour to fall asleep, which I usually find frustrating.

But tonight, listening to Hope drift off beside me, it feels like a gift.

6
SECOND MATE

Wonders of the Caribbean, Day 5

Welcome to Basseterre, St. Kitt's, and Nevis!

Today the *Romance of the Sea* takes you to the white sand shores and verdant mountains of St. Kitts and Nevis. Culture hunters can stroll down the cobblestone streets through the charming colonial architecture and bustling markets of Basseterre, or explore the imposing Brimstone Hill Fortress, a UNESCO World Heritage Site. Intrepid adventurers can fly through the rainforest canopy with a thrilling zip line tour of the jungle, surf the gentle swells of Frigate Bay, or hike to the summit of Mount Liamuiga, an extinct volcano. And don't forget to explore the unspoiled vistas on the St. Kitt's Scenic Railway.

Kick back after your exciting day this evening with the tunes of Billy Joel at the Piano Bar. Or songbirds can provide the entertainment themselves—don't miss karaoke at 21:00 in the Mermaid Club!

Have a wonderful day!

Hope

The only downside to waking up with a boy you can't keep your hands off is having to leave him when your alarm goes off at seven a.m.

Felix stirs at the sound of my phone beeping. "What time is it?" His voice is thick with sleep and he has tousled hair and bedroom eyes. It's one of the better sights I've seen in my lifetime.

"Seven," I tell him.

"Too early. You're not permitted to get out of bed." He throws an arm around me and pulls me close. He's naked, and his body is warm from sleep. All I want to do is nestle up and stay here all day—especially when he starts kissing his way up the side of my neck.

I decide I can spare fifteen minutes. We make good use of it.

"Operation Morning Sex accomplished," I say.

"Vastly superior to a hangover."

I flick him. "Thanks for the compliment?"

He kisses me. "Let's stay in bed all day. You can teach me elevenses sex, teatime sex . . ."

I gently detach from him. "I have to go get ready. My excursion leaves at eight thirty."

"Gutting."

"Surf lessons wait for no man. Think of me while you're zip-lining?"

"That won't be a problem. I'll almost certainly get distracted and crash into a tree."

"Don't do that. Your sisters will make fun of you."

"I will promise to stay safe," he says, "if you promise we can do this again tonight."

I give him one last kiss. "Obviously. I'll text you when I get back."

"Have fun. Avoid sharks. And Hope?"

"Yeah?"

"Thank you for last night. I hope I wasn't too . . . much."

He means when he got a little teary the first time.

That was my favorite part.

"You," I say, "were perfect."

And I mean it. The sex was amazing in its own right. But it was heightened by how vulnerable he was with me. How honest.

I'm already beginning to be pained by the fact that this bliss is temporary. That in a matter of days, we'll have to say goodbye.

But the high I'm feeling is no doubt in large part due to the fact that there's no pressure for this to last. No question of what we are to each other. No time for games or overthinking. Just pure crush jitters and sex endorphins.

It's the sexual equivalent of staying in a hotel ten times nicer than your apartment.

Lauren is on the veranda in a flowing coral caftan and full makeup when I get back to our room.

"Well hello, my little strumpet," she says, taking a sip of cold brew.

"Where did you get that?" I ask. I'm dying for caffeine. Felix and I didn't do much sleeping.

"Saint Crisanto," she says. "He brought one for you too. And there are almond croissants." She gestures at a small spread on the patio table and I grab a pastry and wolf it down in three bites.

"Worked up an appetite?" she asks dryly.

"I think I burned more calories last night than I did last year."

"Sounds X-rated."

"Oh my *God*, Lauren. I went, like, full Sonic the Hedgehog on him."

She snorts. "Don't make me choke on my coffee."

"Sorry."

"Was he a generous lover?" she asks.

"Only you can say 'generous lover' with a straight face."

"Don't avoid the question."

"Without getting into details, *generous* is not an adequate word," I say, remembering the miracles he performed with his tongue in the middle of the night.

"Good," she says. "You need a man you can use for his body."

"I know. And it's great because we also have a real connection. Like all these honest things just come out of me when I talk to him."

The cat-who-ate-the-cream look fades from her face. She scrunches up her lips, like she wants to say something and is looking for the right words.

"What?" I ask.

"That's exactly what you said about Gabe."

"Gabe lived in the same country as me. This is different."

"Is it?"

"You've already given me this lecture. I'm really not in the mood to hear it again. And anyway, all of this don't-fall-in-love-on-a-cruise-ship business is a bit rich coming from a girl who's here to meet a husband."

"Darling, when's the last time I got my heart broken? I'm strategic when it comes to men. You're pure emotion, and you know it."

"I'm not falling in love, I promise. I only meant that I actually like him, which is the icing on the cake. Like, I could see us being friends after this."

She sighs. "Oh, Lord."

This irritates me. But I'm not going to take the bait.

"Anyway, I should get dressed," I say. "We have to leave for surfing in twenty-five minutes."

"Um, so about that."

"Oh God. What now?"

"Colin asked me to go with him on a food tour, so I switched at the last minute."

I should have known something was suspicious when she wasn't wearing a designer rash guard.

"Lauren! Surfing was your idea in the first place! You said it would attract fit men with coastal homes."

"And it will. Felix is probably going. He looks like the type. Did you ask him?"

"He's zip-lining with his sisters."

"Shit. Sorry. I would have told you I was changing plans but I didn't want to interrupt your date."

"You are a menace."

"Just skip it if you don't want to go."

"No, the beach is supposed to be amazing. I'll go alone."

"Good. And promise you'll come with me to karaoke tonight."

I look her dead in the eyes. "Of course we're going. Together. Do *not* betray me on this."

She puts her hand over her heart. "I swear."

I put on my trusty nip-slip bathing suit, since if it caused a wardrobe malfunction during pool aerobics, how could it go wrong for surfing? I skip makeup, throw on shorts and a T-shirt, and head downstairs to meet the group.

A few people are already there, and most of them are close to my age. I sit down at a table with the attractive young couple I saw when we were checking in. As expected, they're on their honeymoon. It turns out they are also from New York, so we're comparing notes on our jobs and neighborhoods when I see it.

See *him*.

It's Gabe.

Gabe Newhouse.

My ex-boyfriend.

Standing in the doorway to the room, gazing at me, a hand pressed over his heart.

I lurch to my feet involuntarily.

"Hope," he says in a voice so loud every single person in the room turns and looks at him.

He bounds over to me and wraps me in a full body hug before I can react.

"I can't believe this," he says, squeezing me so tight I cough.

I push him off as firmly as I can without making a scene. "Stop," I hiss.

He steps back, eyes shining. "Sorry," he says. "I'm suffocating you. It's just—my God, what are the odds?"

"What are you *doing* here?" I ask shakily. "Are you stalking me?"

This is unlikely, given he so callously broke up with me, but it's no more inconceivable than him being here out of a lust for mass travel to the Caribbean. Gabe is a sailboat-in-Nantucket kind of person, not a cruise ship kind of person.

He laughs. "No, I'm here as a hostage, actually." He rolls his eyes in that conspiratorial way he has, like he's inviting you into a joke. "It's Gran's eighty-fifth birthday. She made me promise I'd take her on a cruise if she lived to see it. As though there was any question. That woman will outlive us all."

This throws me.

"Maeve wanted to go on a cruise?" I ask.

Gabe's grandmother is an intimidatingly patrician Bostonian from a family so old and rich there are hospital wings and Ivy League buildings named after them. Think the Kennedys, minus the political ambitions and tragedies.

I'd have thought she'd want to celebrate her birthday with gin and tonics at the family estate on Martha's Vineyard. Not on a boat called the *Romance of the Sea*.

"She did, oddly," Gabe says. "Highly out of character, I know. She'll die to see you."

"Then I'd better stay away from her," I hear myself say. I am not conscious of actually thinking up the words because I feel like I am observing this scene from outside my body.

"No, she's going to demand an audience," he says. "You know how she is."

I do. He introduced me to his family within a month of our meeting each other. We spent an entire summer commuting to their place on Martha's Vineyard for long weekends.

They were surprisingly welcoming for moneyed WASPs.

Probably because they, like me, thought we were going to get married.

"But what are *you* doing here?" he asks. "I thought you always spent the last two weeks of August in Vermont."

I am paralyzed between the desire to leap off the boat into the harbor to escape him, and the desire to play it cool so he can't tell how completely rocked I am that he's here.

I decide to go with cool.

"My parents are selling the cottage," I say. "And Lauren is doing a sponsorship with the cruise line, so we decided to take a free vacation."

He grins. "Classic Lauren."

He clocks that the couple across from us is looking at us attentively, and because he has perfect manners, he extends his hand graciously to the woman, Nuala.

"Gabe Newhouse," he says.

He always proactively introduces himself, and always uses his first and last name. It's a habit that would come off as obnoxious if he weren't so handsome and friendly.

And he's certainly that. He has the ability to be both refined and exuberant, dripping charisma without coming on too strong. And with his golden blond hair and striking brown eyes, not to mention the perfect tailoring of the expensive clothes on his fit six-foot-two frame, people can't help but be drawn in.

I certainly couldn't.

"How do you two know each other?" Nuala asks.

"It's the damnedest thing," Gabe says. "We used to date."

Nuala glances at me, as if trying to read whether this is a good thing or a bad thing. *Bad*, I telegraph to her with my eyes, as though she can save me.

She can't.

The only thing that can save me is to make an excuse and leave.

I again perform a mental calculation as to the wisdom of this. If I go, I will spare myself the pain of being around the person who has hurt me the most in my life. On the downside, I will have let him run me off, making me seem pathetic or resentful.

My pride finds the latter unacceptable.

But there's something else.

Something that horrifies me.

It's the small part of me that wants to stay because I've *missed* him.

I know. I *know*.

But I can't help it. I loved him so much that his physical nearness is causing a strange, contradictory reaction in my body. I'm both repelled and attracted at once.

So I stay.

Of course I stay.

"Yes, it's a bizarre coincidence," I say to Nuala with a smile. "Gabe, Nuala and Clayton are from New York as well. They live in Fort Greene."

I know this will cause him to hold forth on how much he loves Brooklyn. He does, but in the way of a man with a palatial apartment on the Upper West Side who finds the outer boroughs quaint.

Our tour guide comes in to greet us, then leads us to the pier. Gabe falls into step beside me as we walk to our van.

"How have you been?" he asks. "You look stunning, as always."

I don't know how to react. His manner is so off. He's treating me like an old flame he's pleased to have run into, not like an ex-girlfriend whose heart he broke last fall.

It occurs to me that I could take this opportunity to eviscerate him for what he did to me. To tell him I was exhausted and incoherent with despair. That I had to crash with Lauren for months because, as he knew, I gave up my rent-stabilized apartment and sold all my stuff when I moved in with him.

But that would show weakness. I want to radiate strength.

"I'm fantastic," I say. "How are you?"

"Fabulous, now that I know you're here. How's Lauren? Has she snared a billionaire yet?"

"Still working on it."

"I should introduce her to Alfred Khan, the curator. He just divorced and he's very much her type."

I'm sure any curator friend of Gabe's *is* very much Lauren's type—she once wrangled an internship as a gallery girl at Art Basel to meet men. But Lauren hates Gabe, and by association anyone in his orbit, so I'll pass on her behalf.

"She's got her eye on a handsome Irishman, so I think she's good."

"Are you still working on your collection?" he asks me.

He's referring to the short stories he encouraged me to write when we were together. The ones he said would dazzle the literati and put me on the map as a writer to watch.

I haven't touched them since we broke up.

"Yep," I lie. "Going great."

"I'd love to read them when you're ready."

"Thanks, that's kind of you. How is your work going?"

"We're publishing the new Alex Lho book next month. Incredible novel—I think it's going to win prizes. I'll send you an advance copy if you like."

I hate how small and insecure this conversation is making me feel. Gabe's world was always intimidating, but I felt differently when he assured me so confidently that I was meant to be part of it. That I too was destined for great things.

I feel every bit the broke thirty-one-year-old publicity peon still struggling to get on my feet.

I'm grateful that the van stops, ending this excruciating life update.

We step out onto a beautiful, if crowded, beach occupied by line after line of umbrella-shaded lounge chairs. Our guide leads us to a surf shop and introduces us to our instructors for the day. They divide us into groups according to our experience levels. My level—unathletic with no core strength—is politely called "beginner."

I assume this means Gabe and I will part ways, and I can get some time to collect myself.

Unfortunately, he tells the instructor he's never surfed before. Even more unfortunately, everyone else has some experience, so the two of us are paired off to learn the basics on the shore while the rest of the group starts off in the shallows.

We're given boards and coached on paddling, popping up, and catching a wave. We practice on the sand. Neither of us can master the popping up part. I'm too top-heavy and keep instinctively using my hands. Gabe, who is lithe and strong and always moves athletically, for some reason keeps falling over.

It makes me a little suspicious that he's just doing this to make me feel better about my own clumsiness.

The instructor, Rufio, is patient, but it's clear that our inability to master the fundamentals frustrates him. He suggests we take our boards out into the water to practice paddling, then come back to try standing again. I look longingly past Rufio's shoulders to the people sunning themselves on the lounge chairs.

"Or," Gabe says to me, "we could admit we're terrible at this and catch up at the restaurant."

I follow his gaze past the chairs to a covered patio with a circular bar. Blenders buzz, glasses sweat, ceiling fans whir.

My entire soul *aches* to be there and not here.

I know that hunkering down with Gabe at a bar is, on the surface, a bad move. But having one cold drink in the blissful shade after hauling myself up and down on a hard, sandy surfboard under the glaring sun feels like a justifiable tradeoff.

"You know what, Rufio?" I say. "You've been great but I think we're going to call it a day."

"Thanks, man," Gabe says, handing him a couple of twenties.

Rufio shrugs and tells us to have a good trip.

"And now," Gabe says. "Margaritas."

We perch on high-backed stools and order drinks. Under the shade, I can actually appreciate the beautiful day and idyllic surroundings. The bartender puts two drinks in front of us. Gabe lifts his glass to mine.

"To not surfing," he says.

This, at least, I don't feel conflicted about. "To not *fucking* surfing," I say, clinking.

My drink is amazing—icy and citric in a way that perfectly cuts the humidity. I decide this was the right move.

Until Gabe takes my hand.

I freeze at his touch.

"I've missed you terribly," he says. "I've tried calling you, but I couldn't get through."

"That would be because I blocked you," I say. "Everywhere."

Though not immediately. There were months when the only thing in the world I wanted was for him to say he was sorry and ask to try again. But after an entire fiscal quarter of radio silence, Lauren finally succeeded in convincing me that any shred of hope was counterproductive. It was better not to know.

"I also stopped by Lauren's, but she wouldn't tell me where you were."

I didn't know that. I'm sure she did it to protect me, but it feels like information I was entitled to.

Not that I would say that to *him*.

"That's because you fucked up my life. You get that, right?"

"I do," he says, looking into my eyes. "I understand. I know that I hurt you. I'm so sorry."

Right. He's sorry. Just like he said he was when he did it in the first place. Doesn't change anything.

"It's just . . . us both being here," he says. "Doesn't it feel like fate?"

The sentiment is so overblown that it knocks some coherence back into me.

"It feels like a coincidence," I say, slipping my hand out from under his.

"A *wild* coincidence. I wonder if it's a cosmic sign telling us there's a chance for repair."

Repair?

What would that mean, exactly? Are we going to be friends? Gallivant around at book parties and run into each other in the Hamptons?

Unlikely.

"If by repair you mean in the sense that we can talk civilly over a drink, sure," I say. "Beyond that, I've moved on."

His eyes crinkle with disappointment.

"You mean to someone else?" he asks.

"I mean with my life."

"Are you seeing anyone?"

"I'm not going to discuss that with you."

He holds up his hands. "Oh, right. Of course. I'm sorry for asking. It's only—" He closes his eyes tightly, then rubs his temple. "I made a big mistake, Hope."

My heart clenches.

I don't want it to, but I have *longed* for these words.

"I'd never been so in love with someone before. It terrified me, and I shut down. It was childish and shortsighted, and I'm so ashamed of what I did—how I left you in the lurch. And regretful. Because the thing is—I *did* want it. Everything we dreamed about, everything we planned."

I will my heart not to beat faster at this pronouncement.

"You say that," I say, "but it's only because you can't have it anymore. You romanticized the idea of it. You hated the reality."

"No," he says. "That's not true. I've done extensive therapy since we broke up—"

"Since you left me," I interrupt.

He winces. "Yeah. And what I've realized is that I have a block around giving and receiving real love. You know how cold my family is. I want something better for myself, something like you have with your parents. Like I had with you. I was just too frightened to take it."

I'm trying so hard not to be drawn in. *So* hard. But when someone who has shattered your heart comes and lies down at your feet, it's very difficult to be entirely unmoved.

"I'm not sure why we're having this conversation," I say, straining not to reveal that this is softening me. "Or why *you're* having it."

"You *know* why I'm saying this to you, Hope," Gabe says softly. "Of course you know."

"I honestly don't."

He leans forward and traces his thumb over the line of my jaw.

"Because—" he begins to say.

But he's interrupted by a posh British woman saying, "Is that Hope?"

I dart my eyes toward the voice to see Pear and Prue Segrave looking straight at us. Behind them is Felix. And his eyes are trained on Gabe's hand cradling my face.

Felix

I would not describe myself as a possessive person. But I physically recoil when I see Hope being touched—tenderly caressed, more accurately—by some strange man.

Their posture is so intimate that I feel like I'm seeing something that should be happening in a locked room.

Where the fuck did this person come from? Did she randomly strike up a romance with some guy from surf class in the four hours since she left my bed?

Hope ducks away from the man and waves at us in a fashion that is unnaturally casual for a woman who was just staring into her companion's eyes like a lover.

Prue, who is never at a loss for words, is frozen, looking daggers at this gentleman with whom Hope appeared to have been having a moment.

"Sorry, we're interrupting!" Pear calls. "Don't mind us."

"Not at all!" Hope exclaims. "Join us!"

My sisters glance at me for a cue.

I don't know what to do. If I refuse to say hello I'll look infantile.

I nod, and head in their direction.

"Gabe, these are the Segraves," Hope says. "Prue, Pear, and Felix. They're on the cruise with us."

Us.

Could it be that she met him days ago? That I'm not the only person with whom she's been having a cruise ship flirtation? But where would she find the time?

The guy beams at us and holds out his hand to Pear. "Gabe Newhouse."

Pear inclines her head inquisitively. "Where do I know that name from? Oh! You aren't by chance related to Eliza Newhouse, are you?"

"My sister," he says.

"I knew it! We met during my gap year in Paris. What a star, that one. I'll have to call her to catch up, it's been ages."

She turns to me and Prue. "Eliza's a film producer. She did *Alouette*. A real powerhouse."

Gabe nods, the very picture of a proud sibling. "Nominated for Best Picture last year."

"And they were *robbed*," my sister says.

"And how do you know Hope, Gabe?" Prue asks. Her tone is polite but not friendly. She is clearly not any more pleased to see Hope with this man than I am. "Did you meet on the boat?"

"Oh, no," he says with a laugh. "We're dear friends."

His tone clearly implies they are more than that. Am I to gather that some lover of hers is on the cruise with us, and she didn't think to *mention* it? Surely not. I'm jumping to conclusions. And even if I were correct, I'm not sure I have a right to the hurt that I feel.

But it's there nonetheless.

"Can I get everyone a drink?" Gabe asks.

"Yes, please. What are you having, Hope?" Pear asks, looking covetously at the cocktail glass sweating in front of her.

"Pineapple jalapeño margarita," Hope says. "It's delicious."

"I'll have one of those," Pear says.

"Same for me," Prue echoes.

"And for you?" Gabe asks me.

I'm dying for a Coca-Cola, but I can't stomach the idea of this man ordering me one. "I'm good," I say. "Thanks."

"Nonsense, have a drink," he says affably. "A beer?"

"I'm sober," I say flatly.

This is not something I would normally announce to a stranger, but I hate being pressured to drink. Especially by a charming all-American golden boy who is *dear* friends with the woman I—

I what?

Fucked?

I remind myself I don't have a claim on her. I shouldn't be pugnacious.

"Oh, sorry," Gabe says.

"No worries. I'll have a Coke, actually," I say, straining for an ease I don't feel.

Gabe flags down the bartender and orders a round.

"I thought you guys were zip-lining today," Hope says.

Yes. Clearly.

"We tried," Pear says, "but it was ghastly. Rickety ropes two hundred feet in the air? No thank you. I insisted we leave."

"Prue and I were enjoying ourselves but dear sister here threw such a fit that it was more pleasant to go," I say.

I'm not feeling particularly chatty, but I decide it's better to make conversation than to stand sullenly off to the side and let Hope think I feel threatened.

"I did not *throw a fit*," Pear says primly. "I imposed a boundary. Anyhow, our guide recommended this beach club for lunch. Have you eaten?"

"Not yet," Hope says. "We attempted to surf, but neither of us could get up on the board, even on land. Never made it into the water."

I dislike her use of the word *we*. I also dislike that she seems slightly tipsy. A thing I have no business disapproving of, but which deepens my sense of unease about this whole situation.

My sisters ask Gabe where he lives and what he does, and he says he's a book editor from New York.

My forced chill deserts me.

How many book editors from New York could one woman have dated? This must be *the* guy. The ex who broke her heart. He's here, and he seemed on the verge of kissing her when we ran into them.

I feel absolutely shattered. I'm barely following the conversation—I'm wondering, in fact, if I can come up with an excuse to leave—when I hear my name.

Pear is telling Gabe about my pubs. He reacts as though she's told him I own Noma, and starts peppering me with all sorts of questions about the cuisine and locations with a seeming genuine interest and friendliness that makes it hard to dislike him as much as I'm inclined to.

"Do you happen to know Matthew Reynaldo?" he asks. "We're good friends."

Matthew Reynaldo is a three–Michelin star chef and the owner of Schoolmarm, the most difficult booking to get in town.

"Afraid we haven't met," I say.

"*Great* guy," Gabe says. "If any of you ever need a table send me a word, any time. Hope has my number."

"Yes, *please*," Pear says. "I've been dying to go, but they're booked out five months."

"Oh God, you must go," Gabe says. "The nettle-smoked mackerel terrine is the best thing I've ever eaten."

Another round of drinks is ordered, and Gabe suggests we all sit down for lunch. Since lunch is the reason my sisters and I came here, I don't have a plausible reason to say no.

We migrate over to a table with a view of the sea.

"So how exactly do you two know each other?" Prue asks Hope.

"We used to date," Hope says, flitting her eyes in my direction for the first time since we got here. A silent apology? An acknowledgment of how uncomfortable this all is?

Gabe looks at her fondly. "She's the one that got away."

He says it like it's a joke, but his expression makes me think he's not kidding.

Her face twists like she just bit into a lemon she thought was an orange.

I can't parse it. Is she angry at him? Or moved to hear he longs for her?

Whatever the case, there's some emotion at work between the two of them that is not at all neutral, and it is excruciating to observe.

Hope stands up abruptly. "I'm going to the bathroom," she says. "Can someone order me the snapper if the waiter comes by?"

"Of course," Gabe says, at the same time I say, "Sure."

Gabe's eyes follow her as she walks away.

Pear starts peppering him with questions about books, looking for recommendations. Gabe goes into a monologue about upcoming releases and brilliant debuts with apparent relish, while Pear whips out her phone to write it all down.

My phone buzzes in my pocket. It's a text from Hope.

Hope: This is so awkward. I'm sorry!

My acculturation as a Brit makes it my impulse to write something like "not at all" but I am too frankly pissed to wave it away. I settle on:

Felix: It's a bit weird, yeah.
Hope: I didn't know he was here—he's randomly on the cruise with his grandma.
Hope: Just found out this morning.

It's not generous of me, but I can't help wondering if she's telling the truth. Could she really not have known he was here? Am I a pawn in some sort of revenge game? An effort to make him jealous?

Regardless, I'm not going to ask her via text.

Felix: Got it.
Hope: Coming back. Just wanted to let you know privately.

I don't like the formal nature of her phrasing. I type "thanks."

The food arrives right as Hope returns. The fish appears to be perfect, served blackened with a side of rice and peas and a bright slaw of onion, cabbage, and mango.

I can't taste it.

Gabe looks at his phone and winces. "Hope, we'd better go. Our van leaves to go back to port in five minutes."

She nods and wipes her mouth with a napkin as he throws several hundred-dollar bills on the table.

"My treat," he says. "It was *so* nice to meet you all. Let's do it again on the boat."

"Absolutely!" Pear says.

Hope, standing out of his eyeline, looks at me, clenches her teeth, and shakes her head no.

I know she wants to reassure me. I can see that, whatever is happening here, she feels terrible.

But as I watch them walk away together, I can also see the familiarity between them. The way they fall into step like people who intimately know each other's rhythms.

I can't shake the fear that I've lost something I just barely had.

Hope

"Really nice people," Gabe says as we walk to the meeting point for our ride back to the ship. "And it's wild that Pear's friends with Eliza."

"Yeah," I say dazedly, because I feel like my skull has been beaten with a sledgehammer. "Small world."

"She misses you, you know," he adds.

"Who?"

"Eliza."

Doubtful. She's on the long list of people I haven't heard from since the breakup. I don't say anything. My brain feels like static.

"Is something wrong?" Gabe asks. "You're quiet."

Part of me wants to say: "I'm traumatized because I just had lunch with the ex-boyfriend I have complicated feelings about and the sweet guy I slept with last night."

Instead I say: "Tired from all the sun."

I close my eyes on the trip back to avoid talking. Gabe takes the hint and lets me rest, striking up a conversation with a fit elderly couple about their previous surfing experiences and many grandchildren. It's as though he's trying to remind me how winning he can be.

I don't want to be reminded. I don't want to be back in that headspace.

And I feel terrible about Felix.

I say goodbye to Gabe as soon as we're back on the ship. He touches my arm to stop me. My body has not forgotten how much it likes his touch. I instinctively turn to him.

"Hey," he says. "I don't want to pressure you. But it would be nice if you'd have coffee with Gran. You know how she adores you."

I don't remember Maeve "adoring" anyone—she's more of a towering matriarch than a warm maternal figure—but we did always have a cordial rapport.

"Sure," I say. "I'll text you."

But I'm not sure I will. Given how wobbly I feel in his presence, it's likely unwise.

"Thanks," he says, his eyes lit up like I've just promised to marry him. An irony that is not lost on me.

I go up to my room, praying that Lauren won't be there. I need to process all this before I hear her opinion. Actually, I already know what her opinion will be: feed Gabe to the sharks.

Part of me wants to.

Part of me is fucking enraged that he could be so friendly, affectionate, even proprietary after what he did to me.

But then there is the other part of me that thinks, *thank God*. Thank God he still cares for me. That I didn't just imagine he loved me. That perhaps I've lingered with him the way he's lingered with me.

I have, to be clear, no respect for this part of me. I wish this part of me could be cut out with a scalpel and evacuated in a hazmat truck.

But emotions are emotions. They're just . . . there. Whether you welcome them or not.

And right alongside them are my feelings for Felix. The object of my gooey, previously uncomplicated vacation crush. The guy who still makes me feel fluttery even when he's sitting next to the former love of my life, visibly trying not to glower.

I could tell he was upset, and I get it. I'm upset too.

I feel like I'm fucking with him against my will. That Gabe's very presence—and my reaction to it—is a betrayal.

Okay, obviously I do need to talk to Lauren.

I pick up my phone to ask where she is, and see a missed FaceTime call from my mother. She's the last person I could ever talk to about this, but given how depressed she's been, I don't like to keep her waiting when she reaches out. I go to the balcony to call her back.

"Hello, dear," she says in greeting. She's outside in the garden of the cottage. The sun is streaming against her auburn hair, making her glow. She looks beautiful. And maybe it's just the light, but she looks less tired than usual. Peaceful.

"Oh, you're at the cottage already," I say. "I thought it was Dad's week."

"It is, but there are some decisions we need to make together, so I came up early. The weather is beautiful."

It's odd to think of them sharing a house, however briefly. I haven't seen them in the same place in over a year. The sadness of the situation overtakes me, but my mom seems upbeat—rare these days—and I don't want to bring down her mood.

"I wish I was there," I say.

"No! You're somewhere far more exotic. Tell me all about your adventure!"

It's all I can do to paste on a smile.

"I'm having a surprisingly good time," I say. Because until today, I have been.

She laughs. "Imagine that, a free Caribbean vacation being enjoyable."

"You like anything free." My mother is famously cheap. She buys all her clothes secondhand, reuses tea bags, and still clips actual paper coupons out of the local newspaper.

"So what have you been getting up to on this trip of yours?" she asks.

"Well, let's see. I learned how to cook Antiguan food. I saw a shockingly good Elvis impersonator. And today I failed to learn to surf."

I obviously don't tell her about Gabe.

"Sounds eventful," she says. "How's our Lauren?"

"She's dating everyone on the boat, of course."

"Oh no. Are you lonely?"

I debate telling her about Felix. But I want to talk to *someone* about him.

"Well, actually . . ." I say, "I met a boy."

Her eyebrows go up. "Oh?" she says neutrally.

"He's British. A chef. Very nice. Here with his family. You'd like him."

Her expression could be charitably called "unconvinced."

"How long have you been on this boat?" she asks. "A week?"

"Five days."

"That's awfully quick."

"I didn't say I'm going to marry him, Mother. And didn't you fall in love with Dad in a week?"

Their love story is legendary family lore. They met at the college bookstore the first day of their freshman year, bought overpriced textbooks for a statistics class they both ended up dropping, and never looked back.

"Best money I ever spent," Dad always says.

Said.

Mom frowns, and I belatedly realize now is not the time to mention their romance. Clearly, my wits have deserted me.

"Yeah" is all she says. "Just be careful."

"I will," I assure her, even though, given the mess that I'm in, it's far too late for that.

"Well," Mom says, "we're in the middle of cleaning out the gardening shed, so I'll let you go. I just wanted to check in to see how you're doing."

This is typical. My mother can't stand to be on the phone for longer than five minutes.

"Okay," I say. I don't comment on what occurs to me—that cleaning out a gardening shed seems like an odd reason for two people in the midst of a divorce to spend time together at an isolated country cottage.

"Love you," she says.

"Love you too."

As soon as she hangs up, I text Lauren.

Hope: Hey! When are you coming back. I have VERY BAD drama. Need advice!

There's no response—she must still be on shore.

But there is a new text from an unknown number.

Unknown: Hey, it's me from Maeve's phone.
Unknown: (Not sure if you unblocked me).
Unknown: *So* great seeing you.
Unknown: Would tomorrow work for a coffee?

The fact that this man has to text me through his grandmother's phone hits me like an ice bath.

Welcome back to reality, Hope Lanover. A reality in which you are a strong woman who has moved the fuck on, and who deserves to enjoy her vacation with things that make her happy rather than miserable.

And what makes me happy is Felix.

I need to talk to him right now. I can't stand the thought of him being confused or hurt. I text him.

Hope: Hey, what are you up to? Can we meet up?

Felix: Sorry, can't—busy with the parents until after supper.

I notice he does not sign this text with an "x."

Not that I deserve one.

Hope: Gotcha. See you later?

He doesn't answer.

Well, I can't blame him after what he saw. If I happened upon him having drinks with an ex several hours after sleeping with him, I'd be unhappy too.

I hope I haven't ruined things.

I shower, read a little, and doze off. I must have been tired from the previous night's sex fest and the morning's emotional journey, because when I wake up three hours have passed. Lauren is in the bed next to mine editing photos on her laptop.

"Hi," I croak.

She sits up and clacks her laptop shut.

"Finally you're awake," she says. "I am dying of suspense. What is your *very bad* drama?"

I don't sugarcoat it.

"Gabe is here."

Her jaw drops down comically, like she's a cartoon.

"Gabe *Newhouse*?"

"Yep."

"How is that possible?"

"Apparently he's treating his grandmother to celebrate her birthday."

"That is psycho."

"I know."

"Did you talk to him?"

"I didn't have a choice. He was on the surf expedition."

"Did you push him off his board and drown him and now he's dead and good riddance?"

"I kind of wish. He gave me a big heartfelt speech on how he regrets everything and wants a chance for 'repair.'"

She stares at me. *"Repair?"*

I sigh. "Yeah. I know."

"The only thing that needs repairing is his sense of goddamn decency and, like, his *soul.* Tell me you told him to fuck off."

I collapse into my pillows and groan.

"Hopie!" Lauren says. "*Tell me* you told him to fuck off."

"I panicked. I didn't really know how to feel about it. I was mad but then there was that fraction of me that was like . . . relieved. Or flattered. Or something? Ugh, Lauren, why am I *like* this?"

I'm expecting a lecture—I'm inviting a lecture—but she comes to sit next to me on my bed and strokes my hair. "I get it," she says.

"You do?"

"I do. It's natural to want people to feel badly for hurting you. But remember," she says, tapping me on the shoulder for emphasis, "he was always good at saying the right thing. That's why you fell for him. It's how he treats you once he has you locked down that's the problem."

"I know, I know." I sigh. "Thank you. I needed to hear that."

"That's what I'm here for. Setting your ass straight."

"That's not all of it though," I say.

"Lord deliver us. What now?"

"Felix showed up just as Gabe was basically on the verge of trying to kiss me. And . . . we ended up having lunch with him and his sisters."

"What? How? Why?"

"One of Felix's sisters knows Gabe's sister and they started chatting and—"

"Girl!" she cries. "Are you in a soap opera?"

"Feels like it. Especially after Gabe low-key announced to everyone that he's my ex-boyfriend."

She claps her hand over her mouth. "Oh dear God. What was Felix's reaction?"

"He seemed . . . dismayed."

"Understandable. Have you talked to him?"

"I hid in the bathroom and texted him to try to explain, but it fell kind of flat. And when we got back I asked him to hang out and he said he was busy all day."

"Shit," she says.

"Yeah. Feels not good."

"Well, it's not your fault your ex showed up. And not to be harsh, but you don't owe Felix anything. You just met."

"I know. But I understand him being taken aback. I mean, what he saw looked pretty intense. If I had seen *him* doing that with an ex after last night, I'd have been upset too. I don't want to hurt him."

"Well, you just need to talk to him. And he can't exactly avoid you forever. He lives three doors away."

"I guess I could do a stakeout."

"No ma'am. What you need is a girls' night."

This sounds incredibly soothing. "Yes, please," I say.

"Let's go to the tapas place before we hit karaoke."

We get dressed up. She wears a low-cut, backless, taupe silk dress that only a woman with more clavicles than breasts can pull off. I choose a wide-legged jumpsuit and cinch it at the waist with a narrow vintage belt. I'm pleased when Lauren pronounces it sexy and doesn't even try to make me change.

She downloads me on all her suitors at dinner. Her eyes light up in an unfamiliar way when she gets to Colin, the distiller.

"I think I actually like him. And you'll be pleased to learn he's only forty-six."

"Spring chicken."

"Oh, come on. He meets the age-gap rule!"

"What's the age-gap rule?"

"Half your age plus seven. So if he's forty-eight, the youngest he can date is . . ." She performs a mental calculation, then smiles triumphantly. "Thirty-one."

"You're thirty," I remind her.

"Rounding error."

"Well I'm glad you hit it off."

Usually the men she meets on her "missions" are more for content than real romantic interest.

She waggles her eyebrows. "He booked a private sailing trip for us tomorrow in St. Thomas."

"That sounds lovely. Even if it means I'll be snorkeling alone."

She gives me a look like I'm an utter dunderhead. "Um, no. Invite Felix. Get out your phone and do it right now."

"What if he rejects me?"

"Then you had really good cruise sex with someone you'll never see again like the plan and not worry about it."

I don't believe this is possible, but I obey her.

Hope: Hi again. I was wondering if you have plans tomorrow? I'm doing the catamaran snorkeling trip. Want to come?

He doesn't reply.

"Well, I asked. We'll see."

"He's probably at dinner. Don't worry."

We finish eating, taking our time to linger over an absolutely delicious passionfruit flan, and then head to karaoke. We arrive right on time, but there's already an elderly crowd assembled.

"I bet we're in for a lot of Frank Sinatra," Lauren says.

"Good evening, ladies," a very upbeat gentleman I recognize as a singer from the Broadway revue says to us.

"Hi there," Lauren says.

"The song library is here," he says, handing me an iPad. "Be sure to sign up with me as soon as you look. It's a full house and slots are filling up fast."

"Will do. Thanks," I say.

We look through the selections. Lauren chooses "Heartbreaker" by Pat Benatar.

"I'm going to dedicate it to Colin," she says. "He'll eat it up."

"He's coming?" I ask. I'm a little disappointed to have company on our girls' night.

"Yeah, I want you to meet him again!" she says. "I need a second opinion."

"That I can provide."

I check to make sure they have my go-to karaoke song. They do.

We walk back to the sign-up guy.

"Can I do 'Wuthering Heights' by Kate Bush, please," I ask.

"I'm sorry, ma'am," he says. "I'm afraid that one is already taken."

This is inconceivable. Who other than me would choose a niche art pop song inspired by a nineteenth-century novel, let alone one with that much falsetto?

"Who took it?" I ask.

He points to the front of the room, near the stage. "That gentleman."

I follow the line of his finger to none other than Felix Segrave.

"Oh my actual God," Lauren says. "This is some fated mates shit."

"Should I talk to him?" I ask.

"Duh."

I walk over to where he's standing. He's in conversation with Pear and doesn't see me coming until I tap him on the shoulder.

His face goes tentative.

"Hey," I say.

"Hey," he says back.

It's a little stilted, but he doesn't pull away.

"Can we talk later?" I ask.

"Sure," he says. "After I bring down the house."

"Uh, so, about that. I'm afraid you stole my karaoke song."

"Pardon?" he asks.

"'Wuthering Heights' is my signature number. I'm going to need to politely ask for it back."

His face pulls into the wry smile I love. "No can do. It's also *my* signature number."

"No way. Men cannot hit those notes."

"Felix can," Pear says. "It's uncanny."

I cross my arms. "Not fair. I slay with that song. And I'm the Brontë superfan."

He tsks at me. "You forget the Brontës turned me into the nascent scholar of English literature I am today."

"You well-read *devil*."

"I'll tell you what," he says, "because I'm a compassionate soul, I'll allow you to do a duet with me." He pauses and looks at me severely. "If you promise you can hit the notes, that is."

"Oh, I can demolish the notes."

He offers me his hand. "We have an agreement, Miss Lanover."

I squeeze it.

And I don't care about the song. All I care about is the fact that he squeezes back.

Felix

I'm grateful to the gods of amateur singing for forcing me to see Hope.

I've been avoiding her all day and feeling cowardly about it. But I'm uncomfortable with how much seeing her with her ex affected me. Whether his presence here was an omission or a coincidence, I shouldn't be this thrown by it. This is supposed to be a fling. It's a bad sign that I'm jealous.

I just hope I'm not supposed to be.

Even entertaining the idea that Hope would use me to inspire envy in her ex makes me feel like shit. But I can't help it. The bleakest part of my mind spins a scenario where she started flirting with me as soon as she found out Gabe was on the ship.

But everything between us has happened organically, hasn't it? Reading *Middlemarch*? Showing up for the same dance class? Throwing crab in my hair on day one?

If she had meant to entangle me in some sort of love triangle, surely she would have simply introduced herself, without getting the raw bar involved.

I'm being paranoid. I need to slow down.

This is a cruise hookup after all. Not a love story.

Still, it's reassuring that Gabe's not here with her. And karaoke seems like a light, reasonable way to resume communication. We can hash it out afterwards.

The lights dim and the Australian man who took down our names comes onstage and introduces himself as Theo, our host for the evening. He kicks things off by performing his own number, "You've Lost That Lovin' Feeling" by the Righteous Brothers.

He kills.

"I find this ethically dubious," Hope whispers to me. "It's not fair we should have to follow up a Broadway singer."

"If you're losing your nerve, I'm happy to do my song alone," I whisper back.

"*Your* song? I've loved Kate Bush since my tortured adolescence."

"I'm a year older than you, so I've loved it longer."

I am not trolling her. Kate Bush is one of my top five artists of all time, and my ability to do justice to her anthem is my best hidden talent. I *always* sing it at karaoke.

Theo receives a standing ovation, and introduces the next singer as Mark from Plymouth, Massachusetts. Mark is a portly seventy-something who does "(I Can't Get No) Satisfaction" by The Rolling Stones. He's fine. No Theo, but fine. Nevertheless, we all cheer as though he's Mick Jagger himself. Karaoke is about building up your fellow man, and ignoring when he's slightly pitchy.

Next we get "9 to 5" by a very, very old woman who uses her cane to conduct us for the chorus; "Mr. Brightside" by the lone teenager on the boat, provoking the confusion of the audience averaging fifty years his senior; and "Jagged Little Pill" by Pear. Pear is an absolutely godawful singer, but the crowd hoots and applauds her bravery.

Theo introduces "Colin from Ireland" to come up. He's a handsome, barrel-chested guy in his forties. He begins by dedicating his number to "the dazzling Lauren"—yes, Hope's Lauren—and then proceeds to perform "Pour Some Sugar on Me" by Def Leppard. He not only does it well, he does it filthily, thrusting his hips and getting down on his knees in front of her to throw back his head and wail out the final chorus. She eats it up, rewarding him with a kiss that is far more sloppy than I would have expected of her.

Then Theo announces it is his pleasure to introduce "Hope from New York and Felix from London."

"Last chance to back out," Hope says to me.

I stand up. "Nope. You've made your bed."

"I meant you."

"I'm not worried about me."

The crowd obviously is though. From the second the piercingly high-pitched opening notes begin to play, I see people glancing at me with bemused looks.

Hope meets my eye as we mentally count through the bars of the preamble, waiting for the opening line of the first verse.

We nod at each other and start perfectly in tandem.

And, thank you very much, *perfectly* on pitch.

Hope's eyes nearly bulge out of her head as she realizes I was not kidding about being able to hit these notes. This is one advantage of going to an all-boys school with a very competitive choir: someone has to be the soprano.

That someone, when he was not playing the tuba, was me.

Something beautiful happens. Hope's whole face glows. She doesn't take her eyes off me as she throws herself into the song. She's amazing, though that isn't surprising based on her performance with Elvis. What is surprising is the way we're able to communicate telepathically, trading every other line until we reach the first chorus, at which point we both belt out together: "HEAAAAAAATHCLIFFFFFFF—"

There are literal gasps, and then clapping and laughter, as we fucking nail it. We sing to each other with all the unhinged drama of a woman beckoning a deranged man to dig her out of her grave. We give gothic. We give desperate pining. We give agonized wailing through the windswept moors.

When we reach the last verse we take each other's hands and circle each other as we head into the final chorus. Hope sings to me. I sing to her. We sing to the audience.

And then the music tinkles off, and it's over.

No one in the room will ever be the same again. We have changed them. They, like the Cathy of the song, are ghosts now.

I dip Hope back and she kicks up her leg in triumph.

Lauren, who is recording this with her phone, puts her fingers in her mouth and whistles. The crowd whoops along with her. They love us.

With one exception.

A man whose face I only now notice frowning in the back of the room.

Gabe.

I look away. Whatever is going on with him and Hope, I don't want to be in the middle of it. And I note she did not insist on duetting with *him*.

Theo comes back on stage and takes the mics from Hope and me.

"Ladies and gentlemen, join me in thanking these two for that magnificent number!" he says. We bow and head back to our sofa as he introduces the night's final singer—Lauren, performing "Heartbreaker." She high-fives us as we walk past her.

We're both panting a bit from the exertion and adrenaline of what we've just achieved, and we collapse down on the couch and fall into laughter. Hope puts her head on my shoulder, overcome with giggles.

I would like this, were it not for my awareness of Gabe's eyes on her. I don't know if she's noticed him too. I pray she's not doing this to get a reaction out of him.

But I like her touch too much to move away.

She stays there the entirety of Lauren's performance—which is directed exclusively at Colin. When she's done, he leaps up to give her a one-man standing ovation. I suspect I'm not the only man on this cruise who is feeling immoderate attachment to an American girl he met a few days ago.

Theo returns to the stage and starts to thank us all for coming when Gabe calls out, "Do you have time for one more? Sorry, I was late and didn't have a chance to sign up."

Theo mimes checking his watch. "Ladies and gentlemen, what do you think? Time for one last song?"

Everyone applauds gamely.

Gabe sails up to the stage with charming smiles for the crowd. I resent how handsome and confident he is. He confers with Theo over the iPad, then takes the mic.

"I'd like to dedicate this song to the most beautiful girl on the boat," he says, grinning at Hope. "I'm not a great singer," he confides to the audience. "Bear with me, I beg you."

The room takes to this confession fondly.

I glance at Hope. She has adjusted herself so that we're no longer touching. A tight smile is affixed to her face. And then the song comes on.

It's "Please Forgive Me" by Bryan Adams.

Now, as I just demonstrated, I am the last person in the world to assert that men cannot sing songs in a high register. Some of us are brilliant at it.

Gabe, as promised, is not.

He doesn't seem to care, however. The point of this exercise is obviously not the way he sounds, but the message he wishes to impart.

"Are you in a karaoke battle?" Prue hisses to me.

I really, really hope not.

"If they are, Felix is winning," Pear says. "Mate's butchering this."

"He realizes it's a song about wanting someone back after *treating them like shit*, right?" Lauren says loudly.

"At least he's self-aware," Hope mutters.

I take heart in the fact that she doesn't seem to be enjoying this.

The song finally—mercifully—ends, and the crowd applauds in what I assume is some combination of gratitude that the torture is over and sympathy for the man who has just made such a humbling production of himself.

He bows and hands the mic back to Theo.

An old woman near the aisle touches his wrist. "She must be quite a girl," she says to him.

"The best," Gabe says, looking at Hope.

"Well, that was an, um . . . *memorable* conclusion to the evening," Theo says. "Thank you so much to all our talented entertainers! And don't forget to come back tomorrow night for our magnificent magic show."

Gabe is trying to get to us through the crowd of people exiting the theater.

"Fuck," Hope mutters. She grabs her bag and turns to me. "I need to get out of here. Come with me?"

"Yeah," I say, relieved by the invitation.

She speeds out of the room so fast I have to jog after her.

I catch up to her at the bay to the lifts, where she's punching the up arrow like it's the only thing between her and damnation. Luckily, it arrives right away. We step into it and she jams the "Door Close" button.

When the doors finally obey, leaving us alone, she leans back and bangs her head lightly against the wall.

"That was so embarrassing," she says.

"For him," I say.

"For me."

There's a heaviness between us. I don't know what she's feeling, or how I fit into it.

"Seems like he has some strong feelings," I venture.

"Yeah," she says, sounding exhausted. "Or something."

"You look upset," I say. "If you want to be alone—"

"No!" she exclaims. She straightens her posture and shakes herself out. "Sorry, that just freaked me out. Are you still cool to talk? This is all very bizarre and I really feel like I owe you an explanation."

I was already feeling better about the situation given she fled the karaoke room, but her earnestness heartens me. She doesn't have to give me an explanation, but I appreciate that she's offering one.

"Do you want to come to my room?" I ask.

"Yes," she says. "I want very badly to come to your room."

"I'm happy to hear that." Very, very happy, in fact.

"Tea?" I ask, when we get inside.

"Only if it's exactly eighty-five degrees."

She sits down on the couch while I fill the kettle.

"I wasn't sure you would want me to come over," she says. "After today."

"I wasn't sure you would want to come," I admit.

"I invited you snorkeling. That's girl code for 'please forgive me.'"

"Are you quoting your ex?"

"Poor choice of words."

"Well, is there something to forgive?"

She rubs her temple wearily. "Well, today was uncomfortable. I know you saw me talking to him."

She means I saw him on the verge of kissing her, obviously.

"It seemed like an intense conversation," I say.

"He's the guy I mentioned. The bad breakup. Up until running into him this morning, I hadn't seen him since he ended things."

I can see how shaken up she is, and I feel bad for her.

"I know how tough it is to have to face someone after something like that," I say gently. "Are you okay?"

And I genuinely want to know. But what I also want to know is: *Do you still have feelings for him?*

She lets out a long sigh. "I'm fine. But I certainly would have preferred *not* to be stuck on a boat with him." She pauses. "I'd rather devote my undivided attention to this nice boy I met."

She looks at me searchingly. "If he still wants me to."

Her ex is not my business, and if she says she wants to be with me, I am going to believe her.

"He does," I say. "Very much."

I pour water over the tea bags and bring her a cup. She pats the seat next to her. "Sit with me?"

"Gladly."

She curls up beside me and rests her head on my shoulder. "Karaoke was so much fun. You were amazing."

"*We* were amazing."

She leans up and kisses me. "Yeah," she says. "We were."

I will not report the details of what happened next. Except to say: it was amazing too.

And when I wake up in the morning with Hope beside me, Gabe is the last thing on my mind.

7
THE DEEP END OF THE OCEAN

Wonders of the Caribbean, Day 6

Welcome to St. Thomas, US Virgin Islands!

Today the *Romance of the Sea* takes you to Charlotte Amalie, the picturesque capital of St. Thomas, boasting glimmering bays, powdery sand, rich history, and bountiful wildlife.

For luxurious relaxation, indulge in a day floating on your own personal aqua-cabana at the legendary mile-long Emerald Beach, or take a private catamaran to the beautiful shallows of St. John National Park. Divers and snorkelers can feast their eyes on the vivid coral and colorful fish of Buck Island's Shipwreck Cove—perhaps you will meet a sea turtle or two! And landlubbers might venture into town for a guided tour of historic Fort Christian, followed by a refreshing drink above it all on the Skyride to Paradise Point.

Finish your day back on board with a sunset steel drum performance on the Lido Deck, or Classic Rock Night at the Cosmic Theater. And for those who enjoy a bit of wizardry, disappear to the Mermaid Club for a Spellbinding Magic Show!

Have a wonderful day!

Hope

I would never have predicted that one of the best days of my life would involve a snorkeling trip during a Caribbean cruise.

I wake up naked in Felix's room. The nudity is convenient, as it allows us to repeat some of the better events of last night.

We part ways to shower and get dressed for our outing, then reconvene to walk down to the lounge where the snorkeling group is meeting.

"Make me a promise," I say to Felix.

"Anything."

"Dangerous words."

"I trust you."

"If Gabe happens to be going on this trip, let's just skip it. We can walk into town or something instead."

After last night, I'm nervous about running into him. I don't want any more grand gestures.

Especially not in front of Felix.

Kind Felix, who seems willing to let yesterday go. Sexy Felix, who used his body to tell me everything is okay.

"I lied," Felix says. "I can't promise that. I want to hang out with him."

"Felix!"

"Sorry, but I'm fully invested in spending the day with your unhinged ex-boyfriend."

"Do you want me to text him and personally invite him along?"

"Please."

I take out my phone and he snatches it away, laughing.

"If he's there, I solemnly swear I'll be the first one out the door," Felix says. "I can't watch him karaoke-bomb you again before lunch."

"Ugh, don't remind me. I forgot how much I hated it when he did shit like that."

Felix raises his eyebrows. "He has a history of serenading you in public?"

"No. First time. But he has this thing about making larger-than-life gestures to express his emotions. It's like a psychological tic."

"What do you mean?"

"Well, say you have a fight and he feels bad about it later and wants to get you flowers. Instead of just picking some up at the bodega and apologizing, he'll like make a scavenger hunt leading you to the botanical gardens, where he's arranged a private after-hours sunset tour."

"That's an oddly specific example."

"Yeah, because he literally did that. He did stuff like that all the time. Like, once I got annoyed with him because he canceled a date to an Italian restaurant last minute. I was pissed because it's a hard reservation to get and I'd made it weeks before. The next day, I get to his apartment and the chef is there teaching Gabe how to hand-make pappardelle for cacio e pepe."

"Wow."

"Yeah. I think it has something to do with his upbringing. His family are these really reserved WASPs who primarily express affection by starting trust funds for one another, so he, like, craves something more personal, but then overcorrects."

And overpromises, it occurs to me. Professes love, names your babies, moves you into his apartment. But can't follow through. Like the gesture is so grand because the emotion behind it is performative. Lacking conviction. A show.

This revelation explains so much. How he's capable of such romance and such detached withdrawal.

I feel like I understand what happened between us for the first time. I was not responsible for the failure of my relationship because I couldn't live up to his expectations.

The problem truly was *him*.

I don't say this to Felix, because we've discussed my ex-boyfriend far too much already. But when I take his hand, I feel lighter. More confident. Like the girl I came on this cruise to get back to being.

We stroll to the tender hand in hand, and yet another couple asks us if we're honeymooning.

"Yes," Felix says, squeezing my fingers conspiratorially. It's clear he loves this game.

"Where are you from?" the woman asks.

"New York and London, respectively," Felix says.

"Oh! Is it hard to be in a long-distance relationship?"

"We make it work," he says. "She's worth it."

I know he's kidding, but my mind flashes to a scenario in which that could actually happen. Does his?

"How did you meet?" the woman asks, disrupting my train of thought. "I'm Nancy, by the way, and this is my husband, Tom."

"Felix. And we met when Hope here threw a crab shell in my hair at a buffet."

The woman laughs uproariously.

"How did you meet?" I ask her, because I don't want Felix going so far down the wormhole that he makes up an entire backstory for us.

My heart can't take it.

She smiles at her husband. "On a cruise, actually."

"You're kidding!" I say.

"No," Tom says. "We were sailing from Australia to Singapore."

"Wow," Felix says. "Sounds like an epic trip."

"It was," he says. "Three months. We met at the singles table the first day, in Sydney, and by the time we reached Singapore we were engaged to be married."

"Cruising is a great way to meet someone," Nancy says, putting her hand on her husband's knee. "You can spend so much time together, get to know each other without distractions."

Lauren should interview this woman for her TikTok.

But the thing is, she's not wrong.

I feel like I've known Felix for months, and it's been fewer days than I have fingers.

"What happened when you got off the cruise?" Felix asks Nancy. "Did you live in the same place?"

"No, Tom was in Palm Beach, and I was in Louisville. I moved to Florida. But it doesn't really matter where we're based. We cruise most of the year."

"We did an around-the-world trip last fall," Tom says proudly. "Thirty-one countries in 126 days."

"Sounds blissful," Felix says with a straight face.

They chat to us about their world travels all the way to the catamaran, telling us about the friends they've made on their various maritime trips, the sights they've seen, the cruise lines they prefer. It seems there is an entire subculture of retired people who live semi-permanently at sea.

I try not to convey my horror.

"That was wild," Felix says once we're on the catamaran and out of earshot. "Can you imagine staying on a ship for four months? Ten days is bad enough."

"Whatever floats your boat."

He groans. "Good one, Dad."

"I agree that monthslong cruises sound harrowing," I say. "But I have to confess that I'm enjoying my sojourn with you."

This is probably a little too sweet and sincere to have actually said out loud, but Felix breaks into a smile so big I know I've genuinely pleased him.

"Are you kidding?" he says softly. "Best holiday of my life."

This makes me so happy that I have to reset the tone to retain my sanity. So I say, "Unless we die snorkeling."

"I don't think you can die snorkeling," he says.

"It's actually one of the most deadly vacation activities there is," I inform him.

"You're thinking of scuba diving. You can't get the bends from going two feet underwater."

"I'm not kidding. People get disoriented and can't find their way back to the boat and drown. Or they get swept up in undercurrents and become too exhausted to keep swimming. I read a whole article about it. It's the leading cause of tourist deaths in Hawaii."

"Good thing we're not in Hawaii."

"We'll have to go there on our next cruise," I say solemnly.

"Uh-oh. Have you been converted?"

"Afraid so. I'm easily susceptible to cults."

"Are you trying to tell me you're a Scientologist?" he asks.

"I'm trying to tell you that I'd endure no end of Broadway musicals, turbulent waters, and midnight buffets if it meant getting to do it with you."

I worry I have once again tiptoed into saccharine town, but he leans in and kisses me.

"Same," he says.

I'm pleased to report that neither of us dies while snorkeling. We do see an enormous stingray, which Felix finds majestic and I find so terrifying I immediately swim back to the boat.

When the catamaran returns us to port, we're both hungry and decide to take a taxi into town for lunch. We ask the driver to take us to a good Caribbean restaurant, and he drops us at a bright turquoise seafood shack with tables on the beach. We order a feast of grilled grouper, jerk mahi, and spicy curry fritters.

"I'm starving," I say, licking fritter grease off my fingers. "Who knew snorkeling was so strenuous."

"You have a pattern of underestimating water sports," Felix says.

"My toxic trait."

"Well, if that's the worst you can do, you're pretty harmless."

"What's yours?"

"Gullibility."

"Pardon?"

"I'm completely gullible," he says. "My sisters spent my entire youth tricking me."

"Like telling you that you were adopted?"

"No, they're far more Machiavellian than that. Most of their schemes involved absconding with my money."

He looks so dismayed that I laugh. "Give me an example."

"Hmm. Okay, here's one: at primary, Pear convinced me this very unpleasant girl named Jemima in year four was going to tell everyone Pear was a bedwetter if Pear didn't give her fifty pounds. She said she couldn't tell our parents because then Mum would call Jemima's mother and Jemima would bully her even more for grassing up."

"So you gave her the money?"

"Of course. Fancied myself quite the hero. Until I found out there *was* no Jemima in grade four."

"Poor boy."

"Tragic, I know," he says. "And of course, to this day it hasn't stopped."

"Dare I ask?"

"Two months ago Prue was pestering me to come to hers for a dinner party. She wanted to set me up with a woman from her book club. I told her I wasn't looking to date, and in any case I had a private event at the pub that night and wouldn't be able to make it—all true."

"Uh-oh."

"The night of the party Pear called me in hysterics saying Prue had been taken to A&E with appendicitis and she was picking me up right away so we could get to hospital. I, of course, left the pub and went with her. Whereupon she drove halfway there before informing me with great glee we were actually going to Prue's house for supper."

"My God!"

"I know," he says ruefully. "They're wicked. But you'd think after thirty-odd goes around the sun I'd be on to them."

"Did you at least like the woman from the book club?"

"I was in far too bad a temper to make proper conversation. Though I must admit she was gorgeous."

I become briefly, ludicrously jealous that this woman has earned such a compliment. I need to cool my jets.

"Well, maybe Prue will trick you into going to another party and you'll get a second chance," I say lightly.

"No need. I'm decidedly single." He pauses, and smiles at me shyly. "Unless of course you decide to move to England, and I change my mind."

My jets are decidedly not cool. *He's just flirting*, I remind myself. But it scares me how much I light up at these words.

My enthusiasm comes burbling out before I can stop it. "That's actually always been my dream," I say.

"To move to London?"

"No, not London. I have this fantasy about living in the English countryside. Buying one of those rambling old stone cottages with a beautiful garden full of roses and fruit trees where I can spend my days writing novels." I shake my head at myself, embarrassed. "You know. The full Jane Austen experience."

"Have you looked into moving?" he asks.

"Oh God no, it's just a fantasy. I read lots of Regency romance novels to scratch the itch."

He frowns at me. "It's not silly to have dreams, Hope."

He's right.

And maybe I need to say mine out loud more often.

"What's your dream life?" I ask.

"Not so far from yours, actually," he says. "I've been toying with the idea of opening a pub with rooms in the country. Somewhere on the coast, maybe. Cornwall, or Devon. Eventually get married. Raise a family there."

I cannot help imagining myself as the woman he builds this life with.

"What about your businesses in London?" I ask, hoping he won't see the wistfulness that's overtaken me.

"Let my sisters sell them to Pizza Express."

"You wouldn't."

"No. But I'm sure I could run them remotely. Pop in twice a month. I don't give her enough credit, but my food and bev manager is brilliant. She could probably take over operations, with some training."

"So what's stopping you?"

"Fear," he says flatly.

"Fear of what?"

"My whole life is structured around my routines. Work, gym, AA, meditation, sleep. I truly believe it's saved me from relapse. Opening something new would blow that all up. I'm not ready."

"But you might do it someday?"

"I don't know," he says. "I don't know that I'll ever be ready. My sobriety is the most important thing to me. I'm not willing to do anything that would threaten it."

His eyes have gone rather far away and his jaw is set. He looks . . . grim.

"It's good that you know what you need," I say, worried I've led him into something he isn't ready to talk about.

"Anyway," he says. "No one needs to hear me prattle on about my boring life. Let's talk about something more interesting."

We settle on books. He says his favorite Jane Austen novel is *Sense and Sensibility*, while I profess mine is *Persuasion*.

"That makes sense," he says.

"Why?"

"It's about unfulfilled dreams of having a home of one's own in the English countryside."

"Well, she wants it with one specific person," I say. "That part's kind of important."

"Do you want it with another person?" he asks.

So much for light territory. It's hard to talk casually about dreams with someone who is rapidly, unwisely, becoming one of them.

"I'd be open to that," I say as breezily as possible.

I leave out the part where a handsome British man I adore, and who loves me beyond reason, shares my rambling cottage with me.

And maybe, just maybe, he owns a pub with rooms.

Felix

I would never have predicted that one of the best days of my life would involve a snorkeling trip during a Caribbean cruise.

But I like Hope Lanover so much it scares me. I like her so much I'm picturing her writing her novel in a hotel I design with a room just for her, overlooking her rose garden.

Or better yet, the sea.

I need to get a fucking grip.

I'm not doing myself any favors, spinning fantasies of some storybook life I can never have. Odds are I'll never leave London. Odds are, I *am* living my dream life. The dream was surviving my old one.

I'm not sure I could handle more.

I'm not sure I deserve to.

But damn is it nice to indulge for a few minutes in the vision of an existence unencumbered by my real circumstances.

When we get back to the ship, Hope yawns and professes a deep desire "for a snooze."

"Want to join me?" she asks.

I do, but I know I need to get my head together.

"I think I might go to the gym. And then I have a booking for a sports massage at six. Late supper?"

She yawns again. "I doubt I'll be very hungry after that lunch. But why don't we go on a date to the magic show?"

"I *hate* magic shows."

"How?" she exclaims. "They're the best."

"I don't like to stare into the face of evil."

"Card tricks are hardly evil."

"Fine," I say. "But I *will* intercede if a magician tries to saw you in half."

"My knight in shining armor. Pick me up at eight forty-five?"

I kiss her on the cheek. "See you then."

And I truly can't wait. I'm pained by the idea of four hours away from her. *Stop it*, I command myself. *This is ending in four days.*

Working out and getting pounded into raw meat by a petite Thai woman helps clear my head. I feel less woozy with infatuation when I knock on Hope's door.

Of course, all my feelings rush back when I see her. Tonight she's in a flouncy, vintage, pink cocktail dress that would not be out of place at the Copacabana. I want to pull her onto my lap on a leather banquette while we watch Frank Sinatra croon in front of a big band.

Unfortunately, we're headed to a magic show on a cruise ship instead.

Which does nothing to reduce the fact that I'm thunderstruck.

"You look amazing," I say.

She twirls happily. "Thanks. I only wear this for very special occasions."

"So, to see and be seen by magicians?"

"I love how deeply you understand me."

Despite finding magic tedious—I truly do not care if a scarf turns into an egg—Hope's unbridled delight at the performance brings me great joy.

She gasps when the magician whips his white cravat in the air and it turns into three doves. She squeals when, at the end of the show, the three doves are transformed into a small white Pomeranian.

"I wonder what the customs logistics of having pets on a ship are," I muse.

"Um, they're not pets. They're manifestations of forces we can't see."

"And I thought *I* was the gullible one."

The night's host steps onto the stage and asks us to give a thunderous applause to the magician. When we do, the magician takes off his top hat and throws it in the air, at which point it turns into a large white cockatiel, who flies toward the crowd, circles back, and lands on the magician's shoulder.

"Abracadabra!" the bird squawks.

The magician gives it an affectionate kiss on the head.

Hope basically swoons.

"I think I found the man I'm going to marry," she says.

"Trying to make me jealous?"

"No. That's what Gabe's for."

I laugh in shock, but the quip reassures me. If it were true, surely she wouldn't crack jokes about it. Besides, the way she was talking about his antics earlier seemed infused with relief that they were behind her.

"For those of you who want an extra dose of the occult," the host intones, "I encourage you to go down to the Cigar Lounge, where our very own psychic, Madame Olenska, will be pleased to read your tarot cards."

"Oh, we have to do that," Hope says, shooting up.

"Um, I think I've had enough magic for one evening. Let's go upstairs and watch the cruise ambassadors seduce their clients instead."

She grabs my hand. "No way you're getting out of this. Come on."

She pulls me up and drags me out of the room.

We go down the stairs to the cigar bar, which is choked with the smell of smoke. (Despite being someone who smoked cigarettes for years and is currently addicted to nicotine gum, I can't stand cigar smoke.)

"Ugh, I can scarcely breathe in here," I complain. "Can I *please* be excused?"

"Afraid not. Look, there she is."

She points to a horseshoe-shaped booth where a woman with a cloud of witchy gray hair is seated before an array of large crystals.

Hope charges toward her.

"Madame Olenska?" she asks.

"That is me, my dear. And who might you be?"

"Shouldn't she know that already?" I say under my breath.

Hope kicks my shoe.

"I'm Hope," she says. "And this is Felix. We were hoping you could read our cards."

"It would be my pleasure," she says. "Have a seat."

We settle into the booth across from her.

"Who would like to go first?"

"He would," Hope says with an evil grin.

"Ah, the skeptic," she says.

"Sorry, is it that obvious?" I ask.

"I can sense you don't trust the divine," Madame Olenska says.

"I just don't like magic tricks."

She raises her brows at me imperiously. "The cards are not magic, or a trick. The cards merely reflect what's inside you, apparent or not."

"Good to know."

"You will see. Do you have a question you would like me to focus on? An issue of concern?"

"Uh, no," I say. "Not really."

"You are new lovers," she says, apropos of nothing.

"We are," Hope says. She gives me a triumphant look like, *see?*

"We will focus then on matters of the heart," Madame Olenska says authoritatively.

"Great," I mutter.

"Now, I prepare the cards," she says.

She closes her eyes and shuffles the deck with the dexterity of a dealer in Vegas. Eyes shut tight, she places both hands on top of the deck and hums. At length.

Just when I'm wondering if we've accidentally stumbled onto a very bad a cappella concert, she opens her eyes and spreads the cards out into an arc on the table.

"Pick one. Whichever calls to you."

Nothing calls to me save for the door leading out of this room, so I slide out a card at random.

"Very good," she says. "Now turn it over without reversing it."

I do, and reveal a bright red heart with three evil-looking swords plunged into it.

"Jesus," I say.

"Ah," Madame Olenska murmurs. "The three of swords."

"Doesn't look auspicious."

"A card of heartbreak," she confirms.

I glance at Hope, whose brow is furrowed.

"The card signifies a betrayed connection," Madame Olenska says. "Perhaps in the past, perhaps in the future. Maybe romantic, maybe not."

"How conveniently vague," I mutter, thoroughly unimpressed.

"We're not finished. Choose another card to unveil further meaning," Madame Olenska says.

I consider declining, but Hope looks eager for me to keep going, so I comply.

I take a card and turn it over. It's a man holding two fistfuls of swords by their blades, attempting to sneak off as he looks over his shoulder at two more swords plunged into the ground behind him.

"Ah," Madame Olenska says, as though this clears up everything. "Another card hearkening betrayal, but in the context of the three of swords, the betrayal itself is the cause of the heartache. Were you cheated on by a lover, perhaps, my dear? For if not, the cards may point to a deep-seated fear that you will be, or—"

Yeah, enough of this shit.

"All right," I interrupt her. "That's me sorted. Hope's turn."

Hope looks at me with concern.

"Are you all right?"

"Fine," I say brusquely. I don't want to be rude but I don't feel like getting into a conversation about my demons with a woman doing a carnival act.

Madame Olenska looks askance at Hope. "Do you want a reading, dear?" she asks.

"I do," Hope says. "But, Felix, if you'd rather go—"

I'm conscious I'm causing a small drama with my reaction to this irritating farce, so I wave this away. "Please, go ahead," I say.

Madame Olenska repeats her ritual with the humming and shuffling, then spreads the deck out again on the table.

Hope holds her hand over the deck, moving it back and forth before finally picking a card.

It's an upside-down image of an old man and a family, overlaid with approximately one million gold circles with stars in the middle.

If the meaning is meant to be "chaotic nonsense," it's dead on.

"The ten of pentacles," Madame Olenska says. "Upright, the card symbolizes prosperity and wealth. But here it is reversed, signifying financial strain or debt."

I glance at Hope.

She looks stressed.

"I thought we were talking about matters of the heart," I say to Madame Olenska. "This is about money."

"Yes," she says sagely. "But the two are often intertwined, are they not? The card could be a warning not to be seduced by the riches of a lover. Or a warning that you already have been. Let's explore this. Pull another card, dear."

Hope shakes her head and abruptly scoots out of the booth. "No, that's okay. We're late to meet our friends. Thank you very much for the reading."

"It is when the cards provoke a strong reaction that they have the most to say," Madame Olenska says sternly.

"You've been great," I tell her, following Hope.

"Thanks again!" Hope calls over her shoulder.

"Well that was a crock of bullshit," I say as soon as we're out of earshot.

I expect her to laugh, but she screws up her mouth.

"Actually," she says, "I don't think it was. Can we get some air? I can hardly breathe in here."

Hope

I march us straight out of the cigar bar and through the corridor to the doors leading outside to the deck.

"Wait up!" Felix calls.

I slow down. "Sorry. It was getting claustrophobic in there."

He's looking at me like I'm a sudoku puzzle.

"What is happening?" he asks. "You seem freaked out."

"I didn't like what she was seeing in my card," I confess.

"Hope," he says, with kindly amusement. "Dear. You can't think a psychic actually just read your future."

"Not my future," I say, feeling too weary to even bother denying it. "My present."

"What do you mean?" Felix asks. "Money's causing you relationship troubles? Aren't you single?"

He's kidding, I know, but I don't have anyone to talk to about this particular problem, and I feel like if I don't get it off my chest I'll explode.

"I think it's about me and Lauren," I say. "She makes a lot of money, and I don't, and sometimes that causes conflict."

"Oh," he says. There's a pause, during which I realize he was not the right person to say this to, and now he's uncomfortable. But I'm too embarrassed to think of a way to recover, so I don't fill the silence, and we both just stand there.

"Uh, what is it Lauren does?" he finally asks.

"She's a lifestyle influencer," I say, not wanting to get into the details of the "finding a rich man" angle, which could sound alarming out of context. If I get into it then I'll have to give the whole backstory, and that's not the point.

"She always wants to do these fabulous things," I go on. "Vacations, spa treatments, expensive restaurants. And I can't afford it—like, at all—so she's always offering to pay. She's very generous, but I feel guilty that I can't reciprocate. And then last fall I had to borrow money from her to put a deposit on an apartment after my breakup, and I haven't been able to pay it back yet. She keeps telling me not to worry about it, that it was a gift. But I feel uncomfortable she had to bail me out."

I know I'm saying too much. Felix isn't my therapist or my financial advisor, and I'd rather he not think of me as some impoverished waif in debt to her best friend.

I don't even get into how the card could also be about Gabe. The pressure I felt to fit into his upper-class world, and my insecurity about not belonging there. The way he too insisted on paying for everything.

I don't want to be seen as someone with a pattern of being a charity case.

"Anyway, it's not that important," I say. "It just resonated for a second."

Felix accepts this without argument, looking a little relieved I'm not pursuing the topic. I know I've said too much already.

"It's nice out here," he says. "Do you want to take a walk around the deck?"

"Sure," I say.

We wander for a few minutes in the moonlight. It's getting late, and there aren't many people around. We stop and look up at the stars.

He's quiet, and I wonder if he's still put off by my oversharing.

"Sorry for getting stressed about tarot," I say. "Didn't mean to bring down the tone."

"Ha," he says. "Not your fault. Wasn't much to like in my cards either, was there? I blame Olenska."

It did not occur to me his bad mood could be about *his* cards.

"Is what she said true?" I ask. "Have you been cheated on?"

"Not that I know of," he says. "But I suppose I've felt badly used."

"How so?"

He groans. "This will make me sound like *such* a prat," he says.

"Well, I already know you're a prat. Your sisters have made it very clear."

"Bless them."

"Anyway, you were saying?"

He rubs his temple, like this conversation is giving him a headache. I'm about to rescind the question, but he says: "Several of my exes were quite . . . how to put it? Socially ambitious. I had a bit of notoriety in the tabs as a kid—bad posh boy about London and all that—and my first girlfriend, Emma, wanted to be in *Tatler* a bit more than she actually wanted to be with me. Took me a while to figure it out. Which didn't stop me from repeating the pattern a few more times."

"Oof," I say. "I'm sorry."

It does not escape me that we are from diametrically opposite worlds. His, where just being seen with him can get you into a society magazine. Mine, where $1.50-a-slice pizza plays heavily into my diet.

Still, it's nice that we can confide in each other. I wonder if we'd be as forthcoming if we were actually dating.

"Well, so much for tarot being a fun diversion," I say. "I was hoping to pull the Empress card."

"What's the Empress card?" he asks.

"It's basically like drawing Beyoncé. She's this beautiful woman in robes sitting on a red throne, holding a gold wand into the sky. She's a symbol of fertility—but not just the babies kind. Like everything. The fulfillment of passion, the power of creativity, abundance, prosperity, romantic love. The whole deal."

"Wow," he says. "I didn't know that was an option. Better that than a bunch of swords plunged into you."

"Yeah. I've always wanted to draw her, and I strike out every time."

He takes my hand and squeezes it. "You're every bit Beyoncé to me," he says.

"Thanks. Finally someone notices."

"I do nothing but notice you."

Emotion wells up in me. "Same," I whisper. "Same."

Slow down, I tell my heart. *Slow down.*

I am so grateful for this man, who is such a good listener, and so willing to be vulnerable with me about his disappointments. Under different circumstances, I'd revel in this easy intimacy.

But that's not what this is about, and I don't want to waste our limited time wallowing in painful topics. We're already halfway through this cruise, and we're under the stars on a beautiful night, and we should be making the most of what we *can* be to each other: lovers.

I wrap my arms around him and put my lips softly to his neck.

He tilts his head back, giving me access to his throat. There must be something about this stretch of the body that exudes pheromones, because electricity shoots through me.

He leans down and takes my mouth, and there's an edge to it. His stubble grazes me, amplifying my wattage. I close my eyes and tip my head back to give him access to the space between my ear and jaw. When he kisses me there, I shudder.

I slip my hand under his shirt, enjoying how his abs reflexively tense, then release, beneath my touch. It's like his muscles are alive for me. Like he wants me deep under the skin.

I slip my hand lower, beneath his waistband.

His cock is as alive as the rest of him—hard enough to fuck. I grip it, enjoying its velvet heat pulsing beneath my hand.

"Fuck," he groans, pressing himself against my palm. I give him a bit more pressure and he puts a hand to the railing to brace himself.

"Not here," he says. "Someone could see us."

"That's what makes it fun," I say. "Turn around and pretend to be stargazing."

He hesitates, but only for a moment.

Then he turns his back to me, and I catch him around the waist, like I'm innocently hugging him. But with my free hand, in the shadows, I unzip his pants.

I grip his cock, teasing it until he gasps. Every little breath he takes lights up a spark inside of me. I feel like I'm made of fireflies.

In the distance, I hear faint voices. A couple is rounding the deck from the other side of the ship. Not close enough to see us yet, but they will be in about a minute.

I stroke Felix fast and hard. "Hurry, baby," I whisper in his ear. "Or they'll catch us."

Whether it's the increased friction or excitement at the danger, he tenses against me. "Fuck," he rasps out. "Oh fuck, I'm going to—"

"That's it," I whisper. "Come for me. Right now."

He does.

I love the way he grips the handrail as his body rocks with pleasure, like what I've done to him would send him overboard if it wasn't there.

Because that's how he makes me feel too.

Like I'm about to fall.

He tucks himself back into his pants and steps away from me just as the couple moves into the light.

"Well, if it isn't the lovebirds!" the woman calls. As they move closer, I see they are Tom and Nancy, the couple we met snorkeling.

"Gorgeous evening, isn't it?" Tom says.

"Yes," I say. "We were just enjoying the breeze."

"Nothing like an ocean breeze to stimulate the senses, is there?" Nancy says. She winks at Felix.

Now he looks like he might fall off the ship for different reasons.

"Nothing like it," he agrees weakly.

They bid us goodnight and step inside.

Felix turns to me with a horrified expression. "Did they know? Because it seems like they knew."

I grin at him. "I think Nancy approves."

He laughs and shakes his head at me. "I need to get you into bed before we get arrested."

"Your bed?" I ask.

"My bed."

"I'm going to stop in my room and change first," I say.

"Don't take too long," he says. "The bed and I have plans for you."

I take a shower and slip into pajamas, then pad over to Felix's room and knock on the door.

He answers shirtless, with a towel wrapped around his waist.

He gives me a lopsided grin. "Hey."

I give him one back. Not that I have a choice. My face just smiles when it sees him. "Hey."

"I'm finishing up," he says. "Warm up the bed?"

I walk into the bedroom. The bed is pristinely made, but there's a piece of paper over the pillow on the side I've been sleeping on.

It's a sketch—a line drawing in the same style as Felix's tattoos.

In it, a woman in robes sits on a throne, holding a wand up into the sky. Below it the word *EMPRESS* is scrawled in all caps.

The woman has my face.

My heart throbs. Do *not* cry, I instruct myself. Whatever you do, *do not cry*.

Felix emerges from the bathroom.

"Hey," I say, holding up the sketch. "Did you draw this for me?"

He sits down next to me and kisses my cheek. "You deserve to have everything you want," he says.

I lean into him, still damp and warm from the shower.

"You're who I want."

I didn't mean to say that. I meant to say "what I want." "Who I want" sounds too personal.

It sounds long-term.

His eyes go dark, possessive.

He puts his hand flat to my chest, above my breasts, and pushes me down onto the mattress. "You're who I want too," he rumbles.

I gasp as he parts my legs with his knee. The drawing I'm still holding flutters to the floor. I make a mental note not to forget it, and then my brain is unable to focus on anything except his hands, gripped on my wrists, lifting them above my head and pinning them in place.

I arch up to him, because our interlude al fresco left me very ready to go and I want to speed this along.

But he doesn't let me.

"No," he says. "Tonight, I'm going to take you."

"Take me?"

"Yeah. Take you," he says in a very low voice.

He dims the lights and tenderly takes off my clothes. Every time I try to help, he stops me.

When I'm naked, he pulls my hands above my head again, covers my whole body with his, and kisses me. It's so deep and thorough and yearning that it feels like falling down a tunnel to the center of the earth. It's how you would kiss if there were no chance of escalation. If first were the only base. If kissing were the greatest bliss, the deepest connection, in the universe.

He kisses me like that even as he slides into me.

He kisses me like that even as I come.

We've slept together, but this is the first time we've made love.

8

MUTINY

Wonders of the Caribbean, Day 7

Welcome to Nassau, Bahamas!

Today the *Romance of the Sea* will dock upon the crystal clear waters of the Bahamas' beautiful capital city. Walk along white sand beaches, dine on the local conch delicacies, admire the colonial architecture of the historical Old Town, and prepare for exhilarating excursions—whether you plan to sunbathe for the day at the world-famous Atlantis resort, swim with the pigs on Rose Island, or explore underwater reefs and shipwrecks on our four-hour snorkeling tour!

Enjoy your day in Paradise!

Felix

The emotion I feel watching Hope when I wake up is not a "cruise ship hookup" feeling.

It's the same feeling that sprang up in me last night as I was fucking her. This deep desire to be inside her. Not just physically—but emotionally. Intellectually. To truly *know* her.

It's something soft I haven't felt in ages.

Maybe ever.

I can't believe how soon I'm going to have to let go of it.

Not one sliver of me wants to.

So instead, I let myself imagine her walking around my flat in London in one of my old T-shirts. Sitting in a booth at the Smoke and Gun with my mates after we close, laughing with them over a pint and a bag of crisps. Coming to Sunday lunch in Hampshire and eating my mother's roast lamb and duck fat potatoes as we banter with my sisters.

Driving down to the coast to look at country inns. Living out her fantasy in the English countryside. The one that could merge so easily with my own dreams for the future.

I get out my phone and go on Rightmove to search for historic houses for sale near Devon.

Just to see.

I discover I could afford one.

My pubs have done very well, and I keep my expenses low and put my savings in the market, investing with the advice of my sisters. I have a solid nest egg.

What if I *did* use it to radically transform my life?

And what if there was some farfetched configuration of the future where that life involved Hope?

I tell myself I'm being ridiculous, but that doesn't stop excitement from tingling through my fingertips when I see the listing for a large manor house that's currently being run as an inn. I click on the hotel's website, which leads me to its Instagram account. I rarely use social media, but I do occasionally log on to see pictures of friends' weddings and babies, so I open the app.

I have a notification for an unread DM. It's from someone called @FYIFelixSegrave.

Weird.

I open it. There's no message, just a repost of a reel from someone named @LaurenLuvRose.

I click on it, and a video starts playing.

In it, Lauren—Hope's Lauren—is sitting in an airy flat holding up a glossy *Romance of the Sea* brochure.

"Hey girlies!" she says. "Lordy Lordy, do I have an update. So you know we're always on a quest to find the most eligible bachelors in the land, right? Well, I have a new idea, and I think it might be my best one yet. Have you heard of luxury cruises? You know, the elegant kind where they serve food on fine china and give you a butler and sail to paradise? Well, guess what else they tend to have? An older clientele. A *well-heeled* older clientele that includes many lonely singles."

She winks. "So guess what? I'm leaving for one in two weeks. The ship is called the *Romance of the Sea*, so how could I not fall in love? I'm going with my bestie and we are going to find us some wealthy husbands, babydoll!" A picture of the *Romance* sailing pops up above her head, and "Gold Digger" by Kanye West starts playing.

"Follow my journey!" Lauren says. "I'll share all my tips for beguiling single gentlemen of means at sea. And wish us luck!"

The fuck?

They're here to meet rich husbands?

This must be a joke.

I click on Lauren's account and see that she's been posting furiously the whole time we've been on the cruise. Every post has tens of thousands of likes.

There's one of her posing seductively in front of the pool in her swim kit. The caption reads: "Aquacise might sound boring, but it's a great way to get just the right kind of attention. Men love a hot girl bouncing in the water." It's followed by a multitude of smiling devil emojis, followed by a multitude of splash emojis.

Okay, this can't be real. It's so over-the-top it's parody. Lauren is obviously playing a prank.

And here I am falling for it, same as always.

I'm about to wake up Hope to tell her I've almost been had.

But there's so many more posts that it gives me pause. I keep scrolling.

I scan over Lauren in revealing gym clothes, remarking that outdoor sports are a great way of finding fit men. Beach selfies and sunset selfies, with makeup and styling tutorials tagged to various brands, all of them with tips for looking your most attractive when on the hunt for "eligible suitors," which seems to be Lauren's code for rich guys. The "snagging" of which appears to be Lauren's *entire* purpose.

Hope mentioned Lauren was an influencer, but she conveniently did not mention this.

And then I see a photo of Hope.

She's in the outfit she wore the day of the cooking class, making eyes at the camera. There's a caption: "My girl going out to snag a man looking smashing in #DiorCruise #ad.

What?

It's one thing for Lauren to make a mockery of herself online.

But Hope? Hope is a *sponsored post* on an account about *luring rich husbands*?

This can't be real. It can't.

I scan faster, looking for Hope's face. Praying I don't find it again.

But a few posts down there she is. She's lying in bed in a turquoise and gold-printed caftan and dark sunglasses, looking impossibly glamorous. The caption reads: "Bestie had a bout of seasickness, but her cruise beau came to her aid in the most romantic of ways. Never underestimate the power of needing rescue. Brings out a man's desire to be a knight in shining armor." #romanceofthesea #versace #ad

The nausea sets in. I keep going.

And then I see my own bloody face.

It's a video of me and Hope singing "Wuthering Heights" at karaoke. It's overlaid with text reading: "It's official! Bestie is in a shipmance with a HOT ENGLISH LORD. Can you even??? This has potential. Let's root for their happily ever after!" #romanceofthesea #ad

I feel like I've been kicked in the stomach.

I look over at Hope, who's still sleeping peacefully.

She's all creamy skin, long lashes brushing against soft cheeks, hair splayed over the pillow, naked shoulders exposed, because beneath the covers she's not wearing any clothes.

I would know.

I'm the guy who took them off her.

Lovingly, tenderly, while imagining that maybe we were meant to meet.

I can feel that tenderness receding like a flower closing with the dimming of the sun.

Details of the past week come back to me in bilious waves. All the chatter at supper about my family's private equity fund. My sisters boasting of Dad's connections, nattering on about yachts and £40,000 handbags.

Hope talking about her debt. Her frustration at her low-paying job. Her stress over money.

Her delight at my title.

Her dream of living in England—my home.

I feel myself reduced from a person into a juicy fucking mark.

"Hope," I say. My voice comes out in a rasp.

She doesn't stir.

I touch her shoulder. "Hope," I say again.

Her eyelids flutter open, and those eyes that just hours ago I was so lost in look at me groggily.

She smiles at me. It's the kind of smile you only give to a lover.

It almost makes me ill.

"Good morning," she says.

I hold up my phone, my hand shaking. "What the *fuck* is going on here?"

Hope

I'm disoriented—yanked abruptly from dappled, abstract morning dreams to Felix's voice urgently saying my name.

I can see that something is wrong—very wrong—but I have no idea what. Only that he's holding his phone up to my face, his fingers trembling and his jaw so taut it reminds me of a slingshot.

"Hmm?" I say sleepily, scrunching my eyes together and then apart to try to make out what's on the phone.

Blearily, I see that it's one of Lauren's Instagram posts.

"Did you think I wasn't going to find out about this?" he asks quietly.

I truly have no idea what he's talking about. Lauren posts like ten videos a day, and I barely use social media.

I sit up. "What's going on?"

"Play it," he says, handing me his phone. "Right now."

I tap the reel, and watch.

My confusion quickly turns into disbelief at her words: "I'm going with my bestie and we are going to find us some wealthy husbands, baby!" I jolt up. And then "Gold Digger" starts playing, and all I feel is panic.

Why is she including me in this? What is she *thinking*?

Felix is staring at me intently. "Keep scrolling," he says.

With horror, I tap through her chronicle of the past week.

I see photos of me tagged with brand names, like I'm some kind of influencer too.

And then I see Felix.

I read the caption.

I feel ill.

But not as ill as Felix looks.

It dawns on me that it isn't Lauren that he's disgusted with.

It's *me.*

"I didn't know about this!" I sputter, because my brain is a kinetic mess of fear and I can barely formulate a thought. "She's not allowed to post about me."

Felix looks at me with searching eyes.

"It's not the posts that are the issue though, is it, Hope? It's what you're apparently here for."

"Whoa, whoa, wait," I say as calmly as I can. I get why he's upset by this. But he *knows* me. "Please, I understand how this looks," I say. "But will you just let me explain?"

He sighs. "Please."

"This is not—" I begin, but I have trouble speaking coherently. I try again. "This gold digger stuff is just Lauren's schtick. It's a bit. She's a reality star. She's only half serious. And it has nothing to do with me. I had no idea she even posted this. She's not supposed to put me in her videos. Let alone *you.*"

He closes his eyes, pained.

I sit up, pulling the blanket with me to avoid exposing my breasts.

"You *know* me," I say. "Do you really think this tracks with my personality?"

"I want to believe you," he says. "I really do. But there are pages and pages of this shit. You're all over it. She's your best friend. There is no reason for her to deliberately make you look terrible."

Yeah, there's not. And I can't fathom why she's done this. But I'll deal with that later. Right now, I need to salvage this.

"Felix," I say, putting my hand on his shoulder. "I came on this cruise because I wanted a fresh start. I wanted to clear my head. I didn't want to be alone in New York all summer depressed about my breakup and my parents getting divorced. *Not* because I'm trying to find a sugar daddy."

He winces at the words *sugar daddy*.

"Again, why would she say this about you if it weren't true?" he asks. "And why in the fucking *hell* would she include me?"

"I have no idea. Probably because she thinks we're cute and thought it would make good content. I'm so sorry. I could fucking *murder* her."

He says nothing.

It begins to dawn on me that he doesn't believe me.

"My God, just *ask* her," I say. "She'll back me up."

"I'm sure she'll say whatever you want her to," he says. "That's the whole point of this exercise, isn't it? To tell them what they want to hear?" He laughs darkly. "And it worked, didn't it."

I stare at him in disbelief. I can't believe he thinks so little of my character. That after everything we've done and shared, he would trust a few Instagram posts over me. That he would even entertain the idea I've faked everything I've felt for him over the past week. And for *money*.

"You really think I'm a con artist?" I erupt. "We've spent an entire week together. I *confided* in you. I *slept* with you. That's *it*. That's my crime. Wanting to spend time with you. A guy who apparently sees me as some desperate broke girl trying to find a meal ticket."

He laughs humorlessly. "So you can imagine how I feel, having told my entire raw, dark, barely behind me past and all my shaky dreams to someone who likes me for what's in my bank account." He inhales deeply. "I don't want to say something I'll regret," he says with an icy politeness that only a British person could pull off. "So I'm just going to say that I find this upsetting, and I'd like you to leave."

His tone feels like a punch to the gut.

"Okay. Wow. If that's what you think of me, we're done," I say. "This is done."

"Yeah," he says. "I think it is."

I pull the duvet around me, stand up, and start collecting my clothing. I go into the bathroom to change.

When I come out, he's gone.

Which means it's safe to start crying.

I sob as I walk back to my suite.

"Hopie!" Lauren chirps from the bedroom when she hears me come in. "You're back! I have so much to tell you. Come snuggle."

The sound of her voice makes me cry harder.

"Wait, are you crying?" she calls.

She rushes into the room clad in a gauzy blush maxi dress that swirls around her legs.

"Jesus, Hope," she says, doing a double take that would be comical if I weren't verging on hysteria. "What's wrong, baby?"

"Your Instagram posts!" I shout.

She chews her lip. "Oh. The ones with you in them?"

"*Yes*, the ones with me in them."

She winces. "Sorry. I was going to tell you about them once we got off the cruise."

"Why the fuck would you post that stuff?"

"Well, it was supposed to be a surprise. Because you know how you're always feeling guilty about borrowing money? I thought I would tag you in some sponsored posts. That way we're even and you can let it go. In fact, now I owe *you* money." She smiles reassuringly at me.

My anger at her abruptly stops my tears. "So you decided to make me look like a gold digger on the internet for ad dollars? Do you *hear* yourself?"

"Well, I have to stick to the brand messaging. I mean, you work in PR, you know how it works. But it's cute. All my followers are rooting for you!"

"Oh how wonderful. I've gone viral as a conniving sugar baby. Thanks so much."

She looks confused. "You know it's not serious. Most of my followers are in on the joke anyway."

"Yeah, well, you know who isn't? Felix. Who you *also* posted without his permission. How did you not think this through, Lauren?"

Her face wrinkles in distress. "Hopie, don't be mad. I was just trying to do something nice. I didn't realize you'd be upset."

"No? Felix literally kicked me out of his room when he saw these."

She gasps. "Sorry? He did *what* now?"

"You heard me!"

"What a fucking asshole."

"*You're* the asshole," I cry, even though I agree with her. "You made me look like I was targeting him in a fucking scam."

"Okay, you can't talk to me like that. You're my best friend."

"I *thought* I was your best friend," I retort. "But it turns out I'm just the sidekick you use as fodder for clicks."

Her mouth drops open.

"Whoa, hold on. I admit I fucked up but you know it wasn't malicious. You *know* me," she cries.

The same words I used on Felix.

And she's right.

I can be angry, but I'm not going to treat her like he treated me. Whatever she intended, it was not to hurt me.

"Okay, Lauren, yeah. I know you. But I'm unraveling here."

She comes closer and takes my hands in both of hers. "Baby, why are you this upset?"

"Because Felix is the first person I've liked in months," I erupt, pulling my hands away from her. "And now he hates me."

"Look, again, I fucked up, okay?" she says. "I wish to God I hadn't done it. But honey," she makes her voice soft and gentle. "I knew you were so stressed about money and I just wanted to help. I want you to be happy."

I know, deep down, that Lauren means what she says. I trust her. We've loved each other too long and hard for it not to be unconditional.

But I still think her judgment was deranged, and I'm not ready to be over it yet.

"I need some space," I say. "I'm going to breakfast."

I turn around and walk out of the room without even bothering to wash my face or change out of my pajamas. I need carb therapy. Immediately.

I grab a plate as soon as I reach the buffet and start piling it with pastries. I'm not even going to pretend I'm interested in balancing them out with fruit or yogurt. I'm scanning the room for an open table when I hear my name.

I look over to see Gabe standing and waving at me.

And he's with his grandmother.

Gabe approaches me with a huge smile that contains no acknowledgment of the fact that I literally fled from him the last time I saw him. "Good morning!" he says. "Gran and I just sat down. Come join us."

Maeve is looking at me expectantly from the table.

I don't have an elegant out.

But there's no way I can do this.

I cram the rest of my muffin into my mouth.

"Sorry, I have to go," I say. "Give Maeve my best."

But before I can flee, Gabe waves at someone over my shoulder.

I turn, and it's Felix. He nods and walks past, looking at the two of us in something like bitter amusement.

Fantastic. Now I'm sure he has concluded I was lying about Gabe too.

I want to cry again.

"Is something wrong, Hope?" Gabe asks. "You seem upset."

"No," I say. "But I don't want to be late for my excursion." A lie. I have no intention of going through with the day's plan of swimming with the pigs with Felix and his sisters. Another thing that he's ruined.

I really wanted to see those pigs.

"I owe you an apology," Gabe says. "For karaoke. I was hoping to charm you. I can see it didn't land."

If there is one silver lining to the events of this morning, it is that I don't have any patience for bullshit from men. I do not want Gabe's apology or his attention.

Felix was right about one thing: he doesn't deserve me.

Neither of them do.

I need to get away from them. I need to get away from every single person on this boat.

I rush to my room, throw on a bathing suit and a sundress, and go directly to the gangway.

The instant I step down onto the pier in Nassau, I run toward solid ground.

9

PARADISE LOST

Back to the Present, Unfortunately

Felix

I had hoped never to speak to Hope Lanover again.

Judging by the panicked way her eyes are darting between me and the departing ship, the feeling was mutual.

Hope is drenched with sweat and out of breath. She looks like she's been crying.

In fact, she looks like she's been crying for hours.

She looks like she's having the worst day of her life.

She looks the way I feel.

"The boat left," I say.

"Yes, I see that, obviously," she snaps. She gestures to the kiosk. "Did you speak to someone? Is it coming back?"

"The guy at the information desk said there's no way to get back on. We have to contact our embassies."

"Oh, please," she says, like I'm the greatest idiot who has ever lived. "It's *right there*. I'm going to talk to him."

I go sit on a bench and watch her have the same dead-end conversation I just had. She returns a few minutes later looking shell-shocked, carrying two pieces of paper.

She wordlessly hands me one of them.

It's the contact details and hours for the British High Commission in Nassau.

The first thing I notice is that the office closed at five p.m.

"Is your embassy still open?" I ask Hope.

"Nope," she says dully.

She looks so despondent that I almost feel bad for her.

"Fucking nightmare," I say. I pull out my phone to google what to do if you're stranded abroad with no identification. The low battery message pops up. The charge indicator is at six percent.

"Great," I say. "My phone's about to die."

"At least you have one," she mutters.

"What?"

"I forgot mine on the boat."

A push alert pops up on my phone from my credit card company.

It's a potential fraud notification asking me to verify a £3,201.22 charge.

"Fuck," I hiss.

"What?" Hope asks.

"My wallet was stolen and now someone's trying to use my card."

Her eyes go wide. "Was your ID inside?"

"Yep."

"So to recap," she says. "We're both stranded in a foreign country without our passports, and you have no money or ID, and I have no phone."

"And my phone's about to die, for good measure."

"What do we do?" she asks.

I close my eyes. There are so many layers to this catastrophe that I'm not sure which problem to attempt to solve first.

And the fact that there's a "we" here is not helping.

"I don't bloody know," I say.

We both stare off into middle distance, where we can still see the *Romance of the Sea* chugging serenely away.

"To be very clear," she says. "I have no desire to be in your presence. However, under the circumstances, I think we need to work together. If you can convince yourself this isn't part of my master plan to steal your fortune."

I don't have a choice. Hope may be a manipulative person, but she's the only one I've got at present. And all she's missing is her phone. I'm missing money and my entire identity. In the hierarchy of who is more fucked, I'm at the top.

"You're right," I say. "We need to team up."

She rubs her temple with an air both tragic and weary. "All right," she says, "here's the plan. We're not going to be able to apply for passports tonight. And you'll probably need to file a police report to document that your ID was stolen in order to get travel papers. So we need to find a police station."

"Yes," I say. "Which will require my phone not to die. So first, phone charger."

She nods. "Let's ask where the closest place to buy one is."

The kiosk guy directs us to a shop on the high street across from the port. Hope buys a charger, and I ask the clerk if I can plug in my phone for a few minutes. We sit down on the floor next to an outlet. Hope is silent while I methodically cancel my credit cards.

A text message from my sister comes through.

Pear: Where are you? We're waiting.

Fuck, fuck, fuck. I forgot about the dinner. As an anniversary gift to my parents, I arranged a ten-course private tasting menu for my family tonight at the chef's table. We're due to meet for pictures with the cruise ship photographer beforehand.

My family is going to go mental. And I, once again, am the self-destructive twat who can't be trusted not to destroy their happiness, even when I try to do something thoughtful.

I am awash in a shame I haven't felt since about six months into my sobriety, when I finally began to believe I was worthy of earning back their trust.

It's been a torturously slow process to rebuild it.

This will completely ruin my parents' anniversary—my family's whole trip—and it's because of me.

"Don't panic," I type. "But I missed the boat."

I immediately get a FaceTime call. I accept it to see my entire family, all of them trying to talk into the phone. The noise is cacophonous.

"I'm okay," I say loudly. "It's going to be fine. Please, calm down."

They do not calm down.

"Pear, can you give the phone to Dad?" I ask.

My father rarely gets riled about anything—at least not on the surface. This can be a fault, but under these circumstances, I'm hoping his chill will reassure my mother and sisters.

"Felix," he says, stepping away from their noise. "You're still in Nassau?"

"Yeah. I'm so sorry. My wallet was stolen and I wasn't able to get back in time."

"So you have no money?"

"Nor identification. But Hope is here. Between the two of us, we should be able to figure it out."

"Fine, good," he says. I'm very glad I did not tell my family what happened between the two of us this morning. It was going to be self-evident eventually, and I didn't want to talk about it.

If they knew, they would be even more worried about me.

"It might take a couple of days to get the travel documents in order," I say. "I'm really, really sorry."

"I'll call Lord Shanks," Dad says crisply. "He'll have a contact at the High Commission. Perhaps something can be expedited."

I wince. Hope can hear all of this. I'm not excited to add to her impression that I'm a coddled rich boy.

But the sooner this is solved, the better.

"Thanks," I say. "Also, can you wire some cash tomorrow when you get to St. Martin?"

"Of course," he says.

"You'll probably need to send it to Hope since I don't have ID. I'll get you the details in the morning."

"Very good. Take care, son."

"I will. Tell Mum not to worry."

He gives me a wry smile. "Your mum will be apoplectic. Nothing to be done about that."

No. Nothing to be done.

I hang up and hold my phone out to Hope. "Do you want to call Lauren?"

She looks at me blankly, like she hasn't heard me.

"I forgot," she whispers.

"To call Lauren?"

"The press release. Oh fuck. Fuck fuck fuck fuck. What time is it?"

"Just after six."

"Give me your phone."

I hand it to her and she starts frantically tapping it, cursing. She looks like she might have a heart attack.

"What's wrong?" I ask.

She doesn't answer, just taps on the phone like she's diffusing a bomb.

"Fucking finally," she says, and dials a number. "Pick up pick up pick up."

I hear an answer on the other end.

"Lana," Hope says. "Thank God. Okay, are you at the office? Good. I need you to go over to my workstation and log in to my account. The password is DorotheaC@us@bon4598!."

Over the next five minutes, I listen as she gives step-by-step instructions about something work related.

"Okay, it's out? You're sure?" she asks. "Check for bouncebacks. We can't miss anyone." She pauses, nodding. "You're a rock star, thank you. Listen, I'm stranded in the fucking Bahamas with no phone. Yeah, I know. She's going to kill me. Can you text me at this number if anything comes up? I don't know how long I'll be offline. Okay. Yeah. Thank you. Uh-huh. Bye."

She ends the call and drops the phone in her lap, sinking back against the wall.

"What was that?" I ask.

"Oh, just me probably getting myself fired," she says. She bends over and puts her head in her hands. She seems like she's going to stay that way indefinitely and the minutes are ticking by, so eventually I say, "Um, well, if it's all sorted, we should probably look into a hotel. Book something before it gets too late."

"Okay," she says. "Let me just text Lauren first so she's not looking for me."

She takes my phone, types a few messages, and hands it back to me. I deliberately don't look at what she's written. I assume it's something like "trapped with the goblin."

I google hotel availability in the area. "Looks like there are rooms at a Marriott a short cab ride away," I say. "I'll just book—"

And then I realize I can't book anything. I've already canceled my cards.

I clear my throat. "Erm, do you mind paying for it with your card? I'll reimburse you as soon as Dad wires me money."

She looks up from her shell-shocked stupor. "Who's the gold digger now?"

"Yeah. I'm aware of the irony. But I thought we had a truce?"

"It's fine," she says. "Whatever."

"I really appreciate it, Hope. I have no idea what I would do if you weren't here."

"Uh-huh," she says, unmoved by my sincerity.

Well, whatever indeed. We don't have to be friends. We just have to survive the night.

I give her the phone back so she can enter her card details. She lets out a bitter laugh.

"Felix. These rooms are over three hundred dollars a night with taxes and fees."

"Like I said, I'll pay you back tomorrow."

"The problem is, my credit card is almost maxed out, I have nine hundred dollars in my bank account, and I don't get paid until next week, assuming I even still have a job. It could take days to get documents. If for some reason wiring money doesn't work out, I'll be screwed if I spend this much."

I try not to let my shock show.

Clearly I'm not successful, because she narrows her eyes at me. "Don't look so horrified. We can't all be heirs to the baronet."

I refrain from pointing out that my relative financial stability has nothing to do with my family's money, which I haven't taken a quid of since school.

"Is there something cheaper?" I ask.

She scrolls through hotels. "Paradise Fun Guest House," she says. "A hundred bucks a night before fees."

"Sounds about right," I say.

"There's one room. We'll have to share."

I try to keep my face even. There is no point in conveying that I'd really rather sleep at the police station than in the same room as her. I can see by her expression she feels the same way.

"Is that okay with you?" I ask.

"Not really, but we don't have a choice."

"Right."

She pulls out a card and books the hotel.

Hope

I have never been so miserable.

It is swelteringly hot, I have no possessions or access to communication, I'm going to get fired, and I am sharing this joyful experience with a man whose very presence fills me with a singular combination of humiliation and rage.

And it's mutual.

Felix is being civil, but I can tell he dreads it every time he has to speak to me.

He offers to drop me at our hotel before he goes to the police station, but I don't think it's a good idea to split up. We sit in tense silence for ninety minutes until someone is free to take his report.

I spend the time catastrophizing about all the additional things that could go wrong. What if it takes forever to get an emergency passport? What if I can't afford to change my plane ticket? What if Felix murders me in my sleep?

I haven't eaten since breakfast, and my stomach starts audibly rumbling.

"We'll get food after this," Felix says.

"Yeah," I say, annoyed that, on top of everything else, he can hear my intestinal noises.

We leave the station and grab takeaway sandwiches from a cheap conch shack and sit outside on a bench to eat them. They're good, but I am acutely aware that it is my finances that are making this whole thing even worse than if the tables were turned, and I had the phone and he had the money.

I'm trying not to feel ashamed. I've worked hard my whole life, and I'm far more fortunate than many people. But after Felix's accusations this morning, I dearly wish I did not have to reveal to him just how tight a budget I'm on.

It looks damning.

We decide to walk to our hotel to save cab fare, since it's only twenty minutes away. This proves to be a bad decision when a big, fat raindrop plops on my forehead.

"Do you feel rain?" I ask Felix.

"Just a drop or two," he says.

Within thirty seconds the drop or two turns into a tropical deluge. We're still ten minutes from the hotel and now far enough away from the city center that there are no taxis.

We get so drenched so quickly that there's no point stopping somewhere for shelter. Instead, we dash through the dark streets, dodging the spray of passing cars, until we reach Paradise Fun Guest House.

I was worried it might be scary or disgusting given the price point, but it's in a tidy enough yellow stucco building, and the tiny lobby is clean.

A friendly woman welcomes us, clucking in sympathy at our bedraggled state. "Hope Lanover, yes?" she asks. "I've been waiting for you. Last guest of the night."

I give her my credit card and ID, and she hands me a set of keys. "You're in room six. Go out the door and up the stairs. It's the first door on your right. Now get up there and dry off!"

There is nothing I want to do more. The once-cute sundress I'm wearing is clinging sopping wet to my body and is so infused with sweat that it probably needs to be burned.

And then I remember I have nothing to change into.

I want to sob in frustration.

I want to sob even more when I unlock the door to our room to see it is approximately the size of a closet and contains only one double bed.

"Shit," I hiss. "It said online it was a double room. I thought that meant two beds."

Felix does not look any happier than I am.

"I'll go down and see if they have something else," he says.

"This was the last room."

He runs a hand through his hair, which is dripping into his eyes.

"I'll sleep on the floor," he says.

I glower at him. "Be serious."

"I don't mind."

"Of course you mind. It's cement and there's like one foot of space." I pause. Take a breath. This is not the thing to freak out about. Not when there are too many others that might literally ruin my life. "It's fine," I say tersely. "We can share."

I refrain from adding *just don't touch me*. I'm pretty sure it's clear from my tone.

"We should get out of our wet clothes," Felix says.

"And change into what?"

He groans. "Ah. Right. Probably should have bought some T-shirts when we were charging my phone."

I hate the idea of exposing even one extra inch of my body to this man, but I cannot remain in this dress.

"I'm going to take a shower," I say.

"Can you hand me a towel out of the bathroom?" he asks.

I toss him one and close the door. The bathroom is grim, with a flickering fluorescent light and a shower stall that drains into a grate at the center of the room, making the whole floor wet. There's no shampoo, only one tiny bar of soap, and the water quickly runs from tepid to freezing.

I scrub myself down as fast as humanly possible and attempt to dry off, but the towel is scratchy and miniscule. It barely wraps all the way around my boobs, and I have to drape it askew to keep my bits covered.

When I emerge from the bathroom Felix is sitting on the bed shirtless with his towel wrapped around his waist. For once, the sight does not make me weak at the knees.

His wet clothes are draped over the small window unit, and I put my dress and the bikini I was wearing there too. (Yes—*that* bikini. The bright red Jessica Rabbit one I put on this morning because the other suit was dirty. Fuck my life.) Given the humidity, there's no chance any of the clothes will be dry by morning.

Seeming to read my mind, Felix says if they're still wet when we wake up, he'll run out and get us some cheap tourist garb.

This does nothing to remedy the fact that we have nothing to wear to bed tonight.

I slip under the covers in my itchy towel. He disappears into the bathroom and showers. When he comes back he turns off the lights and gets into bed beside me, also wearing a towel. He carefully shifts to the very edge of his side of the bed, which still only leaves a few inches between us.

Being so close to him raises my heart rate.

Not with lust, to be clear.

With anxiety.

I've felt on the verge of breaking down for hours and been proud of myself for keeping it together in front of my enemy. But we are staring down what might be days of this torture, and I simply can't take it.

I start to cry.

I try to do so silently.

"Are you all right?" Felix asks, after about five minutes of this. He sounds resigned, like he has to ask out of politeness.

"Yes," I say tightly.

"You're crying."

I wipe away the tears. Speaking to him has the effect of making me so mad that it overrides all my other emotions.

"Well excuse me for that," I snap. "But some might argue it's the correct reaction to being stranded half-naked in bed with you."

"It's not like I *want* this," he says. "I didn't wake up this morning and pray that I'd get trapped without clothes or a passport or money with a person who hates me. But look, calm down. We'll get cash tomorrow and apply for emergency travel documents. This happens. There's a solution."

His rationalism makes me feel worse.

"Don't tell me to calm down. It's condescending."

He sighs. "Fine. Enjoy your doom spiral. I'm going to sleep."

I'm fairly certain he succeeds at this, as his breath steadies quickly into the somnolent rhythm I recognize from our previous nights together.

I lie awake half the night resenting his every soft snore.

Felix

I wake up naked, curled around Hope.

It feels good for the two seconds it takes my sleep-dulled mind to remember that I'm in a shitty motel room in a foreign country with a woman who will likely call the police if she realizes I'm touching her.

I inch away, fumble under the covers for my towel, which must have come off in the night, and wrap it around my waist.

Hope, to my deep relief, doesn't stir.

I check my phone and have a text from my dad saying his private banker in London is going to wire money as soon as he has Hope's information. I tiptoe over to the air conditioner, wriggle into my damp swim shorts from last night, and then open Hope's purse to find her ID.

The picture on her driver's license is laughably terrible. And when I see her name—Hope Gertrude Lanover—I'm reminded of our conversation about my posh name and background.

It worsens my mood.

Hope opens her eyes and clocks me taking a snap of it.

"Are you trying to steal my identity now?" she asks.

"Well, since I have no proof of mine, my father is wiring money to you. We can pick it up at nine."

"You're dressed. Are our clothes dry?"

"Damp," I report. "But dry enough to wear until the shops open and I can get us something new."

"You're not leaving me here alone with no phone."

"Well, then we can have a romantic date to buy novelty T-shirts."

"I don't need your sarcasm."

I sigh. She's right. Fighting isn't helpful.

"I'm hungry," I say in a nicer tone. "Do you want to find something for breakfast? Then we can procure more respectable attire and go to the embassies to apply for our documents."

"Fine. Toss me my clothes."

I hand her her dress and bikini from yesterday.

Hope wrinkles her nose at she takes them. "Gross. My dress smells like mildew and BO."

It does, but I wasn't going to mention it.

She wriggles around under the covers to put it on anyway.

Despite myself, I'm struck with sadness by this. We so recently reveled in each other's naked bodies, and now it's all we can do to have a civil conversation. It's excruciating to be reminded, in retrospect, how deeply I cared for her.

We walk out into the steamy morning. There's a cafe down the street, and I am unable to resist ordering a classic Bahamian dish called fire engine, which is effectively corned beef hash on grits smothered in hot sauce. It burns my throat pleasantly in a way that distracts me from the pall of disappointment and frustration with Hope. I suspect it will be the best part of my day.

There's a tourist shop on the street that's open by the time we finish breakfast. Hope grabs a long, white sleeveless dress, and I get shorts and a T-shirt that says "CONCH KING, Nassau, Bahamas."

"Very tasteful," Hope says, when I hand it to her to pay. "Your consulate will be so happy to claim you."

"If they even believe who I am," I say, giving voice to my nagging concern that I will have no way of proving my identity and be stuck on this island forever.

"Biometrics," Hope says.

"Let's hope the retina scanner is working."

We pop into a small supermarket for deodorant and toothpaste, which is when something very bad happens.

My guts turn over with a sharp and sudden pang that can presage only one thing.

Sweat immediately beads on my forehead. I mentally calculate how far we are from the hotel.

Too far.

"Um, sorry," I say. "I need the loo."

"We're five minutes from the hotel," Hope says.

"Sorry," I say, already dashing toward the cafe responsible for the situation in my bowels.

"Where are the toilets?" I ask the woman behind the counter.

She points to a door by the soda fountain.

I run there and attempt to pull it open, but it's occupied. My stomach roils. I pound on the door. No one answers. I pound again.

Finally, a woman with a little boy comes out and gives me a dirty look.

I don't have time to apologize. I lock the door and do my unpleasant business.

Twelve full minutes of unpleasant business.

I am not one to be embarrassed by the natural functions of my body. But under these circumstances, I want, just a bit, to die.

I wash my hands and splash water on my face, which has gone pale and clammy. I still don't feel entirely right.

Hope is waiting at an empty table. She looks smug. Unkind, since I was so solicitous of her copious vomiting.

"Hi," I say, not meeting her eyes. "Sorry. Let's go."

"Maybe next time don't order something called *fire engine*," she suggests.

"Thanks. That's so helpful."

We return to our hotel room to change. I let her go first. She emerges looking fresh and pretty in her ten-dollar sundress. I hate that I notice this.

I duck into the toilet so I don't have to look at her.

"All right," I say, when I come out, teeth brushed and body deodorized, in my Conch King shirt. "Let's go pick up the money."

Luckily, the shop is only a few blocks away.

The clerk takes Hope's information and comes back with a thick pile of cash. He then counts it out, hundred by hundred, until he reaches . . . ten thousand dollars.

I try not to grimace.

"Lucky lady," the clerk comments to Hope as he puts the small fortune into an envelope with a grin. "Now don't spend it all in one place."

She thanks him and hands me the cash. "Does your father think you'll have to bribe your way out of the country?" she asks.

"Here, take some," I say, peeling off five hundred dollars.

She immediately hands four hundred back to me. "You only owe me one twenty. Half of the hotel plus your clothes and breakfast."

"Just take it," I say. "You might need cash in case we get separated."

"That, Felix, is what ATMs are for."

"Fine. Whatever."

"You should probably stash your filthy lucre back at the hotel," she says. "It's too much to carry around."

"We are not going back to that hotel. I'll get us rooms at the Marriott."

"I told you. It's the only place I can afford. I reserved another night while you were changing."

"Hope, we are absolutely not sharing that bed again. And I kind of like hot water."

"Then *you* can go somewhere else."

"And leave you without a phone?"

"I can buy one of those prepaid flip phones or something."

"Not a good idea. I doubt they have international data. You need to be able to access the internet."

"I'll go to an internet cafe if I need to."

"Do those even still exist?"

"I don't know. Probably."

I am trying to be a good person here, and her refusal of the most basic decency is increasing the considerable degree to which I am already pissed at her.

"We said we were in this together," I say as patiently as I can. "You bailed me out last night. I'm not abandoning you."

"I don't need your chivalry," she says. "And I'm certainly not going to be in your debt."

And I'm not going to argue endlessly with someone who is clearly taking satisfaction in loathing me.

"Fine," I say. "We'll split up. Make yourself happy. But let's at least get you a phone first."

"Fine," she says.

"And it would be nice if we could bury the hatchet until then."

She gives me a smile so big and fake that it's worse than a scowl.

I look up the nearest electronics store and we walk twenty minutes in the heat, defeating the point of the clean clothes.

She gets the cheapest, shittiest burner phone they have that still has international texting.

"Give me the number," I say. "And take mine. Just in case."

She at least doesn't fight me on this. She also uses my phone to get the number for the colleague she spoke to last night.

Once we've exchanged information we stand awkwardly on the street.

"Well," she says with a shrug. "Goodbye, I guess."

"Uh, yeah. Good luck with the passport."

"Mmmhmm. You too."

I feel like I should hug her, or at least shake her hand or something, but this is a reflex borne out of manners, not something either of us will enjoy.

So I just nod at her and walk off in the direction of the High Commission.

It's anticlimactic.

It makes me impossibly sad.

I commence an exhausting, repetitive, frustrating day navigating the labyrinthian process of securing emergency travel documents. I will not recount the precise details of this, save to say it involved many forms, a succession of beige rooms, less than friendly consular employees, a less than flattering passport photo, and a new travel booking made on an airline app so buggy I was tempted to throw my phone at the wall.

I'm told my documents won't be ready for pickup for forty-eight hours, as they are experiencing a backlog in processing applications. This effectively means three more nights on this island. Since by then the cruise will be almost over, I abandon the idea of meeting the ship at a port and book my flight directly to London.

I then look for a hotel on the beach. I might as well stay somewhere nice while I'm trapped here—this is supposed to be a holiday, after all. I must be every bit the princeling Hope thinks I am, because I physically relax as the cab drives me into a lush resort complex, past a manicured lawn to a grand Colonial-style building with the glint of the ocean behind it. I crave functioning AC, hot water, room service. Which will be all the sweeter in blissful solitude, without the resentful digs of a bellicose travel companion.

At the check-in desk, a very helpful woman says they have a beautiful ocean-front suite available. "I just need your passport and a credit card," she says.

"Oh . . ." I say. "I've actually had my ID stolen and won't be getting new documents from the High Commission for forty-eight hours. But I can pay in cash."

She frowns sympathetically. "I'm sorry, sir," she says. "But I'm not able to check you in without an ID. And we require a credit card to take the deposit."

I curse myself for not thinking this through. Of course they need this. It's standard procedure at every hotel.

But I am not above begging.

"You can't make an exception?" I ask. "I have the police report about my ID. And I'm happy to put down a large cash deposit for incidentals."

She gives me a tight smile, shaking her head. "I'm so sorry, but it's our policy."

"Ma'am, I'm desperate."

I can see that her sympathy is waning.

"I'm truly very sorry," she says. "Perhaps you can find another hotel."

"Right. Thank you."

I trudge to a chair in the lobby and set about calling around to see if other places nearby can check me in with just cash.

I strike out.

Which leaves me only one option.

I dial Hope's number.

Hope

Separating from Felix, while satisfying in the moment, was misguided.

It turns out that to get a temporary passport, you need proof of your travel plans. This means I need to change my airline ticket to depart from the Bahamas. Which requires the internet. Which requires tracking down an internet cafe—yes, they do still exist, although nowhere near the embassy—and then physically printing out forms and trekking back another half hour on foot to stand in line once again. (Did I get lost multiple times without Google Maps? Yes. Yes I did.)

The whole process takes hours, and I'm told it will be at least two days before my passport is ready to pick up. Under other circumstances, killing two days on a tropical island would be heavenly. In actuality, it is tragic. I'm paranoid about money, paranoid about getting fired, and paranoid about braving international travel without a smartphone.

Plus, it is so fucking hot.

I trudge back in the direction of the hotel and stop at a market to buy a pineapple Fanta. I stand under the awning in the shade and down it in three long gulps. It's cold and sugary and makes me feel momentarily better, until I ask directions to Paradise Fun and learn that I've walked in the wrong direction and am now forty-five minutes away.

I buy another Fanta.

As I'm paying, my new phone vibrates in my purse. The only people that have this number are Felix, Lauren, Lana, and the embassy. I pray it's not the embassy reporting some new hiccup that will result in further bureaucratic hell. Even more fervently, I pray that it's not Lana telling me that something went wrong with the media blast.

But it's not.

It's Felix.

At the sight of his name, I feel a mix of irritation that I'm not rid of him, and relief that I am not technically in the Bahamas alone.

I accept the call. "Yes?"

"Hey. It's me."

"So I gathered."

"Look, I know you don't want to hear from me and I truly hate to ask, but I need help." He sounds like these words have been extracted from his throat with pliers. "I can't find a hotel that will let me book a room without ID and a credit card."

I instantly gather what this means.

I'm going to make him say it anyway.

"So . . . ?" I prod.

"So, I was wondering if I could stay with you again. At Paradise Fun."

I consider this. On the one hand, I was looking forward to never seeing him again. On the other, if I do him a favor I'll have the upper hand. And there is the human compassion aspect, or whatever.

"Hope?" he asks.

"Yeah, okay," I say. "Fine. I'm on my way back there now."

"Thank you," he says. There is so much genuine relief in his voice that for a second I feel sorry for him. He has offended me to my core and ruined the high I was feeling at experiencing real, actual joy for the first time since my breakup. But he's not a bad person.

Or maybe he's a moderately bad person, but I don't want him to suffer.

I am therefore feeling quite smug and saintly when I finish the trudge back to Paradise Fun and see him sitting, sweaty and disconsolate, on the stairs outside our door waiting for me. He holds up a single, miserable hand in greeting.

"Hi," he says.

"Hi," I say.

"I'm acutely sorry about this," he says.

"Yep. Me too," I say, walking past him to unlock the door.

"I really will sleep on the floor," he says to my back.

"Sure. Whatever."

He comes in behind me, carrying several shopping bags.

"What's all that?" I ask.

"I got more provisions." He dumps them out on the bed. There is shampoo, conditioner, real body wash, a hairbrush, and a family-sized bottle of SPF 70 sunscreen. Two pairs of Wayfarer sunglasses—one in black, one in hot pink. His and hers cotton pajama sets emblazoned with BAHAMA PAJAMA!!! in a neon airbrushed font. And a selection of bottled water, Coca-Cola, and something called Goombay Punch, all still cold enough to be glistening with condensation.

"Planning to build a new life here?" I ask.

"Well, it's looking like I'm here for three nights," he says. "Might as well indulge in hygiene and sun protection."

I reach down for the Goombay Punch. "What's this?"

"A local specialty, I'm told."

I open it up and try it. It tastes like if pineapple Fanta had even more sugar. I love it.

"Amazing."

He pops open a Coke and holds it out to me. "Cheers," he says. "I guess."

I sigh, and clink bottles.

Then we stand there awkwardly and drink soda in silence.

"Look," he says. "Don't feel like you need to spend time with me."

"Definitely don't feel like I need to," I say.

"But," he goes on, "I owe you a huge favor for this. Can I take you out to dinner or something? I can't speak for you, but it was a pretty shitty day and it might be nice to go, like, be in proper air-conditioning and eat food that isn't out of a vending machine."

I haven't eaten anything that wasn't fried or wrapped in cellophane since my carb feast yesterday morning, and this idea does have a certain appeal. Especially when the alternative is walking around alone in the heat or lying in this mildewy room playing the game of Tetris that came installed on my flip phone.

"Fine," I say. "But I'm going to shower first."

"I'll see if I can find a nice place."

I collect Felix's stash of bath products and wash off the grit of salt and grime that has accumulated on my skin after my day hoofing it across Nassau. When I emerge from the shower he's gone. There's a couple of text notifications on my phone.

Felix: Got us a booking for 7pm. Back in an hour.

It's 5:30, and I have no idea what he could be doing in the meantime, but I'm glad that he's not here. I sprawl out on the hard, lumpy mattress and read my other text.

Lauren: Hey! Did you get a passport???

Hope: Not yet. It's supposed to be ready in two days, and then I can get a flight the next morning. I'm going to fly back to NYC from here as soon as I get it.

Lauren: This is so fucked. I'm so sorry Hope.

Lauren: Like, it's completely my fault.

Lauren: I took down those posts.

Hope: It's ok. I know you weren't trying to hurt me.

Lauren: I should have asked you. It was dumb.

Hope: It was dumb, yes.

Hope: But I forgive you.

Lauren: Love you Hopie.

Hope: Love you too.

Lauren: There's a missed FaceTime from your Mom on your phone. Do you want me to tell her what happened?

I shudder.

Hope: ABSOLUTELY NOT.

Hope: She will panic.

Hope: Can you text her from my number and say wifi on the ship is spotty but I'm having fun and will call her when I get back? Code is 879001.

Lauren: Yep.

Lauren: Are you still with Felix?

Hope: NOT INTENTIONALLY.

Hope: But yes. He can't get a hotel without me bc he doesn't have his ID or credit cards.

Lauren: OMG.

Lauren: So you're stuck with him?

Hope: Yep.

Lauren: Are you going to have torrid hate sex?

Hope: Ugh, stop.

Hope: Too soon for hate sex jokes.

Lauren: Sorry!

Lauren: Did he at least apologize?

Hope: Not really.

Lauren: Well be a bitch to him and make his life miserable.

Hope: That's the plan.

Hope: But first I'm going to take a nap.

Lauren: kk sweet dreams.

I put my phone aside and close my eyes.

When I wake up, it's to pounding on the door.

"Hope?" Felix is calling. "Can you let me in? I don't have a key."

When I open the door, he is once again carrying shopping bags.

"That ten k's really burning a hole in your pocket, huh?" I say.

He steps inside and hands me one of the bags.

"So, I got us a table at this place called the Sopadilla Estate. Supposed to be one of the best restaurants in the country and they had a last-minute cancellation."

He hesitates like there's a catch.

"But?" I prompt.

"It's quite smart. So I got us something to wear."

"Are you Pretty Womaning me?" I ask.

"You might want to reserve judgment until you look in the bag."

I reach in and pull out a swishy floor-length caftan printed with bright orange coral designs embroidered in elaborate gold and silver beading. It has cape sleeves and a plunging neckline and a thigh slit. It's like something Lauren would own if Lauren pulled her wardrobe from the costume archives of *Dallas* instead of Bergdorf Goodman.

"So not Julia Roberts, actually," I say. "You think of me more as Blanche from *The Golden Girls*."

He cocks his head to one side. "Who?"

"Don't worry about it."

"Look, I know it's not exactly your style, but I didn't know what size you were and this said 'one size fits all.' But"—he reaches into his own bag and pulls out a tie with the same bedazzled coral print—"I figured if you had to wear that at least we could match."

I take the bag out of his hands and dig around in it for the rest of the outfit. It's a suit. And it is in a shade I can only describe as "vivid cerulean."

"What possessed you to buy this?" I ask.

"The saleswoman told me the blue is complementary with the orange."

"It is that."

"You don't think I can pull it off?"

"I think you won't need to sleep here tonight after all, the way you'll be beating off women in that outfit."

"A cab is coming in fifteen minutes. I'm going to shower."

While he's in the bathroom I pull on the caftan.

If the foggy mirror behind the door is not deceiving me, I actually look kind of amazing in it. It swirls appealingly around my curves, glitters in the light, and I like the thigh slit. My hair looks insane but in this equally insane outfit my swarm of curls nearly passes for deliberate eighties glam. I pull the tube of Dior Cruise out of my purse, put it on, and actually giggle at the final effect.

I'm stylish as hell.

I gloat, knowing that Felix is going to look absurd beside me, until he comes out of the bathroom.

Somehow, he *also* looks amazing. His suit is slim cut and much tighter than anything he would wear in real life. The electric blue brings out his tan.

The tie, however, is still ludicrous.

He does a double take when he clocks me.

"That looks remarkably good on you," he says.

"I know," I say. "If you were trying to sabotage me, it didn't work."

"Very little could sabotage your looks. But I was not expecting a sparkly muumuu to enhance them to quite this degree."

I can't help smiling.

"Shall we go?" I ask.

"Just need some shades."

He grabs the black Wayfarers he bought from the nightstand, but I snatch them out of his hands. "No. I want these. You take the pink ones."

I did this just to be churlish, but he doesn't argue. And when he puts them on, he looks like Ryan Gosling in *Barbie*, and I regret my decision.

It's difficult to be deeply carnally attracted to a person you are committed to loathing.

Which makes me wonder if it is perhaps *not* too soon to make hate sex jokes.

And perhaps not even be joking about it.

Felix

I'm in a too-tight suit in a too-hot taxi with a too-smug woman I am too attracted to.

I'm trying to make the best of things—but only because seeming unfussed is the one move I currently have in the stranded ex-lovers playbook. There is a subtle balance of power when people who despise each other must mutually cooperate to survive, and it is currently tipped in Hope's direction.

And she knows it.

She's been gloating since she found me washed up on her doorstep. And now that she improbably looks like a *Vogue* cover, she has the lofty air of someone who ate helium.

"Nice night," I comment disingenuously. It is perhaps one degree cooler than it was at noon. I never want to feel humidity or see sunshine again.

"Is it?" Hope asks, because Hope is not playing the same game as me. She is playing the let-me-enjoy-antagonizing-the-person-I-hate-because-there-is-nothing-he-can-do-but-grin-and-bear-it game.

"You're sweating like you have a wasting illness," she says.

"You're a bit dewy yourself."

"A dewy complexion is considered a mark of youth and beauty."

"I wonder what those buildings are," I say, to change the subject. I point out the window at a structure of five peach towers topped with spires, one side connected to the other with a swooping sky bridge that makes my stomach drop just from looking at it. "You can see them everywhere."

She snorts. "Seriously?"

"You know what it is?"

"Yes, duh. It's Atlantis."

"Not ringing a bell."

"Clearly you never saw the cinematic classic *Holiday in the Sun* starring Mary-Kate and Ashley Olsen."

"Clearly. What is it?"

"It's a massive resort with its own beach and waterpark. Going there was my childhood dream. I kept asking my parents to take me for my birthday."

"Did they?"

She snorts again. "Um, no. They were broke public school teachers. They were like 'yeah right, here's a fifty-dollar gift certificate to Books-A-Million and an ice cream cake.'"

Fell into that one, didn't I.

"Lauren and I used to joke about going there for spring break and having affairs with teenage staff members while searching for smuggled antiquities like the Olsens," she says.

"Is that the plot of the movie?"

"Yep."

"Do they find the antiquities?"

"Just in time."

Our taxi pulls onto a palm-lined drive and stops in front of a gracious pink house lined with French windows and surrounded by lush green gardens. As soon as the valets open our doors, I can hear the tinkle of piano music and conversation trickling out from inside.

It's the sound of people having fun on an upscale holiday. The sound of the *Romance of the Sea*.

A triggering noise if ever there was one.

"Something wrong?" Hope asks, like she's eager to hear the answer is yes.

"Not at all. Let's go in."

I give my name to the host—an old school maître d' in a white dinner jacket.

"Mr. Segrave, welcome," he says. "Your table is almost ready. Let me invite you into the lounge for a cocktail while you wait."

He takes Hope's arm and leads us into what looks like a wealthy family's living room—overstuffed chairs and sofas and a white grand piano under a dramatically vaulted wood ceiling.

"This is so beautiful," Hope says to the host.

"Thank you so much, Mrs. Segrave," he says. "Can I bring you a drink while you wait?"

"Oh, I'm not Mrs. Segrave, thank goodness," she says conspiratorially. "And yes, I'd love a gin and tonic."

"Same for you, sir?" he asks.

"Club soda, please. With a lime."

I settle onto a sofa to look at a menu but Hope doesn't join me. Instead, she swans over to the piano, where a tall and incandescently handsome Black man is playing some jazzy standard I don't know. She starts chatting with him. A waitress with a silver tray stops by and hands Hope her drink. She takes a sip as the pianist winds down the song he's playing, and then starts "Summertime."

He nods at Hope, and she sings the opening line.

As we know, Hope has an incredible voice. So of course, this stops the room in its tracks. The piano player jumps in at the chorus and they harmonize, prompting enthusiastic applause that lifts the tone in the room from pleasantly relaxed to festive. An older couple gets up to dance, and after a minute, a younger one joins them. Hope finishes the song—to more applause—and is making her way over to me when the piano player starts "Fly Me to the Moon." I half expect her to race back and start covering Frank Sinatra but she's waylaid by a handsome white guy old enough to be her father.

"Would you like to dance?" he asks her.

She smiles at him and says loudly, "I'd love to! My date doesn't know how."

He offers her his arm and they turn away, swaying to the music.

I ignore them.

A pair of women in their forties carrying flutes of champagne—a freckly redhead in a white pantsuit and an Asian brunette in a gold cocktail dress—approach me.

"Hello," the redhead says. "Do you mind if we sit?" She gestures at the sofa across from mine. "We're waiting for our table."

"Please," I say.

"I'm Carly," she says. "And this is Amanda. We're here from Toronto on our honeymoon."

"Congratulations," I say.

"Are you here celebrating something?" Amanda asks.

"Stranded, actually," I say.

She inclines her head. "Stranded?"

I tell them about missing the ship. They're agreeably riveted by my tale of misfortune.

"You deserve a stroke of good luck, Felix," Carly says.

"By the way, are you with that woman?" asks Amanda. She's pointing at Hope, who is now walking toward the front doors.

"Uh, sort of. We're—"

She is now walking *out* of the doors.

"Sorry. One second."

I get up and rush after her.

"Hope!" I say as I step outside. She's waving expectantly at a taxi pulling into the drive.

"Oh, hey," she says affably. "This place is kind of stuffy. That guy I was dancing with told me about a great jazz club, so I'm going to check it out."

"You were going to leave without telling me?"

"No, of course not. You seemed occupied so I sent you a text."

I grope in my pocket for my phone and see she has in fact texted me.

Hope: I'm going out on the town. Don't wait up.

"Did it occur to you I don't have a key to the room?" I ask.

"Get one at the desk." She opens the door to the taxi, then pauses to give me a radiant smile. "Enjoy dinner! The food looked great!"

And with that, she climbs in and shuts the door.

Unbelievable.

I stand there watching the car drive away, marveling that she *really* just did that. It's almost heroic in its childish dickishness.

"Mr. Segrave?" the host asks, stepping outside.

"Yeah?" I say distractedly.

"Your table is ready."

"Brilliant."

I let him escort me back through the lounge to the dining room, where he seats me at a window table sumptuously set for two.

"It'll actually just be me tonight," I tell him.

"Of course, sir," he says, valiantly ignoring that I've just been abandoned.

I order Andros Island crab bisque with pork belly and, for my main, grilled spiny lobster. Amanda and Carly are seated at the table beside mine just as my soup arrives.

"You should join us!" Amanda says, waving me over.

"Oh, no, I'm fine," I say. "Thanks."

"Please, I beg you," Carly says. "We're here for another week and we're already sick of each other."

"Doesn't bode well for our marriage," Amanda says.

I like them, and I'd rather make conversation than eat soup alone, so I agree.

The waiter sets up a place for me at their table.

"So, what happened out there?" Carly asks. "With your . . . friend?"

Amanda nudges her. "Don't be rude."

"No, it's fine," I say. "Long story, but fine."

"We have all night."

"Well, that girl—her name is Hope—we met on the ship and had a . . . thing."

Over the course of my soup, then their appetizers, then our mains, and then a truly exquisite soursop and mango mousse we all share, I tell them the whole sordid story.

This, of course, leads them to a deep dive down Lauren's Instagram.

The posts of Hope have been deleted but they dissect the many videos of the cruise that are still up over their third glasses of champagne.

"Okay, hold up, Felix," Amanda says. "This girl is kind of hilarious. Like, I think I love her."

"You don't think what she's doing is gross?" I ask. "Being a professional gold digger?"

Carly scoffs at me. "Felix, she's *obviously* not serious. Come on. She must know that no man is going to marry her if he thinks she's targeting him for money and posting about it on social media. She's playing a character."

"And judging by her number of followers, she's doing it all the way to the bank," Amanda says.

"Um, yes," Carly says. "I can assure you a girl with this many luxury sponsorships doesn't need a sugar daddy. The internet's her sugar daddy."

In the context of two impartial observers being extremely rational, I begin to reconsider things. It does all track with what Hope said.

"God," I say. "Maybe I've been an idiot."

Amanda nods at me sadly. "A big one."

I put my head in my hands as the enormity of what they're saying sinks in.

Hope isn't any of the things I've accused her of being.

She's the lovely person I thought she was.

And I've been a massive prick.

"Fuck," I hiss. "She's right to hate me, isn't she? She told me all this and I refused to believe her."

Carly downs her last sip of fizz. "Well," she says. "Your reaction sort of makes sense. Your feelings were hurt so you weren't thinking clearly—not able to see the humor in it."

"Yes, that's it!" Amanda says. "You overreacted because the idea she was lying to you hurt more than you were prepared for. You didn't want to acknowledge you could be so devastated by what you were telling yourself was an empty fling."

"Because it wasn't an empty fling, was it?" Carly asks.

"No," I admit softly. "It wasn't."

It was something much deeper than that. Something I have now ruined and will not be able to get back.

It's gutting.

"I need to apologize to her," I say, more to myself than to Amanda and Carly.

They nod.

I pick up the check, say goodbye to my dining companions, and take a cab back to Paradise Fun. Hope hasn't returned yet. I lie on the bed under the fluorescent overhead lights, stare at the water-stained popcorn ceiling, and contemplate the words I should use to tell her I'm sorry.

They all sound so insufficient.

The truth—that I was falling for her and reacted in an overblown way—sounds manipulative, like I'm angling for more than forgiveness. But saying I rewatched the videos and simply accepted they aren't serious doesn't feel heartfelt enough.

I must have dozed off, because I'm startled awake by the sound of Hope letting herself into the room.

She leans back against the door, crosses her arms over her chest, and glares at me.

"You're in my bed," she says indignantly.

I jump up. "Sorry. All yours."

She grabs one of the two sad, thin pillows off the bed and tosses it onto the floor.

"Sweet dreams," she says, gesturing at the pillow.

"Hey, listen," I say. "Can we talk? About what happened?"

She looks at me like I've suggested we eat live snakes.

"No, we cannot. It's two in the morning. I'm tired."

She disappears into the bathroom and I hear her brushing her teeth. It sounds angry. Like she's taking her frustration with me out on her gums.

When she comes out, she's wearing her BAHAMAS PAJAMAS!!! She throws herself onto the bed and starfishes so that she takes up every inch of the surface area, making sure that I'm watching this territorial claim before pointedly closing her eyes.

I do not need any more clues that this is not the time for my clumsy apology.

I turn off the light and lower myself onto the hard cement floor.

It's painful. The penance I deserve.

Hope

I wake up face down on the scratchy, not-entirely-clean-smelling coverlet of the hotel bed.

My whole body is sore from last night. I think I rage-danced with every jazz musician, local fisherman, and vacationing frat boy in Nassau. It was fun, but not worth shin splints.

"Good morning," Felix says from the windowsill, where he is perched because there is nowhere else to sit in the room except the bed I'm sprawled out on.

"Hungry?" he asks. "I got guava duffs."

He holds out a pastry box. I take it and descend on a mouthful of tropical sugary goodness. It's amazing. I eat another one.

"There's also coffee," he says, handing me a paper cup.

"Thanks," I say, taking it and drinking it down so fast I burn my mouth.

"Did you have fun last night?" he asks.

He's being awfully nice for a person I abandoned at a restaurant and spitefully made sleep on a cement floor last night.

"Yes," I say.

"That's great. What did you do?"

"You're being weird," I say suspiciously.

"What do you mean."

"Like, pleasant? Solicitous? Not mean?"

He stands up and looks intensely into my eyes.

"That's because I'm really, *really* sorry, Hope."

This doesn't compute.

"Can you clarify what you are talking about?" I ask.

"I'm sorry for jumping to an unfair conclusion about you when I saw Lauren's posts, for refusing to believe you when you explained, and for generally hurting your feelings and misjudging you," he says.

This feels like an insufficient accounting of what he did.

"Misjudging me?" I ask. "You insulted me more than anyone has in my entire life."

He looks pained.

"I'm so sorry I jumped to conclusions," he says. "I felt very hurt, and I was irrational."

"Yeah, I was very hurt too," I snap. "Because you know what? I *am* on a very tight budget. And I *do* want to find a partner. But I have supported myself since I was eighteen years old. I have made *many* sacrifices to make sure that I can do that. And it is degrading to be accused of manipulating someone for money."

"I'm really sorry," he says. "*Really* sorry, Hope. I believe you."

I can tell he means it. What I'm not sure about is why he has had this change of heart.

"Can you please tell me why you suddenly get it? What changed?"

"I looked at the posts again. Not the ones of you—she took them down. But the whole account. And it doesn't seem serious. It seems like Lauren's playing a character."

"I *told* you that."

He sighs. "Yeah. I know. But I couldn't take it in before."

I feel strangely numb to the idea that Felix is truly sorry. Like I've built up too much of an armor of resentment to give a shit about what he thinks of me.

"That doesn't really cut it, Felix," I say. "I shared a lot with you the past week. I was, forgive the therapy speak, vulnerable. And you dismissed every single thing you knew about me and decided I was a monster in four seconds."

"Because I was falling for you," he says. He doesn't say this in a romantic moonlit confession kind of way. He says it guiltily. Like it just slipped out.

It is astounding.

"What?" I ask.

"I was falling for you," he repeats. "You were—are—smart and beautiful and fucking hilarious, and in retrospect I started letting myself feel way too much way too quickly, which is never good but especially not when I've had myself on strict emotional probation for years. So I was in too deep and when I saw those posts I got whiplash. I was mean, and I'm ashamed of myself."

I'm trying not to get stuck on "I was falling for you."

I'm trying not to lose myself in wondering if the past tense is good or bad.

"Is this how you are?" I ask him. "You lash out at people when you're the slightest bit hurt?"

The question seems to throw him.

"I don't know how I am," he finally says. "Not in relationships. I always used to be easygoing, a little numbed out. I didn't feel *anything* very deeply. I'm still navigating what it's like to be conscious of my own emotions. And it was irresponsible to let myself get so tangled up with you. I know I'm not there yet. It's why I don't date. I let my own bullshit burn you, and I feel absolutely dreadful about it."

I believe him. He looks like he does feel dreadful.

The question is whether I forgive him.

I've experienced too many emotions in the past eight days and I'm spent.

"I don't know what to say, Felix," I admit.

"You don't have to say anything. I just wanted you to know."

"I accept the apology, I guess."

"Thank you," he says.

"But beyond that . . ." I shrug.

"I get it," he says. "You don't have to forgive me. I just need you to know that I was wrong and I know it."

"Okay," I say. "Thanks for telling me."

We're both silent.

It's excruciating. Part of me wants to decrease the awkwardness by offering him some reassurance that everything is okay now. Or the opposite, to say I can't get over it and will continue being hostile.

But I simply don't know *how* I feel.

A question pops into my mind.

"Hey, how did you even see Lauren's posts in the first place?" I ask. "Did you look her up?"

"No. Someone DM'd them to me," he says.

"Who?"

He furrows his brow. "Yeah, I don't know, actually. The account was called FYIFelix or something."

I gape at him. "Wait. Some random burner account sent it?"

"I guess?"

"And that didn't set off red flags?"

"It should have. I wasn't thinking clearly. I'm really sorry, Hope."

"But you must have *some* idea of who would send that to you."

He shakes his head helplessly. "I assume someone I know saw me on Lauren's account and wanted to make sure I was aware."

Lauren does have a lot of followers, but this explanation seems off. If I saw that a friend was potentially being catfished, I'd just tell them. I wouldn't create a whole false identity to freak them out even further.

Whatever. Maybe it's a British thing.

My phone chimes with a new text message.

Lauren: I figured out the perfect apology present.

Lauren: You can't be mad and you can't say no.

Lauren: You are the proud new owner of a suite at Atlantis for the next two nights

Lauren: Check in at the Cove entrance with conf # 3761240.

Lauren: It's already paid for and it's my fault you're trapped there so don't argue and just go.

Lauren: Love you.

"Oh my God," I say out loud.

"What is it?" Felix asks.

I laugh in disbelief. The last thing I want is for Lauren to be spending more money on me. But the gesture is so perfect that I can't be annoyed at her.

"Hope?" Felix prods.

"Lauren booked me a room at Atlantis."

"That hotel you were talking about?"

"She knows I used to be obsessed with it."

A strange look passes over his face—like he's sad to hear this.

"Well, that's good, right?" he asks tentatively. "I can keep this room since we're already checked in, and you can have your own space."

"Yep," I say. "I should pack up."

"Need help?" he asks.

"I have like six things."

"Right." He sits down on the bed and turns his attention to his phone.

I move about the room assembling the small pile of possessions I've accrued and stuffing them into plastic shopping bags.

I take my time with it.

I feel a little bit anxious.

I did not feel comfortable getting around without internet access yesterday. As satisfying as it was to leave Felix at the restaurant, I spent most of the evening paranoid about getting home.

I like the security blanket of having Felix, or at least his phone, around for emergencies.

And after what he said . . . maybe I don't want to end on this note. This tentative blankness.

Maybe I should work out my feelings before I say goodbye to him forever.

"Hey, Felix?" I say.

He looks up. "Yeah?"

"The idea of you rotting away in this dank room alone is depressing me."

"No worries. I like Paradise Fun. Especially when I don't have to sleep on the floor."

"No, I feel guilty. Why don't you come with me?"

He looks at me long and hard, like he's not sure what to make of this.

"You really want to keep sharing a room?"

"No. But I really want access to an iPhone."

"Ah, I see how it is."

"Lauren said it's a suite. I'm sure we can get one with two beds."

He gives me a sad smile. "Look, Hope, you don't have to be nice now. You don't owe me anything. I'm fine."

"I'd really be more comfortable if you came," I say. "I kept getting lost yesterday and my phone doesn't get very good signal. We don't have to hang out, I'd just feel safer knowing you're . . . around."

He nods carefully, like he's taking pains to maintain a neutral expression. "Okay. Sure. I'll call a cab."

Felix

As we drive through the gates to Atlantis, it becomes clear this place is less a hotel than its own city. There's a theme park, a casino, a golf course, restaurants, shops, and multiple accommodations. It's essentially a stationary cruise ship.

I almost wish I had stayed at Paradise Fun.

It wouldn't have been right to leave Hope anxious about being alone with no phone, but every fiber of my being is radiating caution.

It seems my anger at her was providing me with a layer of protection. Without it, I feel acutely aware of what I ruined, and the unhealed darkness in me that sabotaged it so easily.

It's not healthy, but my impulse is to be alone. To stew in the company of my own demons.

We check in and take the lifts to the thirteenth floor, where we're greeted by a huge room with two queen-sized beds, a sitting area, and a balcony overlooking the ocean.

"Wow, what a shithole," Hope says, deadpan.

"Dreadful. I miss Paradise Fun," I say.

"I know. Those cinder blocks. I'm definitely giving it five stars on Tripadvisor."

She looks out the window, surveying the complex.

"We have to start at the water park," she says. "Put on your suit."

I don't want to be rude, but I was not anticipating spending the day with her. Especially not at a water park.

"Children's water attractions make me worry about fecal matter," I say. "I think I'll sit this one out."

She rolls her eyes at me. "Oh, come on. I'm sure there's enough chlorine in the water to peel off a layer of skin."

"Not a winning argument."

"Let's get changed."

"No, really. I'll hang back," I say. "Not in a pool mood."

She frowns. "What are you going to do instead?"

Brood.

"Nap," I say.

"I happen to know you don't nap."

"A night of attempting to sleep on cement is enough to overpower my insomnia."

"Yeah, um. Sorry about that."

"It's okay. I deserved it."

She shrugs and disappears into the bathroom to change. She emerges in a red, gravity-defying bikini. I have seen this garment sitting on a windowsill. I have not yet seen it on her body. It knocks the bloody wind out of me.

"Sure you don't want to come?" she asks.

I suspect the invitation is a peace offering, and part of me longs to accept it. But I feel too ill at ease. Every time I look at Hope, I get a fresh stab of regret.

"Don't worry about me," I say. "Go have fun."

As soon as she's gone, I collapse on one of the beds and close my eyes. I really do want to sleep. Between my guilt over Hope and the bracing discomfort of the floor, I spent most of last night staring at the ceiling.

I close my eyes and let exhaustion overpower everything else.

I jolt awake what feels like a few minutes later. Except the light is different, and when I reach for my phone, the clock reads four thirty p.m.

There are also three missed calls from my mother.

Which—fuck.

I realize I haven't updated my family since picking up the money yesterday morning.

Now that things are calm, the extent to which I have fucked up looms large and ominous in my mind.

I feel like I used to in the deepest throws of a hangover, when the fractured events of the last binge filter back in nauseating snippets. The idiotic things that you did. The people you pissed off or worried or hurt.

I open our family's WhatsApp group to almost two days' worth of unread messages.

Pear: Feeeeelix!!!! What is going on???

Prue: Are you a stateless person???

Dad: Were you able to get an emergency travel document? I found a contact at the High Commission who may be able to help.

Mum: Darling we're so worried! Please check in!

Pear: You're missing standup comedy night. Maybe you should try to swim and catch up with us.

Mum: Not funny.

And then, from late last night:

Prue: Felix WTF? Are you ok?? What is going on???

If the likes of Prue is expressing genuine concern for me, they must be very worried indeed.

Just like they were during the years of my failures and disappointments and benders. I can't believe I have done this again.

I should call my mother, but I know she'll hear the tone of my voice and immediately worry I'm backsliding. So I quickly type off a message:

Felix: So sorry, accidentally had my phone on do not disturb.

(A lie, but hopefully one they'll buy.)

Felix: Everything's fine.

Felix: I should have documents in two days, and then I can fly back to London.

Mum: Oh thank God!
Dad: Do you need more money?

I laugh to myself. I don't know what he thinks I could have spent 10K on in thirty-six hours.

Felix: No, I'm good. Thanks.
Mum: At least you have Hope. Is she ok?
Felix: Yeah, we're together.
Prue: Rather romantic, actually, marooned in paradise.

This stings. Under different circumstances, perhaps it would be.

I don't respond.

I click through to a couple other unread texts from this morning. They're from Sophie.

Sophie: Hey mate.
Sophie: Quick update for you.
Sophie: Everything is UNDER CONTROL but wanted you to know that Izzie quit.

"Fuck," I hiss out loud.

Izzie is the manager of the Smoke and Gun. She's worked there for years.

Sophie: I'm filling in and I have a few leads for a replacement.
Sophie: So don't stress.

Don't *stress*? We're already shorthanded with me away. There is no way Sophie has the capacity to run both businesses and cover the day-to-day at S&G.

Felix: Shit.
Felix: I'm coming back early.
Sophie: No! It's all in hand. Enjoy your trip. I just wanted to let you know.
Felix: It's fine. I was already planning on it. Long story.
Sophie: Ok . . . but truly don't worry, it's all sorted!

She knows me well. I keep an iron hand on the business because I'm obsessive about the details. When something goes off, so does my entire psychological balance.

I wish I were home.

I'm beginning to feel claustrophobic.

I reach in my pocket for nicotine gum, which always helps calm me down. But it's not there. I search through our bags, and it's not there either.

Not a great time to start withdrawing from my drug of choice, but I doubt they sell Nicorette at the hotel gift shop.

You could buy a pack of cigarettes, my evil brain suggests.

No. Bad idea. I associate smoking with drinking. If I have one, I might start craving the other.

I step into the shower and turn the water up to a temperature that threatens to scald me. As I shampoo my hair, I miss the "ocean" smell of the cruise ship bath products. What I would give for it to be two days ago, before I fucked everything up.

Or forty-eight hours in the future, when this whole mess will be, God willing, behind me.

Two nights.

I just have to get through two more nights, and I can leave.

Hope

I decide I'm glad Felix doesn't want to explore the water park with me. He seems pensive, and I don't want to live out my childhood fantasy in the shadow of someone else's bad mood.

Besides, I could use some time to process his apology.

Water slides bring out my claustrophobia, so I forgo them in favor of floating on the "rapids river," a mile-long loop through the park the brochure says is filled with steep drops and sudden wave surges. I assume its thrills will be on the mild side, given that it's full of children, but a section of "white water rapids" topples me over, and a group of little boys laugh at me as I go chasing after my inner tube.

I decide to leave the rides to the one million families milling around. I treat myself to a frozen lemonade and grab a spot by a lake-sized pool under an enormous fake Mayan temple.

The problem with lying by a pool when you have neither a smartphone or a book is that it's inherently boring, and you start obsessing over the boy back in your hotel room.

I need to get this out of my system.

I text Lauren.

Hope: I made it to the hotel.

Hope: It's everything.

Lauren: !!!!

Lauren: Send pics!!

Lauren: Oh wait, you don't have data ☹

Lauren: Did you escape Felix?

Hope: Uh, so . . . no.

Lauren: What?!

Hope: He apologized this morning.

Hope: Out of the blue.

Hope: He said he now sees that your persona is a joke and he overreacted.

Lauren: Pretty shitty apology.

Hope: He also said he took it so hard bc he'd been falling for me.

Lauren: Hmmm.

Lauren: Not sure what to think about that.

Hope: Me neither, tbh.

Hope: I'm less mad but more sad? Cuz I really liked him, and if he also felt so much, maybe it could have been something real.

Lauren: Are you trying to make me give you a lecture?

Hope: I'm not saying I'm going to give him another chance.

Hope: And anyway he didn't ask for one.

Hope: But it does make me sad.

Lauren: YOU ARE NOT ALLOWED TO BE SAD AT ATLANTIS.

Hope: Ha ha.

Hope: You're right. I need to go find the aquarium. I fucking love aquariums.

Lauren: IKR? They're like snorkeling except nothing can bite you.

Hope: What's happening on the boat?

Lauren: I've been hanging with Colin mainly.

Lauren: I told him about my hustle and he thinks it's hilarious and wants to play a character who sweeps me off my feet. He keeps begging me to put him in TikToks.

Hope: Cute!

Lauren: Oh, and I ran into Gabe. He knows about you getting stranded. One of Felix's sisters told him.

Lauren: He offered to get off the boat and go rescue you and I might have said you were happily ensconced in Felix's arms just to make him jealous.

Hope: Good. He deserves it.

Lauren: Going for a walk into town with Colin now.

Hope: K have fun!

These updates make me happy. I have a good feeling about Colin and Lauren. And I do not mind the idea of Gabe sulking around imagining me in paradise bliss with a lover.

It's hot, so I take a dip in the pool, and then dry off and wander to The Dig, an aquarium modeled on the ruins of the lost city of Atlantis. There are endless chambers spanning an entire floor of the hotel. I'm struck by a tank holding an eight-hundred-pound goliath grouper that will surely give me nightmares for the rest of my life. The moray eels don't help. But then I wander through alleys filled with moon jellyfish, a coral reef exhibit bursting with gorgeous colors, and a huge population of bright orange clownfish.

We saw clownfish the day I spent snorkeling with Felix, when he laughed at me for dissecting their social patterns, and then made fun of me for running away from a sting ray. It was such good, clean fun. My cheek muscles were tired from smiling by the time we got back to the boat.

I still love that day. Because I haven't laughed that much with someone besides Lauren in years. I haven't felt so much lightness since my breakup. And really, it wasn't just that day. It was the whole week we spent together.

That week was *good*. It was good *for* me.

It got me out of my head. It made me see my ex more clearly for the asshole he is. It returned me to the world of orgasms.

It made me see myself as Felix saw me: amusing and clever and silly and sexy.

The kind of girl you could fall for without meaning to.

The kind of girl who might just have been falling back.

Even if Felix and I fell apart just as spectacularly as we came together, we gave each other something of value. Maybe I needed him to remind myself who I could be—no, who I *am*—when I let myself live in the moment. When I stop giving myself shit for not being enough.

I make a decision: I'm going to let it all go. I'm going to try to spend this next day or so with Felix as friends. Because while he is not a perfect person, and he made a big, hurtful mistake, I'm still very happy I met him.

He gave me that thing I was looking for when I left New York: optimism.

I came on this trip to wake up, to feel alive.

And I do.

I finally do.

And so much of that is because I met him.

Felix

When I emerge from the shower, Hope is lying on her bed, staring at the ceiling and smiling. She looks so content that I feel my own black mood even more acutely.

"Hey!" she says, like she's happy to see me.

"Hey. How was the pool?"

"It was glorious. Although I did nearly capsize into a bunch of mean children on the rapids ride."

I try to smile. "I'm glad you had fun."

"Did you sleep?"

"I did."

"Miraculous. I'm gonna jump in the shower, and then I was thinking of going downstairs and grabbing a bite. Want to come?"

I'm not hungry, but I haven't eaten since breakfast, and I can tell Hope is making an effort to be nice to me. I go with it.

"Yeah, great."

She takes an epically long shower, which is unfortunate because it leaves me alone with my thoughts. I flip on the TV and half watch previews of pay-per-view movies to keep my brain from whirring out of control.

"You're considering watching *Paul Blart, Mall Cop*?" Hope asks when she comes out of the bathroom.

"Looks oddly charming."

"Are you ready to go?" she asks.

"Yep," I say.

"Do you mind eating inside? I've had too much sun."

"Sure."

We go downstairs and wander around getting rejected from restaurant after restaurant because we don't have a booking.

"I didn't realize you needed reservations," Hope says. "Maybe we can eat at a bar."

We find one called Sea Glass. I immediately hate it. It has aggressively patterned maroon carpeting and a wall of slot machines that blare out tinny, annoying music.

"This okay?" Hope asks.

"Sure. Fine."

We grab seats at the bar amidst a crowd of people dressed up to the nines in resort wear.

"This hotel reminds me very much of a cruise ship," I say to Hope.

"I know. There's no escaping it."

The bartender walks over to us and Hope orders a dirty gin martini.

"Excellent choice," the bartender says.

I agree.

God, I'd love a drink right now.

I push the thought down, even as my mouth literally salivates at the idea of Hope's drink. That icy hit of juniper mingled with salt. That immediate throb of alcohol hitting your bloodstream.

The sharpness of my longing is so terrifying it gives me chills. I haven't felt this way in months—not since I attended my first wedding after getting sober and felt painfully envious of the people enjoying cocktails with the dancing. I left early.

I should do that now.

"You know what, I'm actually not hungry," I say, standing abruptly. "Do you mind if I go back to the room?"

Hope looks at me with concern. "Are you feeling okay? You're a little sweaty."

In truth, I'm jonesing for nicotine and the desire for a drink is putting me on the verge of panic. But I'm not going to lay that on Hope.

"Yeah, yeah," I say. "Just exhausted."

She doesn't look convinced. "Do you want me to bring you something back?"

"No, I'll order room service later if I get an appetite."

"Okay then. Get some more rest."

I couldn't rest if you drugged me.

I am electric with adrenaline.

I don't go back to the room.

I ask the hostess where I can buy cigarettes and am directed to a store on one of the plazas ten minutes away. I speed walk there, and between the heat in the air and my brisk pace, I'm sweating through my new shirt by the time I reach the store.

I buy Marlboros and sit on a bench and light one with shaking hands.

The first drag makes me cough violently. Makes my mouth dry. Tastes disgusting.

I don't let that stop me.

I smoke three in rapid succession.

And yeah, I was right about cigarettes making me crave booze, because now I'm fantasizing in lurid detail about an old-fashioned, one with bourbon and orange bitters, how it would cut the taste of ash and tar, flood me with—

I shouldn't have done this. I need to stop. *Must* stop.

I toss the packet of cigarettes in the nearest bin and rush back to the hotel, dodging groups of merry tourists. When I get back to the room, my skin is cold under the sweat and my heart is pounding.

I'm so fucking anxious.

I'd love to call someone from my recovery group, but it's past midnight in the UK. I collapse on the bed and google AA meetings in Nassau. There's one tomorrow morning at ten a.m.

I just need to get through tonight.

I go out to the balcony and pace back and forth, trying to jangle out my nervous energy. The sun's almost down, and I watch its last pink rays glinting off the sea, hating that sea, hating the notion of water itself, that treacherous substance that led me, somehow, to this state of collapse.

I'm so sad.

My eyes are wet—I'm not fully crying but only because I'm too anxious, not because I don't want to. I grip the edge of the balcony and lean forward, trying to draw deeper breaths.

I wish there was someone to tell me this will pass, to take it one second at a time.

I wish there was someone to hold me.

And then, suddenly, someone is.

Hope

"Hey," I say sharply to Felix, putting my arms firmly around his waist and pulling him away from the guardrail. I know he isn't trying to jump or anything, but he looks like he can't breathe. I can feel his heartbeat through his back, thumping urgently.

"Hey," I say again. "What's wrong?"

He shakes his head, like he can't find the words, and then lets out a deep, heaving sob.

"Oh, Felix," I exclaim. I move around so I'm standing in front of him. He's hunched forward, his knuckles balled up to his eyes. He looks so anguished I'm worried someone has died.

"Hey, what is it?" I ask, gathering him in my arms. His body is sweaty and he smells like musk and cigarettes and he's braced so tight it's like hugging a punching bag.

But then he relaxes and rests his head on my shoulder and cries so hard that his tears roll down my neck.

I don't know what to do. Things are so weird between us that this seems like a violation of his privacy. But I can't let him stand here weeping and not comfort him.

So I wrap my arms around his back and just let him cry.

We stand like that until he stops shaking.

He lifts up his head and the tear stains on his cheeks look like the bioluminescence off the ocean. I've never noticed how long his eyelashes are—wet, they're dark and beautiful, like his eyes are lined with kohl.

"God. Sorry," he croaks, breaking away from me. He lowers his head and shakes it. "You don't need to do this. I'm sorry."

"Felix?" I say.

"Yeah?"

"Don't apologize. It's okay."

He takes a deep breath, lets it out. "Shit. Fuck. I need water."

"Sit down," I say, gesturing at a patio table and chairs in the corner. "Breathe. I'll get you some."

I grab him a bottle of water from the room, and then notice a kettle on the dresser. I check to see if there are any tea bags, and there are—mint and Earl Grey, so I pour some of the water into the machine to boil.

I make him a cup of mint tea and bring it out to the balcony.

"Tea," I say. "Not precisely eighty-five degrees I'm afraid, but it's the best I can do."

He smiles at me weakly and accepts the mug. "Thanks."

I sit down in the chair next to him and lean back. I feel strangely unbound, like his cry was cathartic for me. Like a door has been opened in a cold room and a blast of warm, balmy air has burst through.

I hope it was also cathartic for him.

"Do you want to talk about why you're so sad?" I ask.

"I don't want to unload on you."

"I'm here. I'm asking."

He looks up at the sky.

"It all just hit me at once, you know?" he says. "The insanity of being here, the stress and anxiety of trying to wrangle everything, shit happening at home, at work, our fight. Hurting you."

His voice breaks on those last words, and something inside me releases. It's not anger—I let that go earlier. It's something deeper, something tender that was more bruised than I've been acknowledging to myself.

"It's okay," I say. "We can talk about it more later, when you're feeling better, if you want."

"I just feel like I'm falling apart," he says. "And it's so important to me not to be that person anymore. But it's been building and building and then tonight, I don't know, I almost cracked. I really wanted to drink. And I didn't, but it puts the fear of God into me, how tenuous this all is. My stability, my sobriety—this whole rickety life I've built."

I guiltily recall the martini I had at dinner—how he ran off right after I ordered it.

"Oh, God," I say. "I'm so sorry. I shouldn't be drinking in front of you. It's so insensitive. I wasn't thinking—"

"No," he says forcefully. "It's not your fault, it's not about that. I just let myself get overwhelmed, and I know better. I'm good at home, I'm good alone, I'm good in my routine. I shouldn't have come on this trip. I knew better."

He looks like he hates himself.

I can't bear to see it.

"Felix," I say. "I'm so glad you came on this trip. Because if you hadn't, I wouldn't have met you. And no matter what happened between us, meeting you was one of the nicest things that's happened to me in a long time."

He shakes his head. "You don't have to say that."

"I know. I'm choosing to. Because it's true. I needed to get out of my head, to have an adventure, to feel awake again—and you did that for me. Okay? And yes, things went south, and yes, that sucked, but I don't regret it. And you know what? You might get caught up in fear or temptation, you might break down, you might struggle. I don't know much about recovery and won't presume to tell you everything is fine if it's not. But I do know this: you got through it. Everything is wildly out of control, but you're here, breathing, sober, with a cup of tea. You got through it."

I look into his eyes as I say this, and he doesn't break the gaze.

"Thank you," he says. "For being so kind to me even after, well. You're a nice person."

"Is there anything that would make you feel better?" I ask. "Get your mind off things?"

"Well, I'm going to find an AA meeting tomorrow. Call my sponsor."

"That's great. Anything else? Like maybe something food related that would be a fun distraction?"

"Actually, you know what?" he says. "I really did want to take you to swim with those pigs."

I laugh, hard. "Um, okay. I admit I was excited about that, but are you sure that's what *you* need."

"I want to do something that makes you happy. Before we leave. Will you go with me? Tomorrow?"

"Sure," I say.

I think it might be a nice, unloaded way for us to part as friends.

"Done," he says. "I'll set it up in the morning."

"Sounds perfect," I say.

He pulls away from me. "I'm going to shower now. I might have been smoking."

"I might have noticed."

"Sorry."

"Don't apologize to me. Apologize to your lungs."

While he showers, I change into my BAHAMAS PAJAMAS!!! and turn on the television. When he comes out of the bathroom he looks (and smells) much better.

"Are you tired?" I ask.

"No. I have emotional meltdown endorphins."

"Want to watch an overpriced pay-per-view movie?"

"I wouldn't mind something chill."

"Not *Paul Blart*," I say. "Sorry."

"Fine. We can compromise."

I pat the bed beside me. We're clothed and he keeps a few inches of distance, but it feels nice to be near him. Companionable. It occurs to me that watching a movie is probably the most normal thing either of us has done in eight days.

We settle on *Inside Out*, the Pixar movie about personified emotions. When it makes me tear up—all Pixar movies do—he pats my hand like a granny.

"Your turn for an emotional meltdown?" he asks.

"Don't make fun of me. This movie's so sweet."

"You're so sweet," he murmurs.

His eyes are still on the screen, but the words make me seize up.

I don't know how much to read into his affection.

But my brain drifts back to his confession to me last night: "I was falling for you."

I wonder how much of that lingers.

Not just in him.

In me.

I consider snuggling up against him. Seeing how it feels to be close. But I think better of it. We've made peace. We should end it there.

At some point I must have drifted off, because when I wake up it's ten a.m., Felix's bed has been slept in, and he's gone.

He left me a note.

WENT TO A MEETING—BACK BY NOON.

I BOOKED US A PIG EXCURSION LEAVING AT 1 PM.

THANKS FOR LAST NIGHT.

XX

And it's dumb, but at the sight of those two xx's, I wonder if I made the wrong choice last night.

10

THE LAND LOVERS

Felix

I wake up with the light at six a.m. and immediately look over at Hope, who's sleeping peacefully in the other bed. I have an overwhelming longing to crawl in next to her and take her in my arms.

If I was infatuated with her on the cruise ship, last night shifted my feelings into something more solid. I can talk to her about real, painful things. I can trust her in a moment of crisis. I can lie in bed beside her watching a children's movie and feel utterly safe.

But I need to take care not to confuse her kindness to me last night with a rekindling of something romantic. Even if she welcomed my affection, my breakdown yesterday was a blaring siren urging me to be cautious. I need to take care of myself. I need to get steady.

That doesn't make it easy to walk past her without brushing my hand on her arm. Without tucking the covers up around her. Without placing a kiss on her forehead.

It doesn't mean I don't want more. It just means this last day will be bittersweet. A farewell to something that might have been so good, were only the circumstances—and me—different.

I go out on the balcony and ring my sponsor, an Irish guy in his fifties named Nick who's been sober for twenty years.

He answers on the first ring. "Felix, lad."

It's reassuring to hear his voice—both gruff and lilting.

"Heya, Nick," I say.

"And how's the holiday treating you?"

"Oh, I've had better."

"Uh-oh. What's happened?"

I tell him about being stranded, my near slip, breaking down. He tells me to remember to accept what I can't control, to surrender to a higher power. And to do what I can to ground myself in my recovery plan even amidst the chaos: take it a minute at a time. Exercise today. Go to a meeting.

"And Felix," he adds. "You've done well. Remember to take pride in that. You're strong, boyo."

I thank him, then hesitate. "There's something else."

"What is it?" he asks.

"The woman I'm here with—the one I met on the ship. Before we got stranded, we were sleeping together. I think I have feelings for her."

There's a pause as he considers this. He's aware of my fears around dating. How I associate love with ruin. "Is she a drinker?" he asks.

"Well, she's not sober. But she doesn't drink . . . problematically."

"And are you comfortable with that? Take a moment. Think about it."

I do.

"Yeah, that's not the problem," I say. "It's just I haven't felt like this since before—maybe ever. And I know it's too soon for me. And it's devastating, to meet this person and not be able to pursue it."

"Are you certain that you're not being too hard on yourself?" he asks. "You met the girl a few days ago. You could take it slow. You don't have to marry her tomorrow."

I get a wave of anxiety at the idea of marrying anyone and have to take a deep breath. I blow it out slowly. "Well, it's over anyway," I say. "I fucked it up. And even if it wasn't, she's American. Lives in New York."

"You know, Felix," he says, "it's healthy of you to be cautious. To know your patterns. But it would be a shame to see you deny yourself love forever."

"I'm not saying I'm in *love*."

"Nor am I, lad. You may well never see this girl again, or maybe you will.

Not for me to say. The important bit is to figure out what you really want—not just what you're afraid of."

"Right," I say. I don't add that what I actually want has led me to destruction in my past so many times that I don't fully trust myself to know what's healthy from what's reckless.

That's not something Nick can solve for me.

"Listen, Felix," he says, "you're right not to get swept up in something so quickly it will knock you off your feet. But don't close yourself off to things that might make you happy."

Happy.

This is something I've rarely been able to call myself. At home I feel secure, steady. Content, even.

Not happy.

But I did feel happy this week—at least before everything went to shit.

Hope made me happy.

Still does.

Which makes me wonder if I'm being too protective of myself. Ruling out the possibility of joy on the basis of the man I was, rather than the one I've become.

"That's really good advice," I tell Nick. "Thank you."

"Not at all, any time. Now go on and sort yourself out. Call me if you need me, even if it's late."

"I will. Take care."

I follow Nick's advice to the letter. I go down to a coffee shop for espresso and breakfast, then take a long, fast walk on the beach, during which I call Sophie to check in on how things are going. She's chipper and clearly has the business under control. Hearing her confidence and her updates about this and that assuages my nagging sense that things must be going wrong without me.

"We're quite all right here, mate," she says. "You're the one stuck in the Bahamas with no passport, so worry about your own lot."

I laugh. "Fair, enough," I say. "I'll see you soon."

"If His Majesty's government will let you. Good luck at the border."

Next, I stop at the concierge desk to book a trip to see the pigs this afternoon. I go back to the room to tell Hope. She's still sleeping deeply, so I leave her a note.

Went to a meeting—back by noon. I booked us a pig excursion leaving at 1 pm.

It feels . . . insufficient. I add: *Thanks for last night.*

And then I scrawl: *xx.*

It's fairly anodyne as far as declarations of affection go, but it's the safest way to convey the warmth that I feel for her. I leave the room before I'm tempted to wake her up and kiss her for real.

I take a taxi to a meeting on the mainland. I don't speak beyond introducing myself, but I take comfort in being surrounded by likeminded people, all of whom know exactly what it feels like to experience what I've been going through. We recite the serenity prayer at the end of the meeting: "God, grant me the serenity to accept the things I cannot change, the courage to change the things I can, and the wisdom to know the difference."

I know this is something I may always struggle with.

But saying the words is a good reminder of what I'm trying to achieve.

By the time I get back to the hotel room, around noon, I feel centered. Hope is up and dressed and munching on a sandwich.

"Hey!" she says. "How did it go?"

"I feel a lot better," I say.

"Good. Hungry? I got you lunch."

"Famished, actually. Thanks."

She hands me a paper-wrapped ham and cheese toastie, still warm, and a bag of crisps. There is also a shopping bag on the table bulging with green apples.

"Uh-oh. Seasick again?" I ask.

Hope laughs. "For the record, I'm never eating an apple again. These are for the pigs. According to the brochure in the lobby, they like fruit. Apples were all they had at the sandwich shop."

"Kind of you to provide such a feast."

"You know I go big when I order food. And I want the pigs to like me. I'm not above bribery."

"You know, not to dampen your enthusiasm, but I've been around my fair share of pigs, and they're quite smelly. You might not want to get too close."

"And why is it that you hang out with pigs?"

"I meet all my farm suppliers personally. And we Brits cherish our pork."

"Well, anyway, the pigs swim in the ocean all day. They probably smell like mermaids."

"And how do mermaids smell?"

"Briny."

We meet our tour group and trek out to the beach, where we're catching a boat that will take us to Rose Island.

"Excited to get back on the sea?" I ask Hope.

"Honestly it's a bit triggering. I didn't think this through."

"Let's try very hard not to miss the boat back this time."

She shivers. "Don't even joke about that."

The trip to the island is about twenty-five minutes, and when we get there the crystal-clear shallows are teaming with small- to medium-sized swine frolicking about with half-submerged tourists. Many of them are gamely posing for pictures with people holding selfie sticks.

"They seem to enjoy modeling," I observe.

"Oh my God, look at that!" Hope says, pointing to a man hand-feeding a carrot to a speckled pink piglet, who chomps it slowly and with relish. "Come on, let's go make friends."

She wades to the beach with her bag of apples and immediately commences flirting with every pig in sight. She, and the creatures she is so entranced by, are adorable.

"Can you take our picture?" she asks me, as she scratches a brownish-pink pig on the snout.

I take many.

Then she tosses me an apple and demands I feed a pig too. She makes me give my phone to a fellow tourist and requests a picture of both of us with a very large, speckled swine who snorts into Hope's neck.

Once we've thoroughly documented our adventure, I stash my phone back on the boat and we get into the water to swim. The pigs frolic around us.

"They're like especially friendly dogs," I say.

"I've had cats for a decade that have liked me less," she says.

"You have cats?"

"No, not right now. I meant as a kid. Do you have any pets?"

"No. But I've been toying with the idea of getting a dog."

"What kind?"

"A rescue. Something big."

"To scare off burglars?"

"Yes. I'm terrified of burglars."

"I've always wanted a dog. But my apartment's too tiny and I'm gone for so many hours it wouldn't be fair."

"Yeah. I'd take my dog to work with me."

"You can take a dog to a pub?"

"Of course. A resident hound is an enticement to stay and have another pint."

"I suppose I'll add a loyal hound to my English country dream."

Her English country dream. *My* English country dream. The one I was fantasizing about the morning I found the Instagram posts.

How far gone I was in that moment still scares me. But I can't stop myself from asking: "Would you actually move to the UK?"

Her eyes dart to mine, tentative. Like talking about this with me makes her nervous.

"I would," she says slowly. "If I had a reason to. Unfortunately they aren't just handing out visas to random American publicists."

I know I shouldn't, but I briefly imagine a different life. One where I could be her reason.

Which is why it is imperative that I change the subject.

Hope

Something has shifted between me and Felix. Sitting here on this beach with him, discussing my dreams for the future, I feel that flicker he's so good at eliciting. A flare of connection so bright it's impossible to pretend it's not there.

It beckons me as much as it frightens me.

I'm not sure if I should cling to my resolve from last night with my fingernails, or to simply enjoy him.

I want to do the latter.

We're leaving in the morning. Would it be so bad to lean into our chemistry for a few hours?

I wonder if he's thinking the same thing.

I realize he's not when he says: "You never sound terribly enthusiastic about your job."

There is no greater buzzkill than my professional ennui.

"I'm not enthusiastic about it," I say.

"Why is that?"

"It's stressful, and constantly being under pressure to write press releases is depressing. And begging journalists to cover those press releases is even more depressing."

"I'm sorry," he says.

"Don't be. I'm sure I'm fired anyway."

"Really?"

"I don't know. Maybe not. I think mostly I'm disappointed with myself that this is what I've ended up doing with my life. Like I haven't met my potential."

He nods. "You want to write books."

"Very badly," I admit. "But the older I get the more it feels like that dream is delusional. I came on this vacation in part because I've been so dispirited about the whole thing. Like, if it were going to happen for me, wouldn't I have gotten it together by now? At least have something I'm proud of, even if it's not published?"

"But you obviously have the talent," he says. "You wouldn't have gotten a book deal or an MFA if you didn't, right?"

His belief in me is sweet, but not reassuring. Creating art takes vision and inspiration and the time to put in the work to fulfill it. I don't have any of these things. I haven't in a long time.

"I tell myself that in my better moments," I say. "But to be perfectly honest, my job is such a grind, I barely have time to catch my breath. And the pitiful truth is that I don't have such a burning idea for the great American novel that I'm motivated to get up at five a.m. to work on it anyway. I feel stuck. Like what's the point of even trying?"

"To find happiness," he replies. "Fulfillment."

"Right. So easy."

"I'm not saying it's easy. I just think you're brilliant, and it's worth it to keep going."

"I know you're right," I concede. "I guess I've always imagined that some literary masterpiece would just emerge from my brain like magic. And instead, I've stalled out. I think that's why I was with Gabe. I wanted to borrow his literary existence. Get absorbed into his world because I've struggled so much to make one of my own."

I can tell I'm making Felix sad, which in turn is raising the stakes on how pathetic I feel.

Suddenly I'm awash in regret at how much I've disclosed.

"Sorry," I say. "I'm being depressing. But you know, this has helped. Getting away. I'm not bursting with an idea for a book, but I feel so much more like myself. Like I *can* find that inspiration again."

He smiles. "Good."

I take a plunge. I add, "You've helped with that."

He looks at me searchingly. Like he isn't sure how much to read into my words.

Which makes sense, because I'm not sure exactly how much I'm trying to say.

I'm so confused by what I still feel for him.

"You've helped me too," he finally says.

Before he can elaborate, a pig sidles up to us and starts rooting in my bag for the last apple.

Neither of us pursues the subject further.

Instead, Felix starts building a sandcastle, which I find charming. When a pig trots by and tramples it he doubles over with laughter, which I find even more charming.

I find just about everything he does charming.

Which is partly why, as the day wanes, I begin to feel dread. I don't want to return to my real life.

Felix can evidently tell that something is wrong, because on the boat back to Atlantis, he asks, "What's the matter?"

I decide to tell him.

"This is going to sound insane," I say.

"Try me."

"I'm sad I'm going home tomorrow."

"Come again?"

"I know. I *know.*"

"Is it the lack of telecommunications you'll miss? The absence of valid personal identification? The humidity?"

I laugh weakly. *It's you*, I don't say. *I'll miss you.*

"This week has been a dramatic break from normal life," I say. "A true adventure."

"Plus, nonstop relaxation," he says.

"Oh yeah. Like a weeklong massage."

"At least we didn't get norovirus. My episode with the fire engine notwithstanding."

"Some might argue missing the boat is worse."

"I'm glad we missed it together," he says softly. "There is no one I'd rather be stranded in the Caribbean with."

My heart leaps.

Would he have said that if he didn't feel the same tug I do? That desire to be together, if just fleetingly, one last time?

"You're only saying that because I bought you that 'Conch King' shirt," I say lightly, feeling out the moment.

"I think it was a fair exchange, since I provided you with your only ability to contact the outside world."

"We made a good team."

He smiles at me. "We did, didn't we."

There's a wistfulness in his tone that makes me certain this time has meant something to him too.

"We should do something tonight to celebrate our achievements," I say.

"Want to blow seven grand of my father's money at the casino?"

"You realize it's actual legal currency and not Monopoly money, right?"

"We could break into the water park and go on the slides," he suggests.

"Except I don't want to die tonight."

"More conch?"

"Oh, of course. I thought that went without saying. *Always* more conch."

"The problem is we've already done the greatest hits," he says. "We dined. We snorkeled. We ballroom danced."

"*I* ballroom danced," I say. "You toppled over."

"We aquacized," he says.

"*I* aquacized. You just looked at my boobs."

He glances meaningfully at my swimsuit. "And what boobs they are."

I prickle with awareness.

"We saw four minutes of show tunes," I say. "Which was life-changing."

"You duetted with Elvis."

"Not to mention duetted with you."

"Ah, yes," he says with a satisfied grin. "We *slayed* karaoke."

"And," I say, "you were blown away by breathtaking magic."

"Not to mention the psychic—though she forgot to pull the get-left-behind-on-an-island-with-no-passport card."

"She can't know *everything*, Felix."

Now I'm thinking about the other card I didn't pull.

The Empress.

The sweet drawing he made for me.

"Do you know what my favorite night was?" I ask.

"Yes," he says.

"No you don't!"

He looks me dead in the eyes.

"Of course I do. It was when we ordered room service, and then I ravished you."

He's right. It was not only my favorite night of the cruise, it was one of my favorite nights of my life.

"Actually," I say, "I think it was the other way around. I ravished *you*."

"Who can recall?" he says. "It happened so many times."

He's being playful, but he also has a gleam in his eyes.

It says: *I still want you.*

And my God, I want him too.

"What if we did that tonight," I say softly.

He goes very serious. "Hope . . ." he says. "Is that wise?"

No. It's not wise at all. But I want it anyway.

"We're leaving tomorrow and probably won't ever see each other again, right?" I say, putting all my cards on the table. "We've had a rocky go of it. It would be sweet to end on a high note."

He's silent for a long beat. And then he looks at me, his eyes hooded.

"Making love to you would definitely be a high note," he says.

I try not to read too much into those words, *making love to you*. But the intensity in his gaze tells me he means them.

"Then let's do that," I say.

He looks at me even more gravely. "Yes. But first: room service. It's tradition."

"You order this time," I say, trying not to give away how shaky I am. "If you leave me in charge we'll definitely run out of Monopoly money."

"Deal," he says. He takes my hand and shakes it, and I feel his touch with my whole body.

I've missed it. I've missed him.

When we get back to the room, I take a long, sensuous bath, imagining the next few hours. It's like foreplay.

While I'm soaking, Felix orders food. I emerge in a hotel robe to a feast less deranged than the one I ordered on the boat, but also less appetizing.

It should kill the mood, but instead it fills me with affection for him.

"You're no better at this than I am," I say, taking inventory of a congealed pizza, a wan Caesar salad, and a dry brownie under a melting glob of ice cream.

"You can't hold me responsible," he protests. "I didn't cook it."

"And thank God for that. You'd probably end up in the emergency room."

"Just because I injured myself in the kitchen *one* time doesn't mean I can't cook without doing bodily harm."

"So you say."

"Read my reviews online. Not one mention of stray human fingers in the soup."

"Conveniently, I don't have internet access."

"Well," he says, sitting down in front of the food, "feel free to starve, but I don't recommend it. You're going to need energy for what I have planned for you."

That sultry feeling comes back.

The food is as mediocre as it looks. I call down for it to be removed while Felix showers.

He comes out of the bathroom wearing a robe that matches mine.

"Get in bed," he says immediately.

"Which one?" I ask.

"Mine."

His energy is very "imperious duke in a romance novel."

Which is one of my kinks.

He proceeds to lie me down and kiss me ravenously. It's like coming home.

"God, I've missed you," I gasp as I devour him, pressing him down into me, wanting to be consumed.

"You've got me," he murmurs. "You've got me."

When he enters me, I feel it in my heart.

And when it's over, I want it again.

I want it forever.

"You're perfect," he says, stroking my hair. "That was perfect."

I can't reply. I know my voice will come out in a sob.

At my silence, he looks at me with concern.

"Was that okay for you?" he asks.

I find my voice, because I don't want him to see how emotional I am. "You couldn't tell by my physical and auditory clues?" I ask.

"You could have been faking to stroke my ego."

"I don't fake orgasms, *Peregrine*."

"That's very principled of you, *Gertrude*. Come here." He opens his arms to me and I snuggle close against him. I love the way he smells—just the bare scent of his skin.

"I'm going to miss this," he says into my hair.

I trace one of the tattoos on his arm with my finger. "Me too."

I know it's insane to fall for a boy after such a short time—again. I know that the way a person seems on vacation is not representative of who they are in real life. I know that what I'm about to do is reckless.

But I can't not say it.

It's the kind of thing that you have to try, or you'll regret it for the rest of your life.

"What if we didn't stop?" I ask.

"Don't worry," he says. "My plans for you tonight aren't over."

I'm not sure if he really didn't get what I meant, or if he's trying to ignore it. But I want it too badly to take the hint, if that's what he's giving me. I screw up my courage.

"I don't mean sex," I say. "I mean what if we kept this going. You know . . . like long distance."

He stills under my body.

I can instantly tell I've said the wrong thing.

"Hope," he says softly. "I'm not . . ."

"Never mind," I say quickly. "Ignore that."

He puts his arms around me in a way that seems . . . sympathetic.

Sympathy is the very last thing I want from him.

"I'm flattered," he says. "But I thought we said this was a way to say good-bye."

"We did say that," I agree tightly.

He sighs. "I like you, Hope," he says.

The words are so wan he may have said "you're a nice gal, but I'm not that interested." I was not expecting him to profess that he's madly in love with me, but it would perhaps be nice to hear that he still has feelings for me stronger than "like."

That he hasn't stopped falling for me.

"The thing is," he goes on, "I'm not in a place to be in a relationship. Yesterday reminded me that I'm still wobbly. I want to be solid in myself before I try to be solid for someone else."

I know for the sake of my dignity I shouldn't argue, but this line of reasoning doesn't hold water.

"Are any of us ever one hundred percent solid?" I ask.

He sighs. "Maybe not. But I'd like to be closer. I don't want to live in fear of myself."

Not living in fear of myself is what I'm trying to do right now.

I want to take a risk—on him.

It's crushing to know that he doesn't feel the same way.

Then he says, "And maybe you need to take a break from relationships too."

I'm startled by this assertion. "What?"

"Well, I was just thinking about what you were saying earlier—about wanting someone else's more exciting life."

I recoil from him, genuinely shocked. "I'm not trying to lay claim to yours, if that's what you're implying."

"Oh no, of course not," he says. "My life is in no way exciting. But you said that you aren't fulfilled. So maybe this is an opportunity to pursue what you want. You know, write that book. Be happy with yourself before you try to be happy with another person."

"So, a person doesn't deserve love if their life isn't one hundred percent perfect?"

"Hope, you deserve so much love. I just hate to think of you being in a relationship with someone who doesn't value you just to numb yourself against dissatisfaction."

Now I'm *really* pissed off. At him, and at myself for confiding in him.

I did that because I trusted him. Not so he could turn around and use my weaknesses against me.

I roll away from him. "Thanks for the feedback."

"Hey," he says, reaching for me. "Don't go away. I'm not trying to insult you. I just want you to get everything you want."

"Wow, I appreciate that."

"You're angry with me."

"Well, here's the thing. A few days ago you accused me of seducing you to get at your money. And now it sounds like you think I'm some lost little girl who wants you to amuse me out of my pitiful life."

"I didn't say that."

"You did, actually. And it's insulting that you can't give me credit for having genuine feelings for you, just because I'm not living out all my wildest dreams."

"Hope," he says softly, "I have genuine feelings for you too. I do."

I don't believe him.

I know there's going to be a "but"—and that the but will reveal the true way he feels.

"But"—bingo—"we live in different countries. I'm not ready for a relationship. And I would hate to string you along thinking I might be the thing that could make you happy."

"Got it," I say.

He looks at me, aggrieved. "Please don't be angry."

"I'm not angry," I lie, very obviously. "We have to be up early to pick up our passports. We should go to sleep."

If he'd simply said he wasn't ready for a relationship I'd have been sad, but I would have understood. I'd still happily have stayed up all night with him, having sex and talking and relishing our last few hours together.

Now, all I want is to get into my own bed.

Alone.

So I do.

And he doesn't come after me.

Felix

I don't fall asleep for many hours, and I don't think Hope does either.

I feel bloody awful.

I didn't mean to offend her. But I know that I'm right: embracing love as a means of running from your life is no better than running from love to avoid your life falling apart. Neither of us is in a place to make this more than it is.

But Hope wasn't asking for life advice, and I shouldn't have offered it. It's not for me to decide what will make her happy.

It's just that I want her to have a life she's excited about.

We all deserve that.

I don't know why I didn't work harder to claw my way out when I realized I'd put my foot in it.

Except, maybe I do.

Maybe, at the end of the day, I need for this to be over.

What I didn't say to her is that I can't let myself miss her. I can't let myself pine for a girl abroad, to count the months and weeks and days until I can see her again, and reliably focus on healing the things that I need to fix.

And I meant what I said: I don't want to hurt her. I want to protect her heart—including from me. Except it's clear that I've bruised it anyway.

So I toss and turn and dread the early hour when the alarm will go off and thrust us into a day of potential bureaucratic missteps followed by many grueling hours of travel—the reward for which will be never seeing each other again.

When the alarm sounds, Hope says good morning to me coolly, and refrains from speaking any more than necessary. Probably healthier than forced cordiality, but I hate the chill.

We take a taxi to the High Commission in silence, then another to Hope's embassy for her passport. To my shock, everything is in order.

We can actually leave.

We have hours to kill before our flights, but it's obvious Hope doesn't want to spend any more time with me, and I'm tired of fried food and boiling weather. I suggest we head to the airport early.

She agrees.

We stand awkwardly in the departures lounge after checking in. Our flights are leaving from opposite ends of the terminal.

"Well, I hope you have a safe journey home," I say.

"Yeah. You too."

I open my arms for a hug. I'm half afraid she'll dodge it, but she taps me halfheartedly on the back. I give her a kiss on the cheek.

"Take care," I say.

"Bye, Felix."

And with that, she turns around and walks away.

11
TREADING WATER

Hope

The flight from Nassau to New York is somehow only three hours long.

It's dumbfounding that the whole time I was stranded, I was so close to home.

The last week was like a fever dream, and it has left me feeling the way a real fever would—wrung out, weak, and utterly numb.

I don't want to spend what little remains of my money on a taxi, so I juggle my plastic shopping bags of random possessions on a bus and then two subways back to my studio. It's a ten-minute walk from the train station to my building, and it's just as hot and muggy in New York as it was in the Bahamas. I'm thoroughly miserable by the time I'm approaching my block.

And then I see Lauren sitting on my stoop.

I blink.

The *Romance of the Sea* is still sailing through the Caribbean. Lauren isn't due back until tomorrow.

She sees me, stands up, and waves.

The sun gleams off her perfectly blown-out blond hair. She's so tall and beautiful, and she's looking at me with such profound care, that I drop my bags on the sidewalk and run to her. I want to throw myself into her arms and fall completely apart.

She descends the steps. "Hopie," she says. "Hi, sweetheart."

She pulls me into the world's biggest hug. For such a slight person, she has the strength to squeeze the breath out of me.

I squeeze her back.

"What are you doing here?" I ask.

"I left the cruise early so I could meet you. I thought you might need some moral support. Not to mention your phone and your housekeys."

"Oh, I was going to borrow the super's. But thank you."

"I'm so sorry," she says. "I still feel like a complete shithead. But I love you so much."

"I love you too," I say. "Even when you're the absolute worst."

"Are you okay?" she asks me. "You don't look right."

"Yeah," I say, but I feel woozy. Between the heat and my exhaustion and dehydration from the plane and the crying, I feel like I'm going to faint.

Lauren unlocks my apartment, which thankfully is on the garden level, because I don't think I'd have it in me to climb stairs. My studio is hot and stale after ten days of no air-conditioning in the intense August heat. I sit down on my bed. Lauren turns on the window unit and gets me a glass of water.

"It's stifling in here," she says. "Why don't we take an Uber to my place. You can nap in my guest room. Or stay over. As long as you want."

We always hang out in her West Village penthouse rather than my tiny studio. But right now, I want to be in my own space. I want to be home.

To be in *my* life. Not someone else's.

"I think I need to stay here and sleep in my own bed. For like twenty straight hours. The last few days were rough."

"You weren't restored by Atlantis?" she asks.

"That part was nice. Until Felix ruined it."

She holds up a finger. "Um, girl, wait. What happened?"

"God," I groan. "How much time do you have?"

She sits down beside me and takes my hand. "All the time in the world."

I tell her everything that happened, beat by beat, concluding with Felix's assertions about my need to figure out my life.

"I can't *believe* he would say something like that," Lauren fumes.

"Fool me twice, shame on me, though, right? I should have kept my distance after the Instagram thing. Obviously he doesn't think very highly of me. Not sure why I let myself believe that would change in three days."

She shakes her head. "What a dick. And it's shocking because he seemed so infatuated with you. Like totally gone."

"He has a knack for seeming that way right before he assassinates your character."

"Well, he can go straight to hell as far as I'm concerned."

I close my eyes. "I liked him so much, Lauren. What is wrong with me?"

"You're a romantic," she says. "You have a big, fat heart. It's a good thing. And we're going to find you someone who deserves it."

"Not any time soon. Between this and Gabe, my big, fat heart can't take any more."

"Um, so about Gabe . . ." She pauses, like she needs to say something but doesn't want to upset me.

"What about him?" I ask warily.

"It's just . . . I've been thinking about how Felix found my posts. You said someone DM'd them to him, right?"

"Yeah. Some anonymous account."

"Well, it's been nagging at me. It doesn't add up. I mean, if one of his friends happened to follow me and saw his picture, why would they send it anonymously? Wouldn't they just be like 'Hey dude, are you aware you're getting scammed?'"

"I had the same thought," I say.

"So I was thinking . . . and this is kind of dark but I can't get it out of my head . . . Gabe is the only person who definitely follows me that would have known you were on the ship."

I sit bolt upright in bed.

"Holy shit. You're right."

"He was obviously jealous at karaoke. And he saw the two of you leave together."

"Right. Oh my *God*."

She sucks her teeth. "Yeah."

"Do you really think he'd be petty enough to do something like that?"

"Maybe. The karaoke thing was unhinged. It's not like he was the picture of rational stability."

My brain is trying to actively reject the idea that someone I once loved would be so devious. But Lauren's right. Who else?

"If he did that, he's psychotic," I say.

"Do you want me to confront him?"

"God, no. I never want to engage with him again. I want to go to sleep and forget he and Felix and the *Romance of the Sea* ever existed."

"Fair enough," she says. "How about I chill here in case you still feel weak when you get up?"

Her concern for me is sweet, but I desperately want to be alone. I need to process. And before that, I need to pass out.

"No, I'm fine," I say. "I should rest. I didn't sleep last night."

"All right, sugar. Call me when you wake up. Love you."

"Love you too."

I sleep for six hours, wake up and order a whole ass pizza, inhale two thirds of it, and go immediately back to bed.

I'm rudely awakened at noon by the incessant screeching of my buzzer.

Blearily, I go to the intercom. "Who is it?" I ask.

"Gabe."

Jesus fucking Christ.

"What are you doing here?" I ask.

"I need to talk to you. Can I please come in?"

"I don't want to see you."

"Please, Hope? Just for five minutes."

Maybe confronting him is what I need. Yelling at him actually sounds energizing.

"Fine," I say. I buzz him in.

He appears at my door. He has his suitcase.

"Why do you have luggage?" I ask.

"I came straight from the airport. Took the earliest flight. I heard what happened to you. I wanted to make sure you're okay."

"I'm fine," I say curtly. "Go home."

He looks confused. "Are you angry with me or something?"

"I know what you did," I say acidly.

He looks taken aback. "What I did?"

"Yes."

"What did I do?"

"You sent Felix Lauren's video. To make me look bad."

His face goes slack.

Guilty.

"Fuck," he finally says. "How did you know?"

"Process of elimination."

He leans back wearily against the wall. "Okay. Yeah. I did send it."

"What is *wrong* with you? You realize that is batshit behavior, right?"

He slumps down onto the floor.

"What are you doing? Get up."

"Hope, I was desperate," he says. "I went all the way to the Caribbean to see you, just to find you, like, *besotted* with some other guy. I needed a chance."

This doesn't compute.

"What do you mean you went there to see me? I thought you were there for Maeve's birthday."

"Well, that's what I told her. But I knew you were going because Lauren posted about it. I thought if I came along, it would be a good way to reconnect. You know, two people trapped on a boat. Lots of time to talk. To rekindle something."

My veins are like icicles, sharp and freezing. I feel dangerous.

"Are you fucking kidding me?" I ask.

"I thought it would be a romantic gesture."

"It's scary that you think that, Gabe. It's stalkerish."

"It was the only way to get time with you. You blocked me. You moved. Lauren wouldn't tell me anything. You're not on social media. I just wanted to apologize."

"So you decided to entrap me on a boat? Do you not understand that that is frightening and insane?"

"Well, out of context, I guess, but—"

"The context is that you literally did that! I want you to leave or I will call the police."

He holds up his hands. "I will, I will, Jesus," he says. "But first just let me say one thing: I did it because I love you. I'm *in* love with you."

His expression makes it clear that he thinks this declaration will melt me.

It doesn't.

"I miss your laugh. I miss our road trips to Martha's Vineyard. I miss reading your stories and seeing you in the morning and taking walks in Prospect Park and cooking big dinners and—"

"Stop!" I interrupt him. "I get it. And I don't care."

"I want to get back together," he says. "That's all I was trying to communicate by seeing you. I'm sorry if my approach was wrong, but I meant it earnestly."

"Listen," I say. "Even if I were dying for a relationship, there are no circumstances under which I would want one with you. You spun this bullshit dream life that you didn't really want, and then you kicked me out of your apartment and fucked me over. There's no going back from that."

"That dream wasn't bullshit, Hope. We could be so good together. A power couple. You could quit your job and finally write your book."

"I don't want your help. I don't want *you*. What I want is for you to go, and never to contact me again."

He sighs and lowers his head. "Well, I had to try."

I want to shake him. "This was *not* the appropriate way of trying."

He looks at me sadly. "You know," he says, "I really do want you to be happy. Even if it's not with me."

And then he walks out the door and I lock the deadbolt behind him, ever so grateful that I have become the kind of person on whom this type of thing doesn't work.

My phone rings. My mother.

Fucking hell.

I don't want to talk to anyone right now. But I know she's expecting to hear from me now that the cruise is over, and I don't want to worry her.

"Hey Mom," I say brightly, trying not to betray my wrung-out emotional state.

"Hi dear," she says. "I wanted to hear how the rest of your trip went."

I consider lying, because the prospect of telling her the whole story exhausts me. But she'll find out eventually and be hurt that I didn't tell her.

I decide to edit it down.

"It was a bit of a doozy," I say.

"A doozy?" she asks. "What do you mean?"

I tell her the abridged story. Felix. Gabe showing up. Getting stranded. I leave out the torrid sex parts and refrain from mentioning that Felix and I briefly reconciled in the Bahamas, and then parted on bitter terms. But even without those details, the whole tale is so absurd that, by the end of it, we're both laughing in disbelief.

"Well, those are definitely memories that will last a lifetime," Mom says. "You could write a book about it."

"Martha?" a man's voice calls from her side of the phone.

He sounds like my father.

"Talking to my daughter!" she calls back.

"Is that Dad?" I ask. "Are you still at the cottage?"

"No, I'm back in Burlington." She pauses. "It's actually the new man I'm seeing."

"You're *dating*?" I ask. "Since when?"

"Oh, it's recent," she says vaguely. "Nothing serious."

"Anyone I know?"

"No. But he's a wonderful person."

"Good," I say. "I want that for you."

And I want it for myself too.

I want better for myself than Gabe Newhouse, a man who never deserved me.

I want better for myself than Felix Segrave, a man who won't take a chance on me.

And I want better for myself than the person I've become—this girl who has resigned herself to a small, dissatisfying life.

I want happiness. I want fulfillment. I want love.

And right here, in this moment, I resolve that I am going to get it.

Felix

My flight touches down at Heathrow on a cold, rainy morning. The damp chill feels like my soul returning to my body.

I take a taxi straight to the Smoke and Gun.

Sophie is there, doing inventory in the back office. She startles when I walk in. "Felix!"

"Hi, sorry," I say. "Didn't mean to scare you."

"Jesus, mate," she says, taking me in. "You look like hell."

"Just tired. Long flight."

"Yeah, maybe go home and sleep it off? You'll scare away the punters."

"I wanted to see if you needed a hand."

She rolls her eyes at me. "Coulda sent me a text for that, couldn't ya? You wanted to come see if I sank the ship in your absence. I'll have you know everything's fine. Or fine enough that you can go home and take a nap."

I sink down in a chair. "Well, I'm here. Have a minute to go over the books?"

She gives me a long-suffering sigh but slides over her laptop. We spend two hours reviewing staffing schedules, supply orders, P&L. Everything's in perfect order. So much so that my ego's a bit bruised by how little I'm needed.

I return to my carefully structured days and my rigorous routine. I return to micromanaging every last detail in my pubs, to Sophie's obvious irritation. I return to Sunday lunches with the family, Thursday nights out with my mates, Arsenal games whenever I have the time.

I'm steady, yes.

But I'm also joyless. Stuck.

I try to shake off my malaise by adopting a dog. She's a three-year-old Australian shepherd named Priscilla, which I didn't choose but which suits my family's penchant for giving their children bad "P" names. She enjoys long runs in the park and long naps at the pubs. I already cherish her.

But she has not solved the problem of my life.

Every day, as I slog through the rigid order of this existence I'm so protective over, I feel bored and unchallenged. I feel exactly what I accused Hope of being.

Hope, who liked me enough to risk asking me to be more to her than a fling. A move that was heartfelt and brave, and that I rejected out of hand. Out of fear.

I told her I needed to be stronger before I'm capable of being someone's partner. But I feel more like I'm treading water than shoring myself up.

And then, one morning at a coffee shop in Hackney, I run into Annemarie.

I haven't spoken to her since the day I canceled our wedding, on a phone call from rehab.

Her last words to me were "I hope you fucking die."

I immediately turn around to avoid her, but it's too late. She's spotted me and calls my name. "My God, Fe, it's been ages."

"Hi," I say slowly, because it's disorienting to be smiled at by someone who welcomed your death.

"I've been wanting to get in touch," she says. "I texted you, but I think you . . . blocked me?"

"Uh, yeah," I say. "For obvious reasons?"

She grimaces. "Yeah. Hey, could we talk about that? Sit down for a sec?"

I look longingly at the door.

"Please?" she asks. "I won't keep you, I promise."

"Fine," I say. "Let me just grab a coffee."

I go and order a flat white, taking the time to steel myself against whatever she's going to say.

When I get back she's biting at a cuticle on her thumb.

She always bit her cuticles when she was nervous. She still has flecks of angry torn skin around the nailbeds of her otherwise beautiful hands.

She straightens up and puts her palms on the table. "Sit down?" she asks.

I sink onto a wooden bench across from her.

"How are you doing?" she asks. "You look great."

"I'm good," I say. "And you're looking well too."

She is. She's gained a much-needed bit of weight since I last saw her, and her eyes are bright and clear.

"Yeah, I am well," she says. "Certainly better than the last time you saw me. I've been sober for eleven months as of tomorrow."

"God, Annemarie. That's amazing."

"It is, yeah. I'm really proud of myself. Best decision I ever made. But you know all about that. You've been at it how long?"

"Over two years now."

"That's so great."

"Thanks."

"Listen, Fe, the reason I tried to call you was to apologize. For the way I acted when you went into recovery."

Her sincerity eases my tension. I see her kindness, the openheartedness I once fell in love with. And I know that I hurt her. An apology is long overdue.

"I'm sorry too. For everything," I say. "We were both such messes back then."

We have a long conversation. She apologizes to me for her lack of support when I went to rehab. She said it felt like an indictment, like if I was declaring myself an addict then she must be one too. She felt defensive and scared that our engagement would not survive such a profound change in my lifestyle.

Which, of course, it didn't.

"I'm sorry it felt like I was abandoning you," I tell her. "It wasn't my intention, but I know it still hurt. And it was very painful for me to lose you."

"You had to save yourself," she says. "Put your own oxygen mask on first, and all that. But it did break my heart. I still miss you." She gives me a wry smile. "Sometimes."

"Same," I say.

"I do have some news, though. I'm engaged." She holds up her left ring finger, which is adorned with a beautiful opal.

"Wow!" I say. "That's wonderful. Congratulations."

"Yeah, it happened fast. We met in AA. He's been sober for six years."

Conventional wisdom says that you should spend a year or two in recovery before venturing into a serious relationship, so this news makes me nervous for her.

"I know, I know," she says, reading what I'm thinking in the way she was always so good at. "But I figure, in recovery I have to be strong in myself whatever life brings me—good or bad. And this man—his name is Amar—has brought me so much love. So why not take it?"

This philosophy resonates with me. It's what haunts me every time I think about Hope.

Which is every day. Sometimes every hour.

"I'm delighted for you," I say.

"Are you seeing anyone?" she asks.

"No," I say. "I haven't dated since I got sober."

"Why not?"

"Scared to, I guess."

"That's too bad, Fe," she says.

The genuine compassion in her tone moves me to say more.

"I actually did meet a woman recently. On holiday. I fucked it up though. Freaked out."

"Why?"

"I was worried a relationship would make me relapse," I say bluntly.

She widens her eyes. "Do you still feel that way?"

"I don't know." I sigh. "Maybe it's like you said. Anything can be a trigger. You have to take care of yourself, but you can't let fear be an excuse not to live. I regret it a bit, if I'm honest."

"What happened to the girl?" she asks.

"I don't know. We're not in touch. She lives in the US."

"You could call her."

"I said some things that were out of line. I don't think she'd be happy to hear from me."

"You could . . . apologize."

"Yeah. Maybe."

We hug goodbye and I take out my phone. I open WhatsApp to look at the last messages from Hope. They're about meeting up for the magic show.

I start to type something—*Hey, hope you don't mind hearing from me. I was thinking about you and wondered if we could talk*—but then I stop and delete it.

Because what would I say if I called her?

That my life is perfectly ordered, just like I wanted, and I'm miserable?

That I miss her every day?

That she was right?

What is she supposed to do with this information?

Save me by declaring her love? The same thing I told her wasn't possible?

Hearing her voice would be like sprinkling water on a pot of soil with no seeds. Yes, the water is life-giving. But there needs to be something there to take root.

I was right about one thing: I have to create a life that I want before I can share it with someone. I need to take the same advice I gave Hope.

So instead of calling her, I call Ned. He's a commercial estate agent, and also my primary partner in the pubs, albeit as a silent investor.

"Hey mate," I say when he answers. "I have a proposal. What if we bought a hotel?"

12

SEA CHANGE

Hope

I know that I'm getting fired when Stacy, our firm's founder and CEO, calls me into their office the second I walk into work on Monday.

I've been braced for this and try hard not to panic. *You can get a new job*, I reassure myself. *You can apply for unemployment. It's for the best.*

Stacy is in their late forties, rail thin with a platinum pixie cut and arms always clinking in hammered silver bracelets. They're a consummate gaming nerd with a popular Slack channel, and the single most powerful publicist in this sector of tech. I haven't worked with them closely, since they're Magda's boss, but I respect them immensely.

Even though this job was not a good fit, I regret they'll remember me as a fuck-up.

Stacy is all business as they invite me to sit down.

"Hope," they say, "I'll get right to the point. While you were away, Magda was terminated for cause."

It seems I'm not the only person who has noticed that Magda is inconsistent, disrespectful to her employees, and delegates literally all her work to other people. Stacy explains that the Conifer press release that went out late had actually been Magda's deliverable—Stacy had reassigned oversight of the whole project to her weeks ago when I got my approval to go on vacation. So when it wasn't sent out on time, it was Magda who had to account for why—and me being unreachable on vacation was not an acceptable answer.

"It's become evident you've been picking up a lot of slack for her, Hope," Stacy says. "And I regret that I didn't notice the problem sooner. I'm impressed by how you've handled your workload while covering so much of hers. Your writing is fabulous, you have great contacts, you've been securing awesome coverage, and the clients at Conifer love you. So I'm wondering if you'd like the opportunity to step into Magda's role."

They explain it would be on an interim basis, as they are required to open the job to outside candidates. "But I see great potential in you, and I'd strongly encourage you to throw your hat in the ring for the permanent position."

The interim role will come with an increase in responsibilities, but since I was already doing a huge percentage of Magda's work, it won't cut into my time that dramatically. And it comes with a substantial bump in pay.

Enough that I could afford to quit tutoring.

It is not, by any means, my dream job.

But it's a chance to carve out time for myself.

It's a chance to use my evenings to write.

I accept.

At first, I attempt to refine my short stories. Gabe, after all, convinced me they were my path to literary glory, and for all his faults, he's a card-carrying member of the publishing elite.

But when I reread them, they're unconvincing and pretentious, with an affected point of view emblematic of a person I was trying to be, not the person I actually am.

I'm determined to do better.

It's not easy.

I flounder for weeks, spending my nights coming up with bad ideas, stopping and starting, losing confidence and then reconvincing myself the effort will be worth the frustration.

That this—writing fiction—has always been the thing in the world that I'm best at.

That I owe it to myself to try.

And then, late one night, a tiny glimmer comes to me.

I open my laptop and type three words in bold twenty-four-point Times New Roman font: **Doomed Bourgeois Marriage.**

It's not a plot. It's not even a full idea. But the title gives me a little shiver every time I reread it.

I know there's something there.

On the third chilly fall night I spend staring at it, the story finally comes to me: a professor of nineteenth-century British literature has spent her life studying the canon of her field in hopes of pushing scholarship around the marriage plot infinitesimally forward. But she's disillusioned with her dwindling humanities class sizes in the age of STEM, a body of work that increasingly feels like pedantry, and cutthroat palace intrigue among her university colleagues, who circle like sharks around an ever-shrinking number of tenured jobs.

She decides to put herself at the center of a one-woman ethnographic study. She'll marry someone solely for money, and examine the subtle tortures of the heroines she has studied from the inside of the story, rather than from the pages of a book. The results, she hopes, will form the substance of a memoir that will bridge scholarship with lived experience, and transform her from an obscure academic to a literary star.

But when the book doesn't sell, she must grapple with the fact that she's done what so many doomed heroines have done before her: attempted to use a relationship as a means of escaping the disenchanting confines of her life, and ruined what happiness she had in the process.

It's inspired by what might have become of me had I stayed with Gabe—a hard-won theme about which I have something vital to say.

I paste the synopsis into an email to my old agent. I don't know if she'll even reply, it's been so long since I've been in touch. But she writes back the next morning: *Very compelling. Send me pages when you have them.*

It's the boost of confidence I need. The words begin to flow.

Despite not being a morning person, or even a midmorning person, I drag myself out of bed every day at five a.m. to write for an hour. Every evening, when I have more time, I reread what I've written, edit it, and jot down notes about what to write the next day.

That's all the time I can afford. With work, I barely have a minute to think. And that's good for me, because if I had any slack in my day, I would spend it ruminating about Felix.

Three weeks ago, a huge box arrived in the mail. It was so heavy I had to ask my super to help me carry it into my apartment. Inside was every single product made by Maquille. Moisturizers, serums, tonics, sunscreen, masks, even four different flavors of lip balm.

It came with a note.

HI HOPE!
SENDING ALONG OUR NEW PRODUCT LINE, AS WELL AS THE CLASSICS.
THE VITAMIN C SERUM IS ESPECIALLY BRILLIANT. THANK YOU FOR
TAKING CARE OF MY DEAR BROTHER IN THE BAHAMAS. DO DROP A LINE
IF YOU MAKE YOUR WAY TO LONDON! WE'D ALL LOVE TO SEE YOU!
PEAR XX

The skincare products are lovely, as is the gesture. But what floored me is that they arrived at all. Because she had to have gotten my address from Felix. And if she was feeling friendly enough to send them just because she knows I like the brand, she must not know what happened between us.

It's such a scant thread, but I feel connected to him, knowing he must know about this, and did nothing to stop his sister from getting in touch. I examine her last line—*we'd* all *love to see you*—and wonder if that's a hint.

I know this is my pattern. I brood over people I cared about, even when they've hurt me. It's like my heart can't catch up to my head.

But also, my anger has mellowed. You see, I think Felix was a little bit right about me.

I did need to throw myself into a book rather than a relationship.

I do need to find myself.

"You need to let him go, sugar," Lauren tells me when I confess I've been thinking about Felix on our daily FaceTime. She's still shooting in Australia. Her television work has given her a lot of new content to pivot to, which is convenient, as she's now dating Colin and moving away from her sugar baby brand.

"He knows where to find you if he wants to say he's sorry," she says.

"I know," I say. "I'm not going to contact him."

But that doesn't stop me from tracking down Pear's email address from her company website and writing her a note.

Hey Pear! Thank you so much for the box of goodies. I feel radiant just looking at them. No plans to cross the pond soon, but get in touch if you're coming to NYC. All the best to you and your family. —Hope

She writes back within minutes:

Will do, darling. By the way, you didn't hear it from me but Felix is hopeless without you. xx

My stomach flips so violently I feel like I'm back on the cruise ship.

I can't come up with a reply. If I let myself dwell on what it means I'll obsess.

So instead, I bury myself in my story.

Months go by and the manuscript slowly expands into three chapters, then five, then eight. The words not only flow, they overflow far beyond the amount of time I can devote to capturing them. I'm living for Christmas break, when our office closes for two weeks and I can go home to Vermont and use every spare hour not spent with my parents to write. I'm already stressed that I can't just hunker down in one place—that I'll have to spend my time going back and forth between their two couches, navigating the tension between them as the only child of their divorce.

I leave for the airport straight from work and arrive at Burlington International just after seven. As I step onto the jet bridge, my bones immediately snap into the understanding that we are now in Vermont in winter. Brutal, but nostalgic. The feeling of home.

My dad is picking me up, so I text him to let him know I've landed. He says he's parking and he'll meet me at baggage claim. But when I get there, the first person I see is my mom.

My tired eyes cross at the cognitive dissonance, and I wonder if this is a coincidence—if she's here to collect some other relative.

But then my father walks up beside her.

They smile and wave, looking both happy and sheepish.

"Hey," I say, walking up to them, unsure who I should be hugging first. I haven't seen them together since they told me they were separating.

Mom makes the decision for me, pulling me in for a hug.

And then the damnedest thing happens: my father wraps his arms around *both* of us. It's the hug of my childhood. I'd get this same hug—her around me, him around her—every night before I went to bed, every morning before I left for school, every time I was sad or happy or needed comfort.

I never thought I would experience it again.

Which does not change the fact that it pisses me off.

I shrug out from under them. "What's going on?" I ask. "Why are you both here?"

They look at each other, having one of the silent conversations I grew up trying to parse.

"We wanted to tell you in person," Mom says, taking my father's hand. "We're back together."

I gape at them. "Since when?" I ask, feeling childishly outraged. "I thought you had a boyfriend. I thought his name was Harold."

I admit I haven't asked her a lot of questions about her new man over the past few months. The idea of her moving on from my dad made me a little uncomfortable, even if I was happy for her. And given how busy I've been, I haven't been talking to either of my parents as much as usual.

But even so, this is a total blindside.

"We've been finding our way since the summer," Dad says. "We didn't want to tell you in case it didn't work out."

They both look genuinely apologetic. And how nice, that their love story has a happy ending after all. Maybe there's hope for the rest of us who fall fast and hard.

My shock turns into elation.

"I'm so happy for you," I say, wrapping my arms around them again. "This is amazing."

They look relieved.

"We also have a surprise," Mom says.

"You two being back together isn't the surprise?" I ask.

She laughs. "There's more. We're going to drive out to the Kingdom tonight."

Now I'm truly flummoxed. The Northeast Kingdom is where our family's cottage is, on a few acres near Lake Willoughby.

As far as I know it's sitting empty, waiting for some other family to buy it.

"Why would we go to the Kingdom?" I ask.

"To the cottage," my mom says. "For Christmas."

"I thought you were selling it."

"That's the surprise," Dad says. "We decided to hang on to it until we knew what we were doing. We took it off the market. We've decided to move there full-time—together."

"But what about your job?" I ask. My mom is retired, but my dad is still a middle school principal.

"I took early retirement," he says. "Yesterday was my last day."

"Holy shit," I say.

"I know this is a lot to take in," Mom says, biting her lip a bit guiltily.

"Are you fucking kidding me?" I say. I gesture at myself helplessly. "I'm about to fall over."

"Let's get your bags, kid," Dad says. "We can talk it all out on the drive."

The Kingdom is about two hours northeast of Burlington, so we stop for pizza on the way out of town. Over dinner, they give me the CliffsNotes version of their reconciliation. They spent time together at the cottage packing up their things while I was on the cruise. I knew they had been there together. What I did not know is that they had both felt the reality of their separation emptying out that house. They felt like they were ripping apart the life they'd built together, and it was devastating to see it packed away in boxes and sold.

First, they decided to go on some dates. Then they tried living together in my mom's apartment, while still hanging on to my dad's. And then they decided to burn their divorce papers in a ritual fire in the hearth of the cottage, let the leases on their apartments expire, and move there full-time.

That was last month.

They've already moved the furniture back in, so the house is mostly as I remember it, just with fewer knickknacks and forty-year-old copies of *Reader's Digest*. I never minded the clutter, but now the space feels lighter.

My parents seem lighter too.

I go to sleep in my childhood bed and don't wake up for nine hours. When I do, fresh snow has fallen. My parents are in the living room, reading books in front of the fire—a thick biography for him, a slim volume of poetry for her.

"Want some toast, honey?" Mom asks.

"Sure," I say. "Thanks."

While my mom putters in the kitchen I settle in my favorite armchair with my laptop.

"Not work, I hope?" Dad says. "You just got here."

"No," I say. "It's my book."

"I'm so glad you're writing a novel," he says. "I always hoped you would try again."

"Thanks. Me too."

"How's it going?" he asks.

"I love working on it, and I have a lot of ideas," I say. "But it's hard to keep momentum up with my job. Pretty frustrating."

"What's frustrating?" my mother asks, coming in with a mug of tea and a plate of toast for me.

"Hope's book."

"Not the book itself," I clarify. "Just finding the time to write it."

"I'm sorry, sweetie," Mom says. "I wish you didn't have to work so hard."

"It's okay," I say, because I don't want to worry them. "I'll figure it out. I didn't mean to complain."

They exchange one of their loaded glances.

"You aren't complaining," Dad says. "Maybe that's the problem. If you let loose with complaints, what would you say?"

"I'm really okay."

"I had a lot of complaints last year," Mom says. "I was tired of being bored after retiring. Puttering around Burlington, going home to a sad little apartment. So I said to myself, you know what, Martha? You don't want this. What do you actually want? And it was this place. It was the companionship of your dad."

I'm shocked she's confiding this so directly. My parents are usually more private about their personal business.

"She showed up here in the middle of the summer and told me she didn't want to sell the house and wanted to try again," Dad says. "Obviously it was a risk. But if she hadn't . . . we wouldn't be here right now."

"I feel like you're trying to impart a parental message," I say.

"Indulge us," Mom says. "Close your eyes. Think about it. What would you do if you could throw off your worries and responsibilities and do exactly what you wanted?"

It's not something that requires much thought. "I'd quit my job, move to England, and finish my book."

"England!" Mom exclaims.

"Yeah. You know I've always been obsessed with British novels. I have this vision of going to the countryside and writing."

I hesitate to mention Felix, because it feels wrong to include something I probably can't have, even in a dream life.

But if I were being honest, he's part of it.

And I guess that's the point of the exercise.

"There's also a boy there," I decide to admit.

"Oh?" Mom asks.

"That guy I met over the summer, on the cruise. I really liked him, and I asked him to maybe try to date long distance. But he turned me down. Said he didn't think either of us was ready. But I can't get him out of my head."

"Are you still in touch with him?" Dad asks.

"No. But his sister reached out to me recently and said something that made me wonder if he still thinks about me too. There's a part of me that would like to see him again. Just to test the waters. Maybe when I've finished the first draft of my book."

"It sounds to me, Hope, like you know exactly what you want," Mom says. "And like I said: that's the battle."

"It's never easy to make changes," Dad says. "But you're at an age and stage of life where you do have choices. Don't rule them out."

I think about what my choices actually are. They mainly come down to time and money.

My interim role at work is coming to an end in January, and Stacy has told me I'm in the top three for the permanent position. If I quit, I'd lose my benefits, my security, and my foothold in yet another industry. But if I tutored full-time, as a freelancer, I could potentially make up most of my salary with fewer overall hours, since the pay is so much higher, as long as I lined up enough private students. And since the sessions are all on Zoom anyway, I could do it remotely.

I could do a summer in England and write. Give my dream a real chance and see what happens.

I decide in that instant.

I will.

Felix

The property I find is an existing twenty-room inn in a nineteenth-century manor house in Devon.

The building needs a full update and the restaurant is currently just your average country pub—scotch eggs, fish and chips, well-done burgers. But it's spacious, with a beautiful garden and a view of the sea. The second I see it online I know it's what I'm looking for, and pretty much the moment Ned and I walk into the lobby, we're ready to make an offer.

By Christmas, we own a hotel.

There are owner's accommodations in a flat above the lobby, and I move myself and Priscilla into them.

It's a mess.

Renovation is constant stress and faff, and the costs quickly exceed our projections, so we have to scramble to find an additional investor. I don't have time for a rigorous routine. My entire life is chaos and variables.

I love it.

I feel exhilarated. Energized by living a life different from the one I've always had, in some form, in London. When I go back once a month, to meet with Ned and Sophie and my two pub managers, I can't wait to leave.

It's humbling and reassuring at once to see how well the business runs without my daily involvement. I've built something amazing. But it doesn't need me to fret over it. I can let go and expand my remit.

It makes me want to expand myself in other ways too.

When I envision a life in this place, I envision a partner, eventually a family. And when I think of what that partner might be like—one woman always pops into my head.

Hope Lanover.

It's impossible to walk the streets of this quaint seaside village without remembering her dreams of living in just such a place. I wonder if she'd be happy here. I wonder if she'd be happy with me.

I search online for clues of her, but she's not on social media, and Lauren's posts are scrupulously absent of any hint of her.

Which does not stop my sisters from pointedly asking about her every few weeks. It's been so relentless that when Pear demanded her address, I dug it up and gave it to her.

"Would you like to send a little note with the package?" she asked.

"It didn't end well," I finally admitted. "I don't think she'd want to hear from me."

"I think she would," Pear said airily. "A secret about girls is we always want to know when someone is pining for us."

"I'm not pining," I objected.

"Obsessing, then," she said.

"Fuck off, please."

But my sister is not wrong. *Pining* is an appropriate word.

I know Hope's only a text or phone call away, but every time I resolve to get in touch with her, I lose my nerve at the critical moment.

I had my chance, and I squandered it.

I thought I had good reasons for ending things, but the way I did it was clumsy and hurtful.

I don't know that I deserve a third chance, or how I would handle the long-distance hurdle if she gave me one. I don't want to keep causing her pain.

My sisters come to visit the first week of April. I take them to a quaint town a few villages away to shop for books and games for the library at the inn. While they're poring over the self-help offerings in a bookstore, I wander into the esoteric section, looking for a Ouija board. Might be a nice touch in case guests want to fancy the big old house haunted.

I come upon a deck of vintage tarot cards. The same kind of deck Madame Olenska had on the cruise ship. Impulsively, while my sisters are distracted, I buy it.

I make the mistake of leaving it in a shopping bag among our other purchases on the dining table when we get home. Pear finds it immediately.

"Ha! What's this?" she asks, brandishing the deck the same way she did when we were kids and she found my box of secret treasures. "Felix, have you gone woo-woo on us?"

"Just a little fun for the library," I lie.

"You sneaky boy," Prue says. "You never told us you're a *witch*."

"Come off it," I say.

"This reveals untold depths," Pear says to Prue. "Do you think he's more of a Wiccan or an Aleister Crowley type?"

I snatch the deck out of her hands. "Calm down," I say. "Or I'll summon demons to silence you."

"Let's all draw cards," Pear says. "I want to know my fortune."

"Oh, yes, let's," Prue says. "Shuffle the cards, Felix."

"I'll leave you to it," I say, handing her the deck.

I start to walk away but she grabs me by the arm. "No, sir. Your cards, your shuffle. Otherwise I'll be cursed."

I know they're going to whinge and harass me unless I humor them, so I take the cards, shuffle them, and lay them out face down on the table, the way I saw Madame Olenska do.

"Take your pick," I tell them.

"Wait," Prue says. "We have to ask a question first, don't we?"

"Make it tell me my future, Felix," Pear says. She pulls out a card and holds it up. "King of Pentacles. What does it mean?"

"I have no idea, obviously," I say.

"Let's google it," Prue says. She grabs her phone and looks up the card.

"You're destined for material wealth, leadership, and ambition leading to long-term success," she reports to Pear.

Pear smiles smugly. "I knew I was on to something with the Maquille acquisition. Now you do one."

"I want to know the nature of my deepest soul," Prue says, waving her hand over the deck. She selects the Knight of Cups.

"It says here," Pear reads off her phone, "that the card signifies creativity, romance, charm, imagination, and beauty!"

"Eerie, how accurate it is," Prue says. "These cards really are magical. Your turn, dear brother."

"I'm good."

"Nice try. You're doing it. Ask a question."

"Fine," I grumble. "Tarot, please show me what is going to happen when my sisters finally leave me in peace on Monday."

"Lame," Pear says. "Tarot, please tell him his heart's deepest desire."

I pick up a card and turn it over.

It's the Empress.

I'm not one to believe in hocus-pocus. But I get chills all the same.

"Hmm," Pear says. "An odd one, that, since you're so decidedly a man."

"Read the meaning," Prue says.

Pear scrolls through her phone. "*Oooh*, fertility and love," she says.

"I think the universe is telling you to go on Tinder," Prue says.

But that's not it at all.

If the universe is telling me anything, it's: "You're ready. You know what you want. You know *who* you want."

I don't say anything to my sisters, as they will delight in mocking me for the rest of my life. Probably deservedly, as it's ridiculous to take such profound meaning from a random piece of paper.

But I also feel like I'd be a twit not to take the hint.

I make a decision: I'm going to call Hope.

Hope

I find the cozy flat in Devon through an English grad school friend whose mother owns a handful of rental properties.

It's in a historic limestone building in the center of Torbay with a private garden. It's a one-bedroom twice as large as my studio in New York, and $800 a month cheaper. I sublet my apartment in Brooklyn and use the difference in rent to pay for my plane ticket to Heathrow.

All I bring with me is a large suitcase and a laptop.

I've booked tutoring sessions every weekday afternoon to keep money coming in. The rest of the time is my own, and I am going to finish my book.

When I arrive, I spend the first three days in London with friends. I don't reach out to Felix or Pear. I need my brain fully focused on my writing while I have this precious time to myself.

As soon as I get to Torbay, I develop a routine. I open my laptop first thing in the morning—after the last eight months of predawn writing, I've rewired myself into a morning person—and, with a cup of tea and a plate of toast, pour all my energy into my book. It's such a luxury to do this at a desk facing the garden in the warm yellow light of my living room, rather than in the dark in my bed in New York. I keep the windows open and let breeze and birdsong float in.

Even if this book never comes to anything, I know I've made the right decision. I needed this. My *soul* needed this.

The writing comes easily. Thousands of words a day—whole chapters done in one sitting. And the work is good. The sentences are sharp and my protagonist is vivid to me. Plot twists I hadn't outlined unspool, themes I wasn't aware I was interested in emerge. For the first time in years, I feel like a real writer.

At lunchtime I go into the village and eat at a cute local cafe. I begin to see the same people regularly, and they give me tips on all the best things to do—beaches to explore, coastal paths to wander, restaurants to try. I don't know anyone here, yet I feel so much less lonely than I do at home in Bushwick. By the time I get back, it's morning in New York, so I log on to Zoom to work with my tutoring clients.

After work, I take long walks, have pints at pubs while reading. On the weekends, after I do my morning writing, I take buses to other villages and beaches. My favorite activity is hiking along the paths that trail the seaside cliffs.

One Saturday I decide to do the three-mile hike in Maidencombe. It starts on a sandy beach, and from there you climb into a beautiful forest and walk along red cliffs over the sea. I'm famished by the time I finish the loop, so I decide to walk into the village to get something to eat. I find a cute thatched-roof tavern, order a Brixham crab and cucumber sandwich and a glass of rosé, and sit in the garden in the sunshine.

I realize that for the first time in a long time, I'm happy.

Not "content." Not "doing fine."

Happy.

I realize something else: I'm not going to renew the lease on my studio. I'm going to stay here as long as my tourist visa allows and finish my book.

I sit there smiling to myself, doing absolutely nothing except breathing in the sea air and relishing certainty. Making plans in my head.

And then I hear familiar voices.

"I think I'll have the plaice goujons with saffron aioli, and we'd like the Provençal vegetable platter for the table," one of the Segrave sisters says.

"A quinoa burger with chips for me, please," the other one says.

I turn my head just in time to see Felix Segrave ask a waiter: "And what's the shortcrust pie of the day?"

"Venison, stilton, and rosemary," the waiter replies.

"One of those, please," Felix says.

They are approximately ten feet away from me, at a table near the garden doors. It's oriented so none of them are facing me. They have no idea I'm here.

My food hasn't arrived yet, so I can't leave. And even if I tried, I'd have to walk past them on my way out. My options are to sit here and hope they don't notice me or go say hello.

I think of the question my mom asked me last Christmas. *What would you do if you could throw off your worries and responsibilities and do exactly what you wanted?*

I get up and walk over to the Segraves' table.

Pear sees me first. She claps a hand over her mouth.

"What is it?" Prue asks with alarm.

"Hope!" Pear says, standing up. "Oh my God, darling. Felix, look who it is!"

He turns around.

Our eyes meet.

And his face crinkles into the most beautiful smile I've ever seen.

Felix

I'm at the tavern in town, half-listening to my sisters' chatter and counting down the minutes until lunch arrives, because as soon as we get back to the hotel, I am going to call Hope, and it's all I can think about.

But I don't get the chance.

Because here she is, in this tiny village in Devon, standing in front of me like a vision my heart has conjured.

I leap up. "Hope," I say. "My God."

I can't get anything else out. I don't know what to do. Should I hug her? Kiss her? Propose?

She clearly doesn't know what to do either.

So I stand up, kiss her cheek, and when she doesn't pull away, wrap her in a hug and squeeze her for much longer than is normal.

I know I'm being weird. I can't let go. And when I glance down at her face, she's looking up at me, grinning.

There are no assurances in life, of course. But that smile tells me she's happy to see me. And that's enough for this moment.

"Hi," I say into her ear.

"Hi," she whispers back.

"What brings you to the hinterlands of England, Hope?" Prue asks, either not clocking that I'm having a moment or hoping to break my moment because the way I am holding Hope is not socially acceptable for a family restaurant.

"I'm here for the summer," Hope says, turning to her. "I'm staying nearby, in Torbay."

"Felix, you didn't tell us Hope was here!" Pear says.

"I had no idea," I say.

"Are you guys on vacation?" Hope asks.

"Just a little weekend break to visit Felix's inn. He needs a feminine touch, lest the whole thing be decorated in leather and stag horns."

"I have not purchased a single stag horn," I say.

"Wait, you have an inn?" Hope asks.

"I bought an old pub with rooms to fix up," I say.

"Not a pub with rooms," Pear says. "He bought a dilapidated country hotel in an old manor house that happens to have a pub. He's renovating it into a hipster hotel."

"It will not be a hipster hotel," I clarify. "It will simply have an updated aesthetic. And a gastropub. Hopefully a good one."

Hope beams at me. "I'm so happy for you. Are you living here?"

"Mostly. Going back and forth between here and London. I still have the pubs."

"Too stubborn to let us sell them to Pizza Express, alas," Prue says.

"Would you join us for lunch?" I ask Hope, praying she'll say yes.

"Sure," she says. "Let me just tell the waiter I'm moving tables."

While she retrieves her wine and tracks down the server, Pear and Prue whisper instructions to me.

"We know you still like her," Pear says.

"You're inviting her over tonight," Prue says. "We'll make ourselves scarce."

"Or take her on a walk along the seaside," Pear suggests. "Do it after lunch so she can't escape."

"Ah, yes, much more pragmatic," Prue says. "Do that. And *then* invite her to yours."

Before they can offer more unsolicited advice on courtship, Hope returns and takes the empty chair at our table.

"What did you order?" Prue asks.

"Crab sandwich," Hope says. "I'm obsessed with the crab here."

"Throw some in Felix's hair," Prue says. "Just like when you met."

Hope laughs. "I think you can only get away with that once."

"I don't mind," I say. "You have crab blanche."

"What made you decide on Devon for the summer?" Pear asks.

"Well, I'm working on a book set in England, and I thought it might help to come here. Take in the vibe, get out of New York for a while. And a friend was able to get me a good deal on a flat here."

"How brilliant," Prue exclaims. "Tell us about your book."

Hope explains the plot. It reminds me of the conversation we had when we parted. I don't know if that's good or bad.

I wonder if she thinks about me while she works on it, the way I think of her when I picture my life at the inn.

The food arrives, and we all catch up as we eat. When the pudding has been cleared away, Pear looks at her phone.

"Oh, no," she says. "Milo texted—apparently there's trouble with the Maynards deal. We should get back and hop on a video call."

"Oh, too bad!" Hope says, rising to her feet. "Maybe we can all meet for a drink some time before you leave."

Pear and Prue each give her kisses on the cheek. I know they are lying about an emergency—as far as I know there is no such thing as a Maynards deal—but I'm grateful for their interference.

As soon as they leave, I invite Hope on a walk.

"I'd love to," she says.

"So, this is going to sound convenient," I say. "But I had planned to call you. Today."

She rolls her eyes at me.

"I mean it. I've wanted to do it for months, but I wasn't sure you'd want to hear from me."

She doesn't deny this. She just asks: "What changed?"

"It's quite absurd," I warn her. "Actually, I don't even want to tell you."

"Well, now you have to," she says.

"Prue and Pear made me pull a tarot card from this deck we found. And I got the Empress."

Her eyes widen.

"I thought it was a sign," I go on. "Because I haven't stopped thinking about you since we left the Bahamas."

She takes a deep breath. "I'm going to say something terrifying," she says.

"Try me."

"I haven't stopped thinking about you either."

Hope

There are so many things I've wanted to say to Felix since last summer. But now, in his presence, they escape me.

We're both silent as we walk to the beach.

I wonder if all the time apart was too much for us. If, for all my happiness at seeing him, that spark that burned so hot died from lack of oxygen.

"I'm sorry I'm quiet," he says. "I'm nervous."

I'm grateful for his directness. It's a quality that drew me to him from the start.

"Same," I admit.

"I wanted to call you last year, when I got back to London. Very badly. But I thought it would be unfair to contact you, after the way things ended. That I should leave the ball in your court."

"I didn't realize there was still a court at all," I say. "You said you didn't want to stay in touch. I'm not one for chasing balls I can't catch."

He turns to me and stops walking. "I was scared."

"Of what?"

"That if I let myself acknowledge how much I felt for you, I'd be lost."

My breath catches. "And what did you feel for me?"

"I was falling in love with you, Hope."

"Felix," I say softly.

"I'm sure that sounds dramatic or manipulative or—"

"No," I say. "I was too."

We search each other's eyes.

"And how do you feel now?" he finally asks.

"Like it's hard to tell if this conversation is a beginning, or an ending."

Pain flashes through his eyes. But then it fades into something more reflective. More hopeful.

"What if it's not either one? What if it's—what's that expression you writers use? A turning point in the story."

"I suppose we'll have to see how the plot unfolds." I take his hand. "Let's walk."

We make it to the beach and climb the stairs up the side of the rocks until we're at the top of the cliff. It's slightly overcast, and the sun is peeking behind a flat gray bank of clouds, glinting pale off the sea.

It's beautiful.

"Do you know that song 'God Moving Over the Face of the Waters'?" Felix asks.

"Never heard of it."

"A Moby track from the nineties. Can I play it for you?"

"Sure."

He takes out his phone and opens Spotify. "Here it is."

The song that starts playing is instrumental. It begins quietly, mournful and wistful, and slowly builds to something joyful and powerful that I can only describe as the music of wonder. Of quiet, hopeful possibility.

"This song sounds like I feel," I say.

He squeezes my hand. "Me too," he says. And then he pulls me toward him, puts his hand delicately against my neck, and kisses me.

"I'm sorry," he says, when we part.

I know he's not apologizing for the kiss. He's apologizing for everything else.

"It's okay," I say. "You know, if we'd done what I wanted—stayed in touch, tried to be something—it wouldn't have worked."

"Why do you say that?"

"Because I was in a bad place. I was lost, and unhappy, and looking for anything to drag me out of it." I pause. "You were right. You couldn't be the thing to drag me. I needed to get there on my own."

"Have you?"

"I don't know that I've solved the puzzle of my life. Maybe no one ever does. But I've figured out what I want, and what I don't. I've decided to give up my lease. Stay here through the autumn."

"Wow," he says. "What will you do?"

"Tutor full-time. Finish my book. And then when my tourist visa runs out, I don't know. Maybe spend the winter at my parents' cottage in Vermont."

"Didn't you say they were selling it in the divorce?"

I smile at him. "They got back together. Kept it."

"That's wonderful."

"It is. I'm happy for them."

"I'm happy for you," he says. "That you've found your way."

"Have you? Found your way?"

"I've stepped out onto a ledge. Let go of my paranoia about needing my hand in every pot at work. Tried to be a bit more courageous. Trust myself more."

"That's why you bought the inn."

He smiles. "That's why I bought the inn. Can I show it to you?"

"I'd love that."

A soft rain begins to fall as we walk back to the village. We follow a narrow country road up a hill until we reach a beautiful Georgian-era limestone manor on a bluff with sweeping views out to sea.

It doesn't look as dilapidated as Pear and Prue implied. You can see the age and wear, the life the place has lived. But it's beautiful.

"This is unbelievable," I say.

"You think?"

"I love it. Show me everything."

He leads me inside the front doors into a lobby that looks more like the great room of a country lord's house than a hotel. Which makes sense, given the place's origins. From there he shows me the restaurant—already renovated into a beautiful, clubby room. We walk up the grand staircase to the third floor—which has been finished, unlike the second, which is still under construction.

"Where are you staying, if there's no furniture?" I ask him.

"I'll show you."

He takes me to an apartment at the far west of the building, above the pub.

"My flat," he says, opening the door to a lovely sitting room with a view of the ocean. "Sisters?" he calls out. "Hope and I are here."

No one answers.

He looks confused, then takes out his phone. A smile breaks across his face.

"They've gone back to London," he says. "Apparently they have a crisis with the so-called Maynards deal."

"So-called?"

"It's obviously a ruse. They wanted to give us privacy."

"Do we need privacy?" I ask.

"I hope so," he says.

He pulls me into his arms.

I put my hands around his waist.

We stand that way for a long time.

"Let's have a summer romance, Hope," he says. "Properly, this time."

I lean up and kiss him. "Yeah," I say. "Let's."

Felix

I fell for Hope Lanover in six days and ruined it twice in three more, so it stands to reason that taking more days to ease into things—many more days—is in our best interest.

We resolve to pace ourselves. To spend the summer dating for real. Maximum three "hangs" per week. No sex until we're sure.

That works for about two weeks.

It turns out Hope and I are not meant for slow and steady. After so many months apart, we're ravenous for each other's company. Each other's bodies. Each other's minds and souls and hearts.

Our dates become torturous exercises in tearing ourselves apart.

So we bend the rules. Sex is okay but no sleepovers. Four times a week is permitted. Then "not every night."

"I feel like I de facto live here now," Hope says to me one night when we're making supper in my flat.

"Do you want to?" I ask. It just slips out.

She looks at me with wide eyes, and I know I've stepped in it.

Until she shrugs and grins at me. "Kinda."

She doesn't extend the let on her cottage and one morning I pick her and her single suitcase up. We enter the hotel unceremoniously, like it's any other day. We call the arrangement temporary. After all, she's immersed in polishing the last third of her book, and still figuring out what she'll do when her tourist visa expires in three months.

Another fortnight passes and I do the math on how much time she has left, to the day.

It's not enough.

"What's going on with you?" she asks that night. "You seem bummed out."

"Did you know you have to leave the country in seventy-two days?"

She sighs. "Oh. That. Yeah."

"It's kind of . . . killing me," I say.

She reaches over and strokes some hair out of my eyes. "Me too. But I won't be eligible to apply for an artist's visa unless I, you know, publish something."

"You know how you had that vision of living in rural England and being a writer?" I venture.

"Oh, you mean my lifelong dream? That?"

"Yeah. Well, what if you also did some innkeeping in your spare time."

"You want to hire me?"

"No," I say. And then I take the greatest plunge of my life. "I want to marry you."

She nods, solemnly.

"Well, we did say we'd take it slow," she says with a straight face.

"And it's been seven weeks, so."

"About seven times slower than usual."

"I can't let you go again," I whisper. "I love you too much."

I know it's a risk. I know there are a thousand variables I can't control, and she can't either, despite our best intentions. That it will be work and compromise and might end badly.

But I want it anyway.

She snuggles up to me. "I love you too much too. And maybe this is just how we roll. Fast and furious."

"I do have one stipulation," I say.

"What's that?"

"The wedding must be on a cruise ship."

She nods seriously. "Officiated by an Elvis impersonator."

"Only conch on the menu."

"I'll wear my coral caftan as a wedding dress."

"Honeymoon at Atlantis."

She rolls her eyes back into her head. "All my dreams really *are* coming true."

I pull her close to me. "I'm dead serious about this."

She looks me in the eyes. "Me too."

EPILOGUE

Two Years Later

LONDON

Hope

Do you know what's really great about having a best friend who's a minor celebrity? She can get a *lot* of people to buy your debut novel. So many, in fact, that it hits number eight on the *Sunday Times* bestseller list the third week it's out.

And do you know what's great about having a husband who owns a pub? He can furnish a free place to throw your book party.

And it's a good thing that the Smoke and Gun moved to a bigger space last year, because we need both floors and the whole garden to accommodate all our guests. My friends and teachers from the literary fellowship I did last year in London. Fellow authors from the writer's retreat in Cornwall where I finished the final draft of my book. New friends I've made through Felix, Pear, and Prue and old ones I met in grad school. My team from my publisher. My parents, here from Vermont. Lauren and Colin, here from Ireland. All the Segraves, and their cousins, and their godparents, and probably their neighbors.

I didn't have a wedding, but this kind of feels like one.

My editor, the legendary Aurora Smythe-Pines, launches herself ass-first onto the bar and dings a bottle of champagne with a fork. "Gather, gather, people!" she commands. "Fill your glasses, for I'm afraid I'm about to indulge in a toast."

No one would dare defy Aurora Smythe-Pines. People cram in from outside and upstairs until it's hot and standing room only.

"I am thrilled," Aurora says, "to be here today to celebrate the brilliant Hope Lanover and her tour-de-force novel, *Doomed Bourgeois Marriage*. From the instant this manuscript arrived on my desk I knew I had to have it, and that is why I, forgive the boast, outbid five less fortunate editors to acquire it. And I'm absolutely chuffed to tell you that we expect even greater things for it come awards season."

I blush as she goes on about my searing insights into professional frustration, domestic ennui, and the perils of romantic love, the propulsive nature of my writing, and the gorgeous but always playful styling of my prose.

It's the kind of praise from the kind of person I have craved respect from since I was a teenager, and I feel like I'm floating.

But it's not just the book.

It's the people around me, who bring me connection and laughter and joy every day.

It's the extended family, big and warm, that I never thought I'd have.

It's my best friend, who is livecasting this from the corner beside her charming partner, who donated all the whiskey.

It's our dog, Priscilla, running around between people's legs, excited to have so many hands to lick.

It's the home I'll return to tomorrow, in the quiet of Devon, where I can stare at the sea and work on my next novel.

And it's the man beside me, with whom I live fast and furious, fighting for ever more dreams to come true.

Acknowledgments

Like Hope and Felix, I am not a cruise person. Deciding to write a book about one was therefore one of the stranger decisions of my life—topped perhaps only by my subsequent decision to take a weeklong Caribbean cruise alone as research. Yes, it was on a boutique luxury ship catering to a "mature" clientele—and, yes, I dined with cruise ship ambassadors and attended rousing performances (hat tip to fake Frank Sinatra) and ate my weight at the fancy buffet. For this, I owe thanks to Crystal Cruises, whose absolutely wonderful crew provided such pampering that I was a little sad to go home. (This is not an ad, as I am not, tragically, an Instagram influencer. Yet.)

This book is as much about friendship as it is about romance, and I owe a great debt to the amazing people who keep me afloat as a human. Writer friends—you know who you are—I'm looking at you with stars in my eyes. I am particularly grateful to my beloved Lauren, who contributed her name to the fictional Lauren, and who assured me, upon reading the first draft of this book, that it had sea legs.

It is also about family, and mine is a little bit like the Segraves: dreamily supportive, very close, and relentlessly fond of demonstrating their biting wit in the family group text. I love you and am grateful to you, and I also credit the disastrous cruise we all took together in 2019 with the genesis of this idea.

Speaking of love, I am, as always, eternally grateful to my husband, Chris, for his ecstatic support of my writing endeavors, not to mention his great personality and other ludicrously winning attributes. Thank you for being the love of my life and my biggest fan.

And finally, thank you to the people who help me when I'm stuck, encourage me when I'm feeling like a hack, and whip my books into shape until they are seaworthy. Thank you in particular to my editor Caroline, who swooned for Hope and Felix from day one and helped them become real people, and to my agent, Sarah, for infusing romance into the pages and zinging up Act III with her zest for brainstorming travel disasters. And thank you to the whole team at Flatiron, for everything. Without you there would not be a *Romance of the Sea.*

About the Author

Katelyn Doyle is the author of the contemporary rom-coms *Just Some Stupid Love Story* and *Total Dreamboat*, and she also writes as the *USA Today* best-selling historical romance novelist Scarlett Peckham. She lives in Los Angeles with her husband and very small cat.